ALONG THE MYSTIC RIVER

LISE GOLD

D1564593

Cover design by Lise Gold Books

Editing by Debbie McGowan

For Sanya
My Monday bestie

Old houses, I thought, do not belong to people ever,
not really, people belong to them.

— GLADYS TABER

1

RILEY

Welcome to Historic Mystic. Settled 1654. The round wooden sign with carved inscription on the outskirts of downtown Mystic held a promise of charm and community, but Riley felt little excitement. She was a city girl, and leaving her beloved New York behind was painful and didn't feel right. The idea was to start over, with a new and slower pace of living that would benefit her health and keep her heart ticking steadily, but driving through the sleepy town, she couldn't imagine building a life here.

Only a handful of cars had passed her so far, and everything was closed. It was still early, she supposed, and this wasn't the big city where some shops were open around the clock. Riley was an early riser, and she'd insisted on picking up the keys to her new home first thing Saturday morning, but the drive from Manhattan had only taken her two hours and now she'd have to wait around for the realtor to open. *Slow down.* Her doctor's words echoed in the back of her mind. *Take a step back and slow down.*

Why had she wanted to be here so early? To check if her

things had arrived in the house that she'd purchased last week? To unpack and clean the place? Her assistant had most likely already done that. And then what? That was a scary thought because Riley had no idea what to do with her life if she wasn't working twenty-four seven.

Her satnav indicated she was close to the realtor's office, but instead of parking in front, she continued to drive through the town to kill time. She passed pretty New England coastal-style houses with big porches and generous yards, small independent restaurants and coffee shops, and a gas station where villagers were congregated outside drinking coffee. There were a couple of churches and a sweet little harbor with a long, wooden pier lined with fishing boats. A drawbridge over Mystic River divided the village in two, and as she crossed it, she saw vessels approaching from either side. The river reflected the sweet houses along the waterfront, most of them painted red or white, with private docks and colorful boats. Sure, it was a cute village, some would even call it picturesque, but Mystic was a getaway, somewhere to spend a weekend or perhaps have a second home.

Riley didn't know which side of the river her new house was on. She could go through her documents on the passenger's seat and find out, but the truth was, she didn't care all that much; it could wait until she got her keys. She hadn't even chosen Mystic herself; her assistant had recommended it to her, as it was pretty, quiet, and rural but not too far from New York and close to a good hospital. After that, Riley had scrolled the local realtor's website and picked a house. With only three properties on the market close to the center—if you could call it that—there wasn't much choice, so she'd gone for the biggest one and settled on a great price as it had been on the market for a while.

To others, it may have seemed a ridiculous way to start over, but after she'd nearly worked herself to death and then sold her company, she couldn't care less where she was. She just needed a place to rest and come up with a plan on how to move forward, and Mystic was as good a place as any to do that. At least the name had a nice ring to it; it sounded kind of spiritual.

The town was quieter on the other side of the river, and after driving past an art museum and a small library, there wasn't much to see. More pretty houses, two farms, and a park entrance lined the road, which was broken up with occasional roundabouts that served as focal point for statues of what she assumed to be high-standing historical town figures. Before she knew it, she'd driven out of the village and was nearing Groton, the neighboring town.

"This is ridiculous," she murmured, turning the car on a church driveway. What was she going to do here all day, every day? She was highly intelligent, intensely driven, and anything she touched practically turned into gold, yet now she'd have to take it easy for the rest of her life, and she was only forty. Used to working between fourteen and sixteen hours a day, Riley wondered what people with too much time on their hands did with their lives because she couldn't think of a single thing that she enjoyed more than being successful. Without her PR business to focus on, who was she?

Noting the realtor would be open now, she drove back toward the drawbridge, then cursed as the lights turned red. Her first reaction was to slam her hand on the horn, but she doubted anyone would hold the bridge down just because she needed to be somewhere. *Take it easy,* she told herself once again. *Deep breaths.* She called the realtor; a woman's voice sounded over the speakers.

"Mystic Estates, Lindsey speaking. How can I help you?"

"Hi, it's Riley Moore. I was meant to meet you at nine-thirty to pick up the keys to the Aster House, but the drawbridge is up, and it's taking forever, so I just wanted to let you know I'll be late."

"No problem, that happens regularly," the woman said in a cheerful tone. "And I have the keys here. Your assistant dropped them off last night. Are you in a hurry?"

Riley hesitated for a moment, then sighed. "No, there's no rush," she said, wondering if she'd ever uttered those words before.

"Great. Stay where you are, and I'll come your way as soon as the bridge is down. Aster House is on the Groton side. You're not far, but it's a little hard to find, so I was planning on taking you there anyway."

"Thank you, that's very kind of you. I'll see you soon."

Riley turned off her engine, pushed her seat back, and took a couple of deep breaths. It was only just starting to sink in. She'd arrived, and this was it; her new life, void of direction or any form of excitement. Even worse, she'd be living on the quiet side of the river. Not that the other side had much going for it, but at least there were shops there. And now she'd have to wait every time the bridge was up.

2

QUINN

*Q*uinn got out of her pickup and headed for the ice cream parlor at the base of the drawbridge. Grabbing a coffee while the bridge was drawn was a welcome break to her morning, as she'd been up for a while doing renovation work in one of the houses along the harbor. She preferred to keep her weekends free, but with the looming deadline, she'd decided to wake up early and get ahead of schedule for next week. Passing the queue of cars in front of the bridge, she spotted her friend Lindsey and tapped the roof of her car, giving her a wave.

Lindsey smiled and rolled down her window. "Hey there! Good morning. Are you getting coffee?"

"Yeah, they just opened. Want one?"

"Please." Lindsey handed her a note. "Skinny latte, no sugar. Thank you so much."

"No problem." Quinn ordered a skinny latte for Lindsey, a black coffee for herself, and a slice of carrot cake for them to share. She didn't mind waiting for the bridge and neither did anyone else in Mystic. Most locals knew each other, and it was a great excuse to catch up.

Lindsey shielded her eyes from the sun as she took her coffee. "Where are you heading?"

"Wholesalers in Groton," Quinn said. "I need some more wood to finish up the staircase for the Dalton house."

"Ah. Nearly finished?" Lindsey asked. "I heard it's looking spectacular already and they're giving me the listing. I can't wait to see it."

"Yup. Nearly done." Quinn smiled. "And good for you about the listing."

"Thanks. Things are finally starting to look up after winter." Lindsey sipped her coffee with one arm out of the window, holding on to the roof. "I sold Aster House. Did you hear about that?"

Quinn's stomach dropped, and she steadied herself against Lindsey's car. "What?" she stared at her. "I thought you said it was overpriced and wouldn't sell in a million years."

"Yeah, but the owners were desperate, so they dropped the price. And then this woman from New York showed interest, and she bought it without a single viewing. Just like that. Two point nine million, as if it was nothing."

"So it's gone..."

"Yes." Lindsey shot her a sweet smile. "Hey, that's life. I know you love that house, but let's be realistic. It would take you at least another five to ten years to get the down payment for that mortgage together." She shrugged. "Anyway, she may not stick around, so who knows? Maybe it'll come up for sale again in a few years' time and by then, you might have won the lottery."

Quinn nodded and managed a chuckle. Lindsey was right; it was unrealistic of her to think that house would be hers anytime soon, but it still stung because it felt like hers. "She's from New York, you said?"

"Uh-huh. New York City. Her name is Riley Moore, and that's all I know about her. She wasn't exactly the chatty type on the phone. I'm meeting her on the other side." Lindsey started her car when the bridge lowered and winked at Quinn. "I'll let you know if she's hot. If she's from the city, there might be a tiny chance she plays for your team."

"Shut up." Quinn rolled her eyes and laughed, threw the paper bag with carrot cake through the window, and tapped the roof of Lindsey's car again before she walked back to her pickup truck.

"Hey! Is this for me? We always share," Lindsey called after her.

"Have it," she yelled back with another wave. Aster House had once again slipped through her fingers, and she wasn't hungry anymore. Even though she couldn't afford the house right now—and maybe she never would—she'd liked that it had stood empty since the previous owners put it up for sale and moved away two years ago. As strange as it sounded, it felt like the house had been waiting for her to come back. It looked so sad that it made her stop each time she passed, its big shutters closed like eyelids and the huge front door like a gaping mouth, calling to her. *Come back.* She wanted to open those shutters, wake the house from hibernation, and restore it to its old glory, and wander through the rooms where beautiful childhood memories lay. She'd shower the neglected yard with love, so asters could bloom again, and fill the lawn with laughter. If it was hers, everyone would be welcome and the door would always be wide open. Would the new owner appreciate the house for what it was? Probably not. There had been several owners over the past thirty years, and none of them had stayed long enough to fall in love with it. They'd all said they felt lost there, that it was too big to live in, and some even claimed it was haunted.

Quinn didn't believe in ghosts. She believed in history, and with history came a certain palpable energy, but it was good energy. She could feel it, even from outside the gates. Aster House breathed; long, slow breaths. A sleeping beauty.

Engines roared and someone beeped a horn behind her, startling Quinn out of her thoughts. There was little point feeling loss over something that was never hers in the first place, but she'd have her chance again. Maybe in five years, maybe in ten. No one ever stayed in Aster House.

3

RILEY

"Here we are. Welcome to Aster House." Lindsey pushed open the heavy gates so Riley could drive through. It was much more overgrown than in the pictures, but she supposed the previous owners had stopped taking care of the yard the moment they moved out. Following the long driveway up to the big, white manor house, she was shocked by how grand everything was. The trees were old and huge, the yard stretched far and wide with several old fountains dotted around, and the house itself was at least ten times the size of her New York penthouse. What on earth had made her think it was a good idea to buy a house like this? She didn't need the space; it felt intimidating at first sight.

"It's beautiful, isn't it?" Lindsey said as they got out of their cars. "It needs a little TLC, but that's the fun of it, right? Making it your own?"

Riley swallowed hard as she looked up at her new home. She wasn't superstitious, but something told her she'd have trouble sleeping tonight. The sweeping pillared porch expanded the full length of the house, and stone steps led up to an enormous front door. Two floors and a converted attic; six bedrooms, six bathrooms, an office, a kitchen, a living and dining room, a laundry room, and more space than she could fill with her things.

"Yes, it's nice," she said, already anxious at the thought of going in.

"These are yours. I'll leave you to it." Lindsey handed her the keys and shook Riley's hand. "I'm sure you'll be very, very happy here."

"Thank you." Riley managed a smile and waited until Lindsey was gone before she walked up the steps. She rummaged through the keys until she found one labeled "front door."

The hallway was grand, with a wide, wooden staircase that led up to the second floor. She tried the light switch and was relieved when the chandelier sprang on. Her assistant Wendy had arranged the move, and although she would never let her move in without electricity or Wi-Fi, she was all on her own now and she'd have to figure things out for herself.

With double doors both to her right and to her left, Riley tried the right doors first, and they led into the kitchen. She opened them up entirely and secured them, then glanced around the old country-style kitchen that, as expected, needed some work. It had a certain charm to it, though, with a marble worktop and a big, ceramic sink under the middle of the three windows, plenty more workspace, two ovens, a double stove, built-in fridges, and storage against the opposite wall. The peach color of the cabinets was dated, but she could tell it had once been loved. On the kitchen island stood a vase with a big bouquet of colorful flowers, and she smiled sadly as she opened the envelope that was leaning against it.

Dear Riley,

Thank you for everything you've done for me. I've really enjoyed working for you, but I won't deny that I'm looking forward to a long vacation. I hope you'll be very happy in your new home (it's gorgeous!), and that you'll take it easy like you're supposed to. There's a file on the living room table with all the info you'll need, and I added some local takeout leaflets in the back, along with numbers of local tradesmen, as I'm sure you'll want to update the décor. The movers only filled two bedrooms as there wasn't enough furniture for the rest, but both beds are made, so take your pick. Take care of yourself and I'd love to know how you're settling into Mystic.

Big hug, Wendy.

Riley felt emotional as she read it twice. She'd been close to Wendy, much closer than she liked to admit. Never one to make time for close friendships, Wendy and her team in New York had been her family, and standing in a strange kitchen that didn't feel like her own, in a town she'd never visited before, she suddenly felt very, very alone.

She went back into the hallway and through the left doors, where the living room was situated. She'd seen it all in pictures, of course, but the sheer grandness of it still took her aback. Her own, modern furniture looked misplaced around the old fireplace, like it had been thrown back in time and didn't know how to adjust. She didn't have many accessories; her old apartment was slick, minimalist, and free of clutter, but she could do with some clutter now. The carpet was worn, and the walls had to be stripped and painted. She'd need bookcases to fill the alcoves, even though she had no books to put in there. *What have I done?* Riley felt regret of the deepest kind. Why hadn't she just bought a beachside villa in Hawaii or a swanky condo in Florida? She could have gone anywhere, but she'd insisted on being close to New York. That was pointless; she saw that now. What did she have left there, apart from her old teammates, who were now working their asses off for someone else?

Day by day. She'd have to take it day by day. At least decorating would give her something to do and there was no rush, as she doubted she'd get many visitors. Her father? Her sister and her niece maybe? It had been years since she'd seen Jane at their mother's funeral, and they'd barely spoken after. It only hit her then that she'd neglected everyone she'd ever been close to. Wendy was registered as Riley's next of kin, and she'd been the one to get the call both times she'd been admitted to the hospital.

The shutters facing the backyard were open and she had to admit the view over Mystic River was spectacular. She could see the town and the harbor on the other side, and she imagined the evening light would be beautiful in summer. Still, she'd be here all alone. A small, anonymous speck on a huge plot of land along the riverbank.

Riley ran her hand over the thick, maroon-striped wallpaper and wedged a nail under a peeling seam. It came off easily as she pulled at it, and she groaned when she spotted another floral pattern underneath. This was going to take a while, but she had time. So much time.

4

QUINN

No one made risotto like her sister-in-law, and Quinn helped herself to more of the delicious, gooey rice dish generously filled with prawns and mussels. It was always fun to come here on the weekend, when the kids were home from school and the kitchen was noisy and chaotic.

"This is so good, Mary. Thank you."

"You're welcome. At least someone's grateful," Mary said, shooting her kids a warning look.

Quinn's six-year-old niece, Lila, and seven-year-old nephew, Tommy, were less enthusiastic about the food and were complaining they'd been promised pizza.

"I never promised you pizza," Mary said. "At no point have I said we were having pizza tonight. You're making it up."

Lila jutted out her bottom lip. "But we always have pizza on Saturday. It's a tradition."

Quinn, Mary, and Quinn's brother, Rob, couldn't help but laugh.

"A tradition, huh?" Quinn arched a brow at her niece. "Do you even know what that means?"

"It's when you have to eat pizza on the weekend," Lila said in all seriousness. She picked a mussel from her risotto and hid it in her napkin.

Quinn laughed. "How about I take you guys out for pizza tomorrow? We'll go to the harbor, just the three of us, and you can have any pizza you want." She looked up at Mary and Rob, whose eyes widened with excitement as they nodded.

"Yes!" Tommy was grinning from ear to ear. "Can we go see the boats first?"

"We certainly can."

"And can we go to the toy store?" Lila asked.

"Hey, don't push it now." Quinn ruffled a hand through her niece's hair. "Besides, it's Sunday tomorrow. The toy store will be closed." That was a little white lie, but it was the only excuse Lila would accept. "Now finish your food, otherwise we won't go for pizza. You have two minutes. Go."

That was enough for Lila and Tommy to start scooping big spoonfuls of risotto into their mouths, with Lila wincing after she swallowed a mussel by accident.

"Can you come for dinner more often?" Rob joked. "You really have a way with them."

"It's called bribery." Quinn winked. "It works every time."

"Bribery," Lila repeated.

"There you go. Another fancy word." Mary smiled when they showed off their empty bowls. "Well done. You can go and play now."

Quinn watched them in amusement as they sprinted out of the kitchen, racing each other for the TV remote, then turned back to her food. "You really need to teach me how to make this," she said, pointing to her bowl. "Or is it a secret Italian family recipe?"

"No secrets here. Come a bit earlier next time and we'll make it together." Mary poured them more wine and sat back, twirling the Malbec in her glass. "How was your day?"

"I worked this morning," Quinn said. "And I saw Lindsey by the drawbridge. She said she's sold Aster House."

"Oh? That's been on sale for a while, right?"

"Yeah. I was hoping it would stay like that." Quinn shrugged. "But it is what it is."

Rob stared at her. "Will you stop obsessing over that house? It's not in our family anymore and you haven't lived there for twenty-eight years. Most importantly, you'll never be able to buy it, so don't act like you have claim over it."

"You don't understand. You were too young to remember."

"It doesn't matter. It's in the past. Leave it be." Rob let out a sigh of frustration. "You need to move out of that tiny narrowboat and find yourself a decent place to live. There's no point waiting around until you'll finally be able to buy Aster House. You're thirty-eight. Don't you want a place of your own? You can't possibly bring women back where you're living now."

"Sure I can." Quinn smiled mischievously. "And I do. In fact, women find it charming."

"I can see that." Mary got up, took their bowls, and put them into the dishwasher. "I think there's something very cool about living on a boat. It's bohemian."

"There. See?" Quinn gestured to Mary as she turned to her brother. "Nothing wrong with my boat."

"But don't you want to settle down?" Rob asked. "Meet a nice woman and maybe even have kids?"

"I have yours to hang out with, don't I? All the fun and

zero responsibility. And when it comes to women, it's not like there's much choice around here." Quinn cleared the placemats and the cutlery. "I'm not in a rush, and I'm certainly not lonely."

"Another good point," Mary agreed, slamming the dishwasher door shut. "Now, how about I open another bottle of wine? Do you guys want to play a game? Go a little wild on Saturday night?" she joked. "No more talk about Aster House and Quinn's love life. I don't want the two of you to fall out again. It's boring."

Quinn laughed. "How about Jenga?" She loved Mary; she always took Quinn's side. They'd been close in high school, and even after Mary started dating Quinn's younger brother, they'd remained great friends. And now Mary was part of her family and she truly felt like a sister.

"Jenga it is." Mary stuck her head around the living room door and yelled, "Lila, Tommy! We're playing Jenga!"

5

RILEY

*H*ungry but feeling out of sorts and not in the mood to cook in her new kitchen, Riley drove into town, hoping to find a decent restaurant. The chances of finding a good sushi bar—or any sushi bar for that matter—in Mystic were zero, so she'd lowered her standards and settled for anything but fried food. She'd waited in front of the drawbridge for ten minutes while reminding herself that time did not equal money anymore. Time had taken on a different concept altogether. Instead of being valuable, it was her worst enemy, and she fought hard to keep her anxiety at bay. Too much time had given her more opportunity to think than she wished for, and already on her second day in Mystic, she felt gloomy at the conclusions she'd drawn. She'd been selfish. She'd been too caught up in work to think of anything but her company. She'd neglected her family and her old friends, and she had no other close connections. What she did have was a healthy bank account and a big fucking mansion that she hated, in a village where she felt completely out of touch with herself.

Riley hadn't slept much last night. Worrying about how

the new owners of her company would ruin everything she'd worked so hard for, she'd been tossing and turning for hours. Her thoughts made no sense; she'd received a generous payout and it wasn't her problem anymore, but it was hard to accept that she had nothing left to focus on. Her fragile mental state aside, the house was scary at night, and she'd gotten up five times to check if the front and back doors were locked as she kept hearing suspicious noises.

New York had felt like a safe haven compared to Aster House, even with police sirens raging on the streets below her penthouse. Her new home was quiet and noisy at the same time. The eerie silence outside freaked her out after living in a big city for so long, and the house creaked and whistled at night.

Looking at the restaurants along the harbor, Riley slowed down and parked her Mercedes. She didn't care if the food was mediocre; at least it was busy, and that was exactly what she needed right now. A crowd.

It was only five p.m., but the sun hung low over Mystic River as she challenged the wooden pier in her high heels, cursing herself for her choice of footwear. She kept getting stuck between the planks, so she headed into the first restaurant to save herself from an accident.

"Hello there. Welcome to Mystic Pizza," a friendly hostess said. "Do you have a reservation?"

"No. I was just walking past." Riley smiled at her. "Do you have a table for one?"

The hostess smiled back, but she was clearly confused. In New York, there was nothing strange about eating alone —Riley had eaten alone most nights, either in fancy restaurants or in smaller local places near her apartment—but perhaps they didn't get many lone diners here. Mystic was definitely a place where people came together. There were big groups, families, and couples, but she didn't spot a single solo diner.

"You're on your own?" The hostess glanced over the tables. "We're fully booked tonight, but I'm sure we can squeeze you in somewhere if you don't mind a small table."

"Thank you, that would be great." Riley couldn't remember the last time she'd had pizza, but it smelled amazing, and her stomach was rumbling. She waited while the hostess instructed one of the waiters to clear a table by a pillar that held menus and napkins. Within no time, they'd laid it out with a checked cloth, a placemat, cutlery, a candle, and a random fake succulent in a terracotta pot that had no place in an Italian restaurant.

"What can I get you to drink?" a waitress asked her once she was seated and offered her the menu, but Riley waved a hand.

"A red wine, please, and a bottle of sparkling water. And a pizza Margherita with chili oil on the side if you have that, a small green salad, and a portion of olives." She was used to ordering fast, eating fast, doing everything as efficiently as possible to save time, and she kept forgetting there was no point in doing that anymore. "I'm sorry," she added. "I'm not in a rush. I'm just hungry and I know what I want."

"No. That's totally fine." The waitress stared at her for a moment before she continued. "Any preference for red wine?"

Riley leaned back and tried her best to look relaxed. "The best you've got."

"Very well. Give me a minute and I'll be back with an excellent wine and your water." She rushed off nervously, and Riley wondered if she was giving off a bad vibe. She definitely didn't fit in here. Everyone was dressed casually, and she was still in her pantsuit and heels as if she'd come straight from the office. Her wardrobe was the first thing she'd have to change because she didn't own much other than formal attire, and she doubted there was a drycleaner in Mystic. What made her stand out most, though, was the fact that she was alone, and she felt slightly self-conscious as she glanced around the restaurant.

Riley had never been one to care what others thought of her, but now it seemed like all eyes were on her, curiously wondering what she was doing here. A woman with two young kids at a neighboring table kept looking at her; Riley was sure of it but pretended she hadn't noticed. Scruffy, shortish brown hair fell around the woman's face, framing sharp eyebrows and big, hazel eyes. *Curious villagers.* She'd expected Mystic to be an open-minded community since it was so close to New York and popular with tourists, but perhaps it was just like so many other American small towns; suspicious of strangers and protective of their space. The woman glanced at her phone and chuckled, then turned her attention back to her kids, who screeched in excitement when their enormous pizza arrived.

"Here you go." The waitress put down a glass of wine and her water.

"Thank you." Riley inhaled above her glass that was way too full and took a sip. "What is it?" She was used to tasting her wine before she accepted it, but that was clearly not a thing here.

"I think it's a pinot noir but I'm not sure. I have to check with the bar," the waitress said nervously.

Riley shook her head and forced another smile. "No need, it's fine." She had a feeling this was not the place to make a fuss.

6

QUINN

"So, what have you guys been up to today?" Quinn tapped the table and looked from Lila to Tommy and back, then laughed when they fired off at the same time.

"I went to Christina's house," Lila said. "And we dressed up and went into town in our fairy costumes. Christina's mom said we could keep them on while we got ice cream." She grinned widely, exposing her two missing front teeth.

"I went to baseball practice," Tommy shouted, making sure his voice was louder than his sister's. "And we lost, but our coach said it was okay and that we should focus on tomorrow."

Quinn laughed. "That's right. Keep practicing and focus on tomorrow." She turned to Lila. "And good for you, honey. Getting ice cream in a fairy costume sounds like great fun." A waiter brought over two big Cokes for the kids and a beer for Quinn, and as she thanked him, she spotted a woman being seated at the small table by the pillar. She was on her own and looked out of place with her black suit and dark, blow-dried hair that was styled to perfection as she ordered faster than the speed of light, confusing the waitress. She was attractive, for sure, but Riley already had an idea of who she might be and had no intention of going over there and welcoming her to Mystic. *How childish.* Yes, she was being childish, but this flashy New Yorker had just bought Aster House and Quinn was pretty sure she'd rip out all its beautiful imperfections until there was nothing left but a white, characterless carcass.

"Can we have ice cream?" Lila asked.

"I thought you already had ice cream today."

"I didn't," Tommy chipped in. "So, I'll have two and Lila can have one, and then we're even."

"No! That's not fair." Lila stuck her tongue out and was about to head into a tantrum, but Quinn intercepted.

"If you can manage to finish that big-ass pizza I just ordered, you can both have as much ice cream as you like, okay?" Quinn wasn't even making false promises; neither of the kids would be able to finish the biggest pizza on the menu and they'd soon be sleepy and ready to drive back home to bed. Her brother and Mary were on a date tonight, and she'd promised to put the kids to bed and stay there until they came home.

The woman looked up at her, and their eyes met for a moment. The woman's gaze was mildly accusing, as if Quinn were invading on her privacy, and she wondered what she was thinking. Even though she was pretty sure this was Riley Moore, there was no way Riley Moore knew who *she* was.

A message came in on her phone, and she picked it up to check it.

"Is that Mom?" Lila asked.

"No, honey, it's not." Riley chuckled when she read the message from Lindsey.

Sorry! I've been so busy that I completely forgot to fill you in on the details!! Yes, she's seriously hot (Miss Aster House), even by my straight standards. Very corporate though. Probably not your type and anyway, I doubt she swings that way.

The message was followed by a wink emoji and lots of hearts, and Riley turned her phone away from Lila, who was curiously glancing at her screen.

"Who's that?"

"It's Lindsey from the realtor's office. Remember my friend Lindsey? You met her a few times on my boat. We made cakes together."

Lila nodded and grinned again. "I like Lindsey. Daddy says you like her too."

"Oh, does he now?" Quinn arched a brow at her niece. "Of course I like Lindsey. She's a good friend. You like your friends, don't you?" Quinn couldn't help but wonder what kind of conversations took place in her brother's household. Just because she happened to have a close friend who was a woman didn't mean there was any romance between them, but Rob couldn't help himself.

Hot: agree. She's sitting right here, if she is who I think she is (at Mystic Pizza with the kids). And yes, not that I'm interested, but I doubt she swings my way. Drinks tomorrow?

Again, the woman looked at her, but then their larger-than-life pizza arrived, and the kids shrieked in excitement, distracting Quinn from the beautiful, unwelcome stranger.

"It's bigger than the moon!" Tommy said, attacking his side.

"It's bigger than Daddy!" Lila burst out in giggles and reached for the ketchup bottle on their table.

"Bigger than Daddy? Are you sure about that?" Quinn helped her with the ketchup, then handed the bottle to Tommy, who insisted on doing everything himself.

"Yeah." Lila stuffed a huge chunk of pizza into her

mouth and chewed while she stared at the lone stranger. "Aunt Quinn," she said through a mouthful. "That woman is alone. Can I ask if she wants to sit with us?"

"Shh... It's okay, Lila. Some people like to eat alone." Quinn kept her voice down, but the woman had heard them, so Quinn had no choice but to smile at her. "Sorry," she said. "Kids..."

"It's fine, don't worry." The woman turned to Lila. "I'm not lonely, sweetie. I'm just hungry, so I came in for a pizza." She laughed at Lila's full cheeks and ketchup-covered chin. "You certainly look hungry too."

"We're going to eat this whole pizza and then I'm having ice cream," Lila mumbled. "Do you want some pizza?" Quinn tapped Lila's thigh under the table, but Lila didn't get the hint. "You can sit with us."

Sweet, sweet Lila. Always looking out for other people. Quinn loved her heart of gold, but tonight, she wished her niece would concentrate on her food rather than on the woman she was trying to avoid.

"That's very sweet of you, but my food is coming." The woman sipped her red wine and turned to Quinn. "I'm Riley. I'm new to Mystic. I just moved here."

Quinn forced a smile. There was no reason to be rude after all. "Quinn. It's nice to meet you. And these little troublemakers are Lila and Tommy."

"You have wonderful kids."

"Oh, they're not mine. I'm their aunt. I'm just looking after them while their parents are having a date night." Quinn put an arm around them both. "But we like hanging out together, don't we, guys?" Lila and Tommy mumbled their agreement through mouths full of pizza. The woman was still looking at them and Quinn felt like she had to keep the conversation going, so she asked, "How are you liking Mystic?"

"It's very nice," Riley said, but Quinn was sure she detected a subtle flinch in her features. "Beautiful."

"Yes, it's a great place to live, and the community is very friendly." Riley's pizza arrived and Quinn welcomed the opportunity to end their conversation. "Well, enjoy your pizza. I'm sure we'll see each other around."

7

RILEY

*R*iley ripped off another strip of wallpaper before she stopped for a coffee break. One of the living room walls looked like it had been attacked by a tiger and she hadn't gotten very far since she'd started early this morning. In some places, the wallpaper came off easily, in others, it was stuck like there was superglue underneath. She needed some aggressive wallpaper remover and putty knives, which she should have gotten first thing anyway, she supposed, and she could do with a ladder too. She'd been nothing but efficient as a PR consultant, but home improvement was new to her, and she had no idea where to start. She could hire someone to renovate for her, of course, but then what would *she* do? Stand there and watch them work all day?

Staring at the scruffy wall, Riley hated the house even more now. It refused to let go of its layers, desperately clinging to the past. At night, it kept her up because it scared her, and in the day, it overwhelmed her so much she had trouble thinking straight. There was nothing in between.

In need of some fresh air, Riley went outside and sat on

her front steps while she searched for a hardware store nearby. She found one located in a retail park, a few miles from Mystic. She'd never been to a retail park before, but there were going to be many firsts if she'd be here for the foreseeable future, and besides, it would be nice to be among people as it was so quiet in the house. She thought of Quinn, the friendly woman she'd met in the restaurant last night, and regretted not extending their conversation. Making friends was an alien concept to her; she hadn't done that since college, but if she was starting over, it was time that she put herself out there and made some real connections. If she didn't, she might wilt away here and no one would notice.

The yard was begging for attention, and sitting there, looking out over the huge, overgrown lawn was intimidating. That was definitely a job for a professional; there was no way she could do that by herself. From the faint patterns in the tall grass, she could see there was a network of paths between the currently non-active fountains somewhere underneath, but it would be a huge job to groom it back to its original state. The surrounding hedges were getting too high, blocking out the sunlight in places. A piece of rope was hanging off a tree branch, a sad reminder of a swing that had once been there. It was all a bit sad, really, both inside and outside, and Aster House would never make her happy or even remotely relaxed unless it looked like a lived-in home. The backyard was even worse, but she imagined it would be beautiful when the trees and hedges were trimmed back, giving her an unobstructed view over the river.

After twenty minutes of contemplating what she needed for the living room, the shopping list she'd created on her phone was long and included stripper, paints, brushes, rollers, tools, buckets, steps, a ladder, trash bags, and other things such as cheap clothes she didn't mind getting paint on, sneakers, jeans, and some warm sweaters. Although the sun was warm in March, the evenings were still cold, and her designer trench coat and suits made her stand out too much when she went into town. She'd noticed the looks last night; the staff at the restaurant seemed intimidated by her, and she didn't want to feel out of place.

Again, her mind went back to Quinn. She hadn't asked nosey questions, something Riley had expected from towns-people. Weren't they all curious, eager to pass on informa-tion so they had something to talk about in a place where nothing ever happened?

Riley's thoughts were interrupted by her phone ringing, which had been a rare occurrence in the past days. Up until the last day of her handover, it had been ringing nonstop, and although it often annoyed her, she'd missed the sound of contact.

"Riley Moore speaking."

"Hi, Riley. It's Lindsey from Mystic Realtors."

"Oh, hi." Riley paused, confused as to why a realtor would call her. They tended to stay clear of buyers after their purchase in case they had something to complain about. Then a sudden thought filled her with hope. Perhaps the previous owners had changed their minds and wanted to buy it back from her. Maybe they missed the house and were willing to pay what she had paid, or more. That would be a godsend. "What can I do for you?"

"There's a meeting tomorrow, in the town hall. The Parks and Recreations department is presenting their plans for the summer season. Everyone is welcome, and there will be a Q and A and input session after. The invites were sent before you moved into Aster House, and I figured, since I'm the only one who had your number, I'd give you a call to let you know."

"Thank you, that's so kind of you," Riley said, trying to keep the disappointment out of her voice.

"No problem. It might be a good opportunity for you to meet some people." Lindsey hesitated. "How are you settling in?"

There. She'd asked the question. Frankly, it was unheard of, and Riley could hardly believe what she was hearing. Why was she so nice to her? "It's a big job," she said with a chuckle. "But I'm off to the hardware store and ready to get hands-on."

"That's the spirit. Well, good luck and I might see you tomorrow night."

"I'll be there. Oh, by the way, do you happen to know any good yard workers?"

"I'm not surprised you ask. I noticed it was quite over-grown." Lindsey laughed. "I do, actually. My nephew Gareth does yards. He's very young, and he only just started out, but he's got a few clients already and they seem happy with him. I'll send you his number, but if you'd prefer a professional company, I can recommend you some of those too."

"Gareth sounds great. I'll give him a call today." Riley smiled. "Thank you, Lindsey. You've been so sweet."

"Don't mention it. It's the way things work around here."

8

QUINN

*D*riving out of Groton Retail Park with a truck full of slate, Quinn narrowed her eyes as she spotted a woman trying to fit a ladder into her Mercedes. It stuck out of the trunk way too far to be anywhere near safe while driving, even though she'd secured it with ratchet straps.

She slowed down and planned on opening the window to warn the woman, then saw it was Riley, Aster House's new owner. *Fuck.* She drove on, glancing at her through the rearview mirror. Riley walked around her car, seemingly assessing the situation, then tugged at the ladder. It didn't look secure enough, and Quinn's conscience told her to turn around and go back. She wouldn't be able to live with herself if anything happened to Riley, and besides, there was no way she could avoid her in a small community like Mystic. That would make life terribly complicated. She parked her truck next to Riley's car and got out.

"Hey, there." Riley gave her a wide smile. "Quinn, right?"

"Yes. Nice to see you again." Quinn returned her smile, then pointed to the ladder. "You can't drive like that. It's not safe."

"They couldn't deliver this week, and I need a ladder or I'll get nothing done. It's only a short drive and I secured it, so it can't slip out the back. I'll be careful."

"But it could go through your windshield or worse—into your head if another car hits it from the side."

"Oh." Riley sighed. "I suppose you're right. I hadn't thought of that." She looked deflated as she stood there in a tight pencil skirt and white shirt, balancing on her ridiculously high heels.

Quinn's gaze lowered to her calves, and when she realized she was staring, she quickly looked up to meet Riley's eyes. That didn't help either; the woman was simply gorgeous. Her brown eyes had an intensity to them Quinn had rarely seen. Or maybe she was really stressed; it was hard to tell. "I'll take it back in my truck. I'm headed that way anyway."

"Really?" Riley let out a sigh of relief. "Thank you. That's very kind of you." She held her gaze and regarded Quinn. "Is everyone so nice in Mystic?"

"Not everyone." Quinn grinned. "But generally speaking, yes. It's a hell of a lot friendlier than New York."

"How do you know I'm from New York?"

Oops. Quinn felt busted. "People are nice, but they also talk. I'm close friends with Lindsey, the realtor. She told me you'd bought Aster House," she admitted as she unbuckled the ratchet straps and carefully pulled the ladder out of the car. "So I know where we're going."

"Oh, okay..." Riley helped her lift the ladder into the back of her truck. "Lindsey seems lovely. She invited me to the town hall meeting tomorrow. That was so thoughtful of her."

"Yes, she's a peach. Sorry about the gossip, though, but you might as well get used to it. It's rarely malicious."

Riley shook her head as she brushed her hands off on her skirt. "I don't mind. To be honest, I kind of expected it from a small town." She gestured to the truck. "Do you need the straps?"

"No, this will do." Quinn winked at Riley and got into her pickup. "I'll follow you so you can open the gates for me." She was in two minds as she started the engine. She'd be inside those gates again, and that caused a stir of excitement, yet she knew it was just some morbid way of torturing herself, like getting a whiff of a delicious cake she wasn't allowed to eat or crushing on a straight woman.

The road was quiet, and the drive back didn't allow much time to prepare herself for the nostalgia that hit her when she pulled into the driveway. The shutters of the living room windows were open, but the rest were still closed, and the paint on the front door was peeling, she saw, as she slammed the door of her pickup closed and looked up. The whole facade needed a new lick of paint and some TLC, but other than that it stood as sturdy and proud as ever.

"It's so big," Riley said with a sigh as she lifted the ladder out of Quinn's truck and leaned it against one of the porch pillars.

"Too big for you?"

"Honestly, yes. But it's my own fault. I should have viewed it before I bought it." Riley shrugged. "Anyway, it is what it is, and I'll make it work. It's not like I've got anything better to do than doing it up."

"You don't work?" Quinn asked.

"No. Not anymore." Riley didn't elaborate, so Quinn didn't inquire further. From the look on Riley's face, it was a touchy subject.

"Do you need some help with that other stuff in your

car?" she asked, noting bags were stacked up high on the back seat.

"I'll take care of it later, there's no rush." Riley's lips curled up into a smile. "Would you like to come in for a coffee?"

"A coffee?" Quinn stared at her as if she'd never heard the word before. She hadn't expected that question; not from a New Yorker. *Don't torture yourself.* "Sure," she heard herself say. "Let me take this in for you." She took the ladder while Riley opened the door, taking a deep breath before she entered.

The grand hallway hadn't changed much. The feature staircase still had its original red runner, and her grandmother's crystal chandelier, which had been too large to remove, was sparkling overhead. It looked empty and hollow, though, with the lack of basic furniture. There used to be coat stands by the door, a console with a big, gilded mirror against the left wall, and an antique bench next to a big statue of a tiger on the right side. She left the ladder there and followed Riley into the kitchen; here, too, things were pretty much the same.

"It needs updating," Riley said as she turned on her Nespresso coffee maker that stood out like a sore thumb against the original tile backsplash. "But the layout works, and I love the old stove, so I might keep that." She made a coffee for Quinn and put cream and sugar on the kitchen island.

"Are you planning on changing a lot?" Quinn asked.

"As much as I can. I'll hire professionals to do the big jobs, like renovating the kitchen and bathrooms and updating the heating system, but I'm planning on doing everything else myself with the help of YouTube and endless trial and error."

"That's brave."

"I just need something to do." Riley turned back to the coffee maker while she waited for her own cup to fill. "Shall we go into the living room? I don't have any furniture in here yet."

9

RILEY

Quinn was an inquisitive woman, that much was clear. She took in every nook and cranny of the house with intense interest, and even now that they were sitting on the sofas talking, she was still studying the wallpaper where Riley had started to remove it. Riley thought she was attractive but more in a handsome kind of way. Quinn had an androgynous quality to her that suited her. Her shaggy, brown hair was longer at the front and fell over one side of her forehead. She had a sculpted face, almost structural, with high cheekbones and a sharp jawline, and her tall, lean figure looked great in her tight jeans, gray T-shirt, and the denim shirt she wore open.

"So what do you do, Quinn?" she asked.

"I'm a contractor." Quinn smiled as she sipped her coffee, but she didn't seem entirely at ease. Perhaps the big house was as intimidating to her as it was to Riley. "My company does renovations, mostly in the area. I'm just finishing off a house along the river. That's what the slate in my pickup is for."

"Oh?" Riley's eyebrows shot up. "Would you be interested in doing some work here?"

Quinn hesitated, then shook her head. "No." She winced. "I mean, we're fully booked until fall, so I don't have time, I'm afraid. From what you told me, it's going to be a big job, so you'll need someone with long-term availability. I can give you some recommendations for tradespeople, though, if you want."

"Sure, that would be great." As Riley sat back and crossed her legs, she felt Quinn's eyes on them. Was she checking her out? She wasn't used to women looking at her like that. Was she gay? Riley suspected she was; she certainly got that vibe from her.

"Do you live here alone?" Quinn asked.

"Yes. It's just me." Riley pointed to the wall. "And as you can see, I'm new to home improvement, so any tips are welcome."

Quinn chuckled. "Yes, I figured as much. Are you planning on stripping all the walls?"

"I think so. I don't like wallpaper. Not this wallpaper anyway, or the one underneath. It's awful."

"Right."

Right? What did that mean? From the way Quinn said it, she sounded like she disagreed with her, and the smile had dropped from her face.

"Do you think paint would be a bad choice for the walls?" Riley asked, unsure why Quinn's mood suddenly seemed to have turned.

"No, not at all." Quinn held up a hand. "Sorry, I was lost in thought." She finished her coffee and got up. "How about we get the stuff from your car? I assume you bought some wallpaper remover?" She continued when Riley nodded. "I'll show you how to do it properly. It'll save you a lot of time."

"Oh, don't worry about it. You've done enough for me already and—"

"It won't take long," Quinn insisted. "That handiwork of yours is painful to look at. I can't let you continue like that." She lowered her gaze to Riley's feet. "And you might want to wear something other than those heels if you'll be going up and down a ladder."

"There you go. That's how you do it." Twenty minutes later, Quinn clapped her hands together as Riley came down the ladder with a huge chunk of wallpaper in her hand. "See? It's much easier like that."

"Thank you." Riley shuffled on the spot as she looked up at Quinn. She felt short and powerless without her heels, but the sneakers she'd bought were incredibly comfortable and a whole new sensation for her feet. "You have no idea how much you've helped me today."

"It's nothing," Quinn said. "You'll have this room stripped in no time." She checked her watch. "I should go. I have to be back on site. Good luck with everything."

"Thank you," Riley said again, then cleared her throat as Quinn left. "Wait... Can I cook you dinner sometime to thank you?"

Quinn buried her hands in her pockets and shrugged. "As I said, it's nothing, but I never say no to food."

"Great." Riley let out the breath she'd been holding. Why was it so scary to make new friends? She didn't know how to cook either, so how on earth had she come up with that idea? "Are you busy this week?"

"I'm doing long days while we wrap up our last week on the job, but I'm free on Thursday night."

"Okay. See you Thursday, then? Let's say, seven?" Riley cringed at the desperate undertone in her voice.

"That's perfect. I'll see you Thursday." Quinn gave her a smile and a salute and hopped into her truck, then beeped her horn twice before she drove off.

Riley watched her disappear behind the tall hedge and noted she felt a little more hopeful, now that she knew what she was doing with the walls. *What a nice woman.* She felt a strange pull toward Quinn, a desire to befriend her. Perhaps she was just clinging onto the first person she interacted with. After all, someone was better than no one.

10

QUINN

"*L*et's wrap up for today, guys." Quinn patted Ahbed, her electrician, on the shoulder. "The fixtures look great. Tidy job."

The master bath in the five-bedroom house was the last room to be renovated, and her team had worked nonstop over the afternoon to get the slate floor down. There was some tiling work left in the walk-in shower, and the new sink had to be installed, but they were on track to finish the job on time. The house looked beautiful, and Quinn was proud of her team. Her company was one of the few in the area that offered a full package of carpenters and roofers as well as plumbers and electricians, and that enabled her to be time efficient.

Danny, her carpenter, turned to her and stretched his back. "I never thought I'd say this, but I actually wouldn't mind continuing for a bit longer. If I go home now, my wife will want me to go to that town meeting with her." He sighed and shook his head. "They bore me to tears, those meetings. They're like sitting through a three-hour Christmas mass."

"Same here," Ahbed said. "I'll do anything to avoid them."

Quinn burst out in laughter. She'd had similar thoughts herself and loved using work as an excuse to get out of the long presentations followed by hours of bickering about entirely unimportant matters, such as the location of a swing in a new kids' playground or the exact time of a summer concert. "Then how about a beer in the sun?" She pointed through the window to the backyard on the river-side. "I have some in the cooler in my truck. They should still be cold."

"Sure, I'm in." Danny put his tools away.

Ahbed nodded. "Sounds great, boss. If you get the beers, we'll clear up."

Quinn headed for her truck and grabbed the cooler. Although she rarely drank on weekdays, she always carried a few beers with her, along with plenty of cold water. It was the perfect evening for a beer, with the sun hanging low and spring flowers in full bloom along the riverbank. She sat in the grass and leaned back on her elbows facing Mystic River with Aster House on the other side. The shutters were all open now, and she imagined Riley inside, tearing off the wallpaper Quinn's grandmother had chosen. Yes, it was dated, but that didn't make it any less painful to see it go.

Danny and Ahbed helped themselves to a beer and joined her.

"I heard some lady from New York moved here last week," Ahbed said. "Apparently, she bought that place." He pointed to Aster House. "Have you seen her?"

"Yeah, I met her," Quinn said. "She was trying to fit a trade-sized ladder into her Mercedes yesterday." She chuckled. "I was worried she might cause an accident, so I took it back for her."

"What's she doing with a ladder?"

"She's planning on doing a lot of the work on the house herself." Quinn shrugged. "From what I've seen, she has no idea what she's doing."

"You gave her your card, didn't you?" Danny asked. "She's going to need help, for sure."

"I told her she could call me," Quinn lied. She didn't want the men to know she'd declined a job. "But we're pretty fully booked for the coming months, so I doubt we'd even have time."

"I can always make time for more work," Danny said. "I've heard she's a stunner." He glanced at Quinn and arched a brow. "Is she?"

"Yes, she's attractive." Quinn gave him a nudge when he grinned. "Don't you get any ideas. She's straight."

"That's what they all say until they meet you," Ahbed joked. "Why do you think I've never introduced you to my wife?"

"Not funny." Quin rolled her eyes. "That literally only happened one time and it was years ago. I don't see why it needs to be a running joke." The men were referring to Rebecca, the local baker's wife. She and Quinn had had a brief affair and Quinn regretted ever getting involved with her because it had broken up Rebecca's marriage. They were caught, and their affair eventually fizzled out, but Rebecca had no intention of ever going back to men. She divorced her husband, met a woman online, and moved to New Orleans to be with her, leaving Martin, the baker, with a broken heart and Quinn without fresh bread for the rest of her life. Although she'd apologized to him many times and they were on polite terms again, she still avoided his shop, as neither of them liked to be reminded of what had happened.

"I'm afraid it will be a running joke until we find something else to joke about." Danny took a long gulp of his beer. "So, what's her husband like?"

"She's single, I think," Quinn said. "She lives there by herself, and she didn't mention a partner."

"Oh? That's unusual, don't you think?" Ahbed frowned. "Why would someone want to live there all by themselves?"

"Why not? It's a beautiful house." Even though she knew Ahbed had a point, Quinn always got defensive when it came to Aster House. "Don't tell me you believe those haunted stories."

"No. It just seems too big for one person, that's all."

"I believe them. I wouldn't sleep there alone," Danny chipped in. "No way." He narrowed his eyes at Quinn. "Didn't your grandparents live there?"

"Yes." That was the problem with living in a small community. Everyone knew everything about each other. "But that was a long time ago." Quinn didn't want to elaborate on how her family had lost it; it wasn't something she liked talking about. "I doubt the New Yorker will stay there very long. No one does."

11

RILEY

"You came," Lindsey said, joining Riley in the back of the town hall when they finally broke for coffee.

"Of course." Riley smiled. "That was an in-depth presentation." It was the best she could think of to say about it, because the two-hour slideshow had almost sent her to sleep twice, and her back was stiff from the uncomfortable folding chair.

"People here like to know exactly what's happening." Lindsey winked and lowered her voice. "Wait until they start quarrelling about who the new bench by the bridge should be dedicated to. That's the entertaining part and the only reason I'm here."

Riley laughed as she helped herself to a coffee. "In that case, I think I'll stay for part two."

"It's mainly the people on the first row who are highly opinionated," Lindsey said. "Sarah, the librarian, likes to think she's the voice of the town, but when it comes down to it, people rarely agree with her."

"Small-town politics, huh?"

"Exactly. You might as well get used to it." Lindsey reached for a chocolate chip cookie, broke it in half, and offered Riley the other half. It seemed like a strange thing to do, but not wanting to be rude, Riley took it. "Sorry. I always share sweet stuff. It's my way of cutting down on sugar. I usually share with my friend Quinn, but she's not here tonight."

"I met her, actually. She told me she was busy with work," Riley said.

"That'll be an excuse. She hates this kind of stuff. So, you've spoken to her?"

"Yes. She was kind enough to help me take a ladder back from the hardware store. I've invited her for dinner on Thursday. You're very welcome to join us." Riley chuckled. "I can't promise the food will be any good. I generally can't cook, but without tons of takeout places around here, I figured I need to practice my skills. Your husband is welcome too, of course, or your kids if you have any."

"How lovely of you." Lindsey seemed pleasantly surprised at her invitation, but she shook her head. "I'm single, no kids, and I'm sorry, but I'm busy on Thursday. We should definitely meet up some other time, though." She narrowed her eyes as she studied Riley. "What about you? Do you have anyone back in New York?"

"No. I was married a long time ago, and after my divorce, I was married to my job."

"I feel like that sometimes." Lindsey shrugged. "But hey, I love my job, so that's okay, and anyway, it's not like there's much choice of men here in Mystic. The good ones are taken, and the single ones are single for a reason."

"Dating in New York isn't much better," Riley said. "Everyone is out for themselves there." She hesitated. "And Quinn? Is she single?"

"Quinn?" Lindsey's eyes widened. "Are you into her?" she asked in a whisper. "If you are, you can tell me. I promise it will stay between us."

Riley's eyes widened, and she shook her head. "No, I'm not..." She hesitated. "Is Quinn...?"

"I'm so sorry." Lindsey slammed a hand in front of her mouth and giggled. "Yes, she's gay. I just figured you might be too since you asked."

"No, I'm not. I was just curious, that's all."

Lindsey winced. "I'm sorry, I—"

"Hey, it's fine. Don't worry about it." Riley wasn't surprised to hear Quinn was gay. Women didn't normally stare at her legs the way she did. "I was married to a man. We met in college and got hitched way too young. Long-term, it didn't work out because we were too different. He wanted a family, I wanted to build a career."

Lindsey nodded. "Can I ask you a personal question?"

"Sure."

"How does a New York career woman end up in Mystic? Do you have any ties to this town? Family?"

"No. I just randomly picked a place." Riley paused. She'd expected the question and she was aware her answer sounded ridiculous. "Actually, my assistant picked Mystic. I had to stop working for health reasons. The doctor told me to move somewhere with a slower pace of life, and this was close to New York, plus there's a hospital nearby with a great cardiology department."

"It's your heart? I'm so sorry to hear that." Lindsey rubbed her arm. "Are you going to be okay? Is it safe for you to live on your own?"

"If I take it easy, absolutely," Riley said with a smile. "I can do physical stuff, and I can even work out, as long as I avoid stress."

"Well, your assistant picked a good place. We all take care of each other around here, and with that house, you'll have your hands full, hopefully without too much stress."

"I used to work sixteen hours a day, so a bit of home improvement is nothing," Riley said with a brave face. In truth, the house depressed her to no end, but if she gave up on it now and sold it before she'd done it up, she risked losing a lot of money. She had a healthy bank account, but now that she wasn't working anymore, real estate was her security. She'd be stuck in Mystic for at least a year before she could sell it, and making the best of it was her only option.

"Ouch." Lindsey winced. "And I thought I was a workaholic." She waved at a few people who were making their way over to the coffee table. "Less work and more socializing it is, then. Let me introduce you to some friends."

12

QUINN

*C*lutching a bottle of red wine under her arm, a box of chocolates in one hand and a bunch of flowers in the other, Quinn headed up the steps to the front door of Aster House. Perhaps the flowers were a bit over the top, but she thought it might spruce up the place a little, and it wasn't like they were red roses. The bunch of rainbow alstroemeria came from the gas station she'd passed on her way here and weren't remotely romantic.

"Come in," Riley said, opening the door wide. "Aww, flowers. You didn't have to do that."

"Everyone needs flowers." Quinn handed them over along with the wine, followed Riley into the kitchen, and put the chocolates on the kitchen island. "You have a dining table." She was baffled to see how the kitchen had transformed. The new wooden table was laid out with a cloth and candles, and there was already a bouquet of roses next to the lilies on the worktop. A huge abstract painting covered most of the back wall, and there were navy curtains in the windows. With the lights dimmed, music playing, and a delicious smell coming from the oven, she would even go as far as to say it felt homey in here.

"Yes. It arrived this morning. I hope the chairs are safe to sit on because I assembled them myself." Riley chuckled as she put the flowers in a vase. "I thought we should eat here as it's the only part of the house that doesn't echo, and I'm sick of the sound of my own voice."

"I like what you did with it." Quinn looked her over. "You look different too. What happened to your suits?"

"Yeah...the suits." Riley laughed as she glanced at her jeans and sneakers. "They weren't very practical here, so I invested in a new wardrobe."

"You look nice. It suits you." Quinn's eyes lowered to the white shirt that was unbuttoned just far enough to show the edge of Riley's black, lace bra. Her dark hair was pulled up into a messy top-knot, and a few stray locks were loosely pulled behind her ears. She'd clearly tried to change her style, but she was still as elegant as before, with the fine silver necklace and diamond studs in her ears. "Not that the heels and skirt didn't suit you," she clumsily continued. "Those were great too. I mean...never mind." She shook her head and laughed. "Oh my God, I'm babbling, forgive me."

"It's fine. Thank you." Riley looked her over in return and smiled. "You look nice too."

"Thank you." Quinn blushed when their eyes met. She rarely found herself in the company of women as beautiful as Riley, and she couldn't help but stare. Riley's look was inquisitive, as if she was trying to figure her out.

Quinn had changed twice before she came here, and that was crazy. She didn't normally care all that much about how she looked, but apparently, she cared what this woman thought of her. Wearing jeans and sneakers herself, she'd swapped her white shirt for a gray sweatshirt as she didn't want to look too formal, and she was grateful she had or they'd look like twins. "Do you need help with the food?" she asked, filling the silence that was becoming somewhat awkward.

"I think I've got it under control." Riley opened the oven to check on her dish. "Only just. I have no idea how it will taste, so I got a couple of freezer pizzas in case I mess it up."

"It smells good."

"Cannelloni with ricotta and spinach, and my not-so-homemade tomato sauce. I figured stuffing pasta would be a safe option to start with." Riley bit her lip and grinned. "That, and Lindsey told me you like Italian food. I'm also aware that strategy might not work to my advantage, as you may have had a much better version of this dish before."

"I have had it before, but I'm sure it will be delicious." Quinn sat down when Riley gestured to the table. "Are you and Lindsey besties now?"

"I like her. I saw her last night at the town meeting." Riley opened the fridge and took out a bowl of salad, sprinkled some lemon juice and olive oil over it, and tossed it. "I invited her tonight, but she said she was busy."

"Okay." Quinn found it hard to believe Lindsey was busy, as she was usually curled up with her cat and a book at night, but she kept that to herself. "And how was the town meeting?"

Riley put the salad on the table and joined her with a humorous look on her face. "The first part was dreadfully boring," she said. "The second part was hugely entertaining."

"The Q and A part?" Quinn asked.

"Exactly. Wow, there were a lot of opinions on things I

really didn't think mattered. And I mean a lot. There was mainly disagreement, although in essence, they were all saying the same thing. It could have been easily solved with a small compromise, but I decided to stay out of it since I'm new here and I didn't want people to think I'm some pompous New Yorker who's come here to teach them how to make quick, democratic decisions."

"Oh yeah? Are you good at that? Maybe you should try your hand at politics."

"I've been told to steer away from leadership or stressful situations, so best not," Riley said. Quinn could tell she was putting on a brave face, as the humorous twinkle in her eyes was gone. She was still smiling though; a beautiful, wide smile that showed off her neat, white teeth.

"Your heart?"

"You spoke to Lindsey..." Riley opened the bottle of red wine on the table and poured them both a glass.

"Yeah, she filled me in. We speak almost every day. As I said, there's no malicious gossip, but I'm not going to sit here and pretend I don't know." Quinn decided it would be best to be honest. Against all odds, she liked Riley, and it was nice to have someone new to talk to.

"I appreciate that." Riley tilted her head, crossed her arms, and regarded her. "However, does that mean you'll call Lindsey tomorrow to tell her everything we've discussed tonight?"

"No," Quinn said resolutely. "Lindsey gossips, I don't. I might tell her we've had a lovely evening, but I'd never tell her anything about you personally."

"Are you sure about that?"

"I promise. As the only out gay woman in town, I've been the center of gossip too many times to take part in it myself, so no." She leaned in and lowered her voice to a whisper.

"And you already know I'm gay because you asked Lindsey about my love life."

"Oh." Riley winced. "Busted."

Quinn noticed Riley looked embarrassed, so she shot her a sweet smile. "It's okay, Riley. Everyone does it, and it's not a big deal."

13

RILEY

*H*er first home-cooked meal in two decades. Riley was proud of the mediocre dish she'd produced. It wasn't the best food she'd had, but it wasn't the worst either, and Quinn seemed to approve as she cleared her plate for the second time. She was enjoying the company and the strange new concept of cooking for someone in her home, and for the first time since she'd moved in, she didn't hate the house as much. Well, the kitchen, at least.

They'd talked about Mystic and their nonexistent love lives. Quinn had filled her in on her job and steered away from personal questions so far, which Riley appreciated, as it made the night all the more pleasant.

"So where does your love for Italian food come from?" she asked.

"My sister-in-law, Mary, is Italian. I have dinner with her, Rob—my brother—and the kids at least twice a week. Mary's taught me a thing or two about Italian cooking."

"Then I hope my humble dish was up to your standards.

"It was delicious. Thank you." Quinn took Riley's and

her own plate and cutlery and placed it in the sink, then started rinsing them.

"You don't have to do that. I'll clear up later," Riley said. Quinn clearly felt at home in her kitchen, which was nice but also a little strange.

"Sorry, I didn't mean to..." Quinn shrugged. "I was trying to help."

"And I'm grateful, but really, I don't have that much to do, so I'll take care of it." Riley held up the bottle. "Let's polish this off. Would you like another glass to go with those chocolates you brought? Chocolate and red wine are a combo made in heaven."

Quinn went back to the table and chuckled. "Thank you, but I still have to drive home, so I shouldn't."

"You can stay here if you want. My assistant made up two bedrooms before I moved in, so there's another bed waiting upstairs." Riley narrowed her eyes as she dug through her memory. "I think it's the first bedroom on the left." She waved a hand when it hit her that she might be overstepping. "Or don't. You don't know me, and that was a weird thing to propose. I apologize."

"Don't apologize. You apologize a lot."

"I don't know how this whole social thing works," Riley admitted.

"What? You didn't have friends in New York?"

Riley shook her head regretfully. She'd been here almost a week and she hadn't spoken to any of her team members. "No," she finally said. "I guess I didn't have real friends. I was close to my cleaner and my assistant, but as far as real two-way relationships go, I don't think I had any close friends." She felt a stab when a look of pity flashed across Quinn's face. "Not that I needed friends," she quickly added.

"I was a workaholic, which I'm sure you already know, as Lindsey filled you in."

"Yes, I know." Quinn smiled. "By the way, you're doing well with the social thing as you call it. I've had a great night." She glanced around the kitchen then up at the ceiling. "Do you mind if I have a look around?"

"Not at all. Want me to give you a tour?" Riley topped up her own glass and took it with her into the hallway. "You've seen this already," she said, opening the door to the living and dining room. "And you've seen this."

"You've stripped most of it." Quinn ran her hand over the wall, touching the snippets of leftover wallpaper as if they were precious paintings.

"I've been keeping busy." Riley ignored the rest of the living space; she didn't like to be there. "Let's go upstairs."

They went back into the hallway and headed up the wide staircase. "Everything is still in its original state up there," she said, slightly embarrassed about the dusty rooms. As I said, two beds are made, but that's about it."

"It's beautiful." Quinn looked around the square landing where three doors lay ahead of them and one on either side.

"I wouldn't call it beautiful. It's a bit of a dated mess, but I'll deal with it." Riley opened the first door, to her bedroom, which was the biggest one. Like the kitchen, it didn't look quite as depressing as the rest of the house, as it had been lived in. The antique dressing table held her makeup and accessories, and her new clothes were piled onto a chair next to the big, freestanding closet. Wendy had hung her New York living room curtains in here, which added a sense of security, but the gray fabric jarred with the floral wallpaper and the antique four-poster bed that the old owners had left behind. "This is my bedroom," she said, feeling like a stranger in the space. "Needless to say, everything needs updating."

"Why? It's nice." Quinn turned to her. "It breathes history. Don't you love that?"

"It's not my history." Riley arched a brow at her. "If you ask me, they're lucky I didn't sue them. There's a bunch of clutter the previous owners should have removed, and the only reason I didn't complain is because I need that stuff. It makes it less eerie and dampens noise. I'm terrified at night." She glanced at the yellowish paint that was plastered all over the doorframes and any other wood surface on display. "And my next step is to paint everything clean and white. That color is hideous. It looks like chain smokers lived here."

"So you're just going to erase all of it, are you?" Quinn's sharp voice echoed off her bedroom walls. "I knew it. You have no appreciation for this house whatsoever." She locked her eyes with Riley's, and there was anger in them.

"No...I didn't say that." Riley stared at her. "Why are you so passionate about this house? I'm sorry, but I feel like you're overreacting." Shocked that a woman who seemed totally chilled a few minutes ago was suddenly getting worked up about her choice of paint, she had no idea what to think of the situation. "It's my house. I can do whatever I want with it."

"You're right. It's your house." Quinn stepped out of the room and sighed as she shook her head. "I apologize, I didn't mean to be rude. It's probably best if I go now."

"Yeah." Still confused, Riley nodded. There was something strange about this woman, and she didn't like the awkward turn the night had taken. "I'll walk you out."

14

QUINN

Quinn felt deeply ashamed for snapping at Riley, and she cursed herself as she stepped onto her barge. She'd gone to Aster House with the intention of having a nice evening with a new friend, but instead, she'd gotten stuck in the past.

While they ate and talked, she could clearly picture her grandmother cooking in the kitchen and her grandfather sitting at the head of the table, reading his newspaper. The house smelled just like it used to, especially in the hallway, and the crystal chandelier still made the same, beautiful sound when the front door opened, causing the wind to hit the crystals. It had all come back tonight, the good and the bad. The summers she and Rob lived there while their parents worked long days at their restaurant. Happy memories of barbecues and games in the yard. The way her grandfather's walking stick tapped against the wooden floors when he came out of the bedroom in the morning, announcing a new day. Her grandmother humming her favorite tunes while she knitted in front of the fireplace. The presents her grandfather brought back from his business trips to Nevada, and his big, warm smile as he watched them unwrap their gifts.

And then, one summer, her grandfather stopped smiling. No one understood why until the bailiffs showed up on his doorstep. He'd developed a secret habit for gambling while he was away for business and built up a debt so big no one could save him from losing his beloved Aster House that his father had built. Their grandmother had no idea what he'd been up to in Nevada, and although their marriage survived, he never forgave himself and started drinking. Two years later, he died of a heart attack in their one-bedroom apartment.

Quinn's grandmother was in a home now and suffered from Alzheimer's. Quinn visited her once a week, and sometimes, when her grandmother fell back into the past, her face lit up as she talked about Aster House and those summers.

Riley's comment about the clutter had stung. Some of it was her grandparents' clutter, and to her, the few bits of furniture they'd left behind were special and belonged in the home her great-grandfather had built. Quinn used to lock herself in Riley's bedroom closet when she played hide-and-seek as a kid, and her grandmother had varnished the four-poster bed that Riley slept in. Her brother was right; she should stop obsessing over it, but he was seven years younger than her and had little recollection of how perfect Aster House used to be.

Quinn turned on the soft ceiling light, put the kettle on the stove, and sat back on the sofa next to the kitchen unit while she waited for the water to boil. The barge was small, and there was little space for storage, but she liked waking up to the view of Mystic River and the sound of people on the pier. Over the years, she'd learn to live with little and use her space in a smart way. An old chest that held her books served as a coffee table, and her clothes were stored in the drawers under her bed. Her shoes were in cubbyholes underneath the floor, and even her pans had removable handles so she could fit them into the small kitchen cupboard.

"Quinn?"

Quinn looked up find Lindsey in front of the window. "Hey. What are you doing here?" She frowned as she opened the door for her.

"I was crossing the bridge and saw the light was on, so I came to see how your date went." Lindsey got up, brushed off her jeans and stepped inside.

"It wasn't a date. You very well know that."

"It was sort-of a date, wasn't it? She said she was cooking for you." As usual, Lindsey made herself at home. She grabbed two mugs and added tea bags and hot water, then scooped a generous amount of sugar into hers. "Well?" She turned to Quinn and her smile dropped when she saw her expression. "Hey, are you okay?"

"Not really. I messed up."

"Oh?" Lindsey pursed her lips as she stared at her. "What did you do? You didn't get emotional about the house, did you?" She sighed when Quinn didn't answer. "Okay. Seriously, Quinn. You need to get over it, it's her house."

"I know. I'll apologize."

"I have her number if you want it? You could send her a message."

Quinn shook her head. "I'd rather do it in person." She covered her face with her hands and groaned. "God, I'm such an idiot. We were having a really nice time, but then she gave me a tour of the house, and I didn't like the way she talked about my grandparents' stuff, so I snapped and told her she had no appreciation for history."

"And you didn't tell her you used to live there?"

"No."

Lindsey nodded. "Look, I'm going to be very frank with you. Aster House is just a house, yet you've devoted your life to getting it back. It's not healthy. Who says having the house back in your family will make your life complete?" She glanced around Quinn's tiny living space, then peered out of the window. "Do you even realize the only reason you're living on a narrowboat is so that you can look at that damn house twenty-four seven?"

"That's not the reason," Quinn protested. "I like my narrowboat and being on the water."

"Come on, Quinn. There are plenty of spaces to moor a narrowboat in Mystic, yet you chose the most expensive spot on the pier, and it happens to be opposite Aster House. Coincidence? I don't think so."

Quinn didn't have the energy to argue with her, so she ignored the comment. "I'll apologize in person tomorrow."

"You should. Riley's super nice. I'm sure she'll understand." Lindsey opened the kitchen cupboard, got on her tiptoes, and glanced inside.

"Nothing sweet there, I'm afraid." Quinn said, suspecting she was looking for cookies.

"Nothing? How can you not have cookies?"

"You didn't exactly announce your arrival, cookie-monster."

"Fair enough." Lindsey leaned against the counter, blew on her tea, and took a careful sip. "Take her cookies. They're generally the solution to all problems." She grinned. "And while you're at the store, get some for me too."

"Sure." Quinn rolled her eyes. "By the way, why didn't you come tonight? Riley told me she'd invited you too."

"For the obvious reason. I wanted to give you guys privacy."

"Why? Riley's not even gay."

"True. But you're attracted to her, right? And we all know you have a talent for turning straight women. You might have a chance."

"Not that again. I wish everyone would just forget about the Rebecca situation."

"It's not just Rebecca. There was the tourist who rented one of the river houses a few years ago, and that rich lady who moors her boat here every summer," Lindsey said in a teasing tone. "Come on. Just admit it. You're into straight women and you've got the hots for the fancy New Yorker."

"I do not. I was just being nice and thought she could do with a friend," Quinn shot back at her. "She seems lonely."

"Riley seems fine to me. She was really social at the town meeting. I'm sure she'll make friends in no time."

"Hmm..." Quinn let it slide because even though Riley did seem lonely to her, Lindsey was right with her teasing comments. Deep down, she wasn't after friendship. She felt attracted to Riley, and that could only lead to trouble.

15

RILEY

*T*he house was creaking and howling, and Riley had trouble sleeping again. It wasn't just the noise keeping her awake; she'd replayed her last exchange with Quinn over and over, and she couldn't work out why she'd gotten so upset, especially after such a fun night. It wasn't like Riley was going to bulldozer the place—she didn't even plan on changing the layout—and anyone could see the property was dated and needed modernizing.

She regretted not asking Quinn to stay and talk about it. Quinn was one of the few people who had made Riley feel a little more comfortable in Mystic, and she'd hoped they could become friends. Would anyone else in Mystic have a problem with her renovations? Would she now become the most hated person in this little town?

A bang made her shoot up in bed, and she slammed a hand in front of her mouth to stop herself from screaming. She suspected it was one of the doors slamming, caused by the draft from a window she'd left open. That was likely, as she'd been airing the house since she moved in, but she was still shaking on her legs as she quietly snuck out of her room. Standing frozen on the landing, she held her breath as she waited for the banging to continue. It was dark and chilly, but she was too scared to turn on the lights. What if it was a burglar? Could they see her? Was she being watched?

One of the bedroom doors blew open and loudly slammed shut, and Riley's heart was beating wildly as she walked in and turned on the light. Relieved to see her suspicions confirmed, she rushed over to the open window and closed it before it caused her another fright, then let out a long breath as she steadied herself against the wall. *There's no one here, and there's no such thing as ghosts.* Needing distraction and time to recompose, she focused on the room.

It was one of the smaller bedrooms that she'd barely taken a good look at, having decided to concentrate on one space at the time to make the renovation project more manageable. Small wasn't the right way to describe it, though; it was still bigger than her old bedroom in New York. She grimaced as she took in the dark, floral wallpaper for the second time since she'd moved in. It had faded over time, and she could see darker pattern where the bed had been. There was no furniture here, and instead of the ugly carpet she planned on removing from all the other rooms, this one had a wooden floor that creaked under her feet. Perhaps the previous owners hadn't used this space. Riley certainly had no idea what to do with it. A gym? It wouldn't be a bad idea to start working out, now that she had the time, but she preferred the idea of running outside, along the river. A walk-in closet? She didn't have enough clothes and shoes to fill half of it. No. Maybe it was best to keep it as a bedroom; otherwise, the en-suite bathroom would be a wasted space.

Riley wondered if Aster House had ever been used as a guesthouse, as it was perfect for that purpose. All rooms had private bathrooms, the living room had a big dining area, and the yard was huge with plenty of space for parking. The fact that it was on the river was another bonus; people could arrive by boat as well as by car, and the river might even be suitable for swimming. She contemplated that idea and tried to imagine the room done up to hotel standards, with a comfortable king-size bed, hanging closets, and a seating nook by the window. It would look great with heavy drapes, a beautiful rug, and some art on the walls.

That idea distracted her from her fear, so she focused on it. Mystic was popular with tourists, and there was only one hotel in town. She could always rent out rooms in summer; it would be nice to have other people in the house, especially at night. Riley couldn't picture herself working in hospitality, but perhaps it was worth a try. It would give her the focus she so desperately needed, as well as an income. Her savings wouldn't last forever, and at some point, she had to think about her future and come up with a way to generate income. It had to be something that didn't require too much of her time and energy and, most importantly, wouldn't cause her stress. One thing was clear: her current situation wasn't healthy because her fear and anxiety that rose after sunset reached alarming levels, and that was bad for her heart.

Her mind consumed with ideas, she inspected the door that failed to fall into the lock. She'd have to fix that tomorrow or there would undoubtedly be more banging. As she ran a hand down the doorframe, she felt ridges and leaned in to see what they were. Someone had carved into the frame at different heights, and although layers of paint had filled them in over time, she could still make out some of the dates next to them. This had been a children's room, she realized, and the ridges and dates indicated their height at certain dates that she couldn't read through the paint.

Even though it was completely plausible that many children had lived in Aster House, it still caused a chill to run down her spine. Riley had no problem with children; in fact, she took great pleasure in being in their presence, and she loved their energy and spontaneity. However, now living in a big, old house, she was half expecting to hear a child giggle or see a small figure in a white nightgown appear in one of the many dark corners.

There was a strange creaking noise nearby that caused the hairs on her arms to rise, and she rushed back to her bedroom, closed the door behind her and turned on all lights. Slipping under the covers, she pulled them up to her chin and lay still. Her eyes were wide open, darting around the room while clammy sweat seeped from her pores. Tormented by irrational thoughts, she'd never missed New York as much as she did tonight, and she'd do anything for the sound of sirens or club music. The creaking noise continued steadily as if Aster house was deliberately punishing her for stripping it. It was not her friend, and it never would be.

Minutes passed, and knowing she wouldn't sleep, Riley turned on the TV on the console at the end of her bed, then went over to her door to check if she'd locked it properly. Scrolling through the channels, she found an old comedy from the nineties and tried her best to concentrate on the mediocre storyline. She had to find a way to get through the nights or there was no way she could stay here.

16

QUINN

"Hi." Quinn lingered on the doorstep, wishing she'd prepared her speech as she didn't know what to say. Riley looked surprised to see her and had opened the door with a screwdriver in her hand. She was wearing shorts and a tank top, and her bare legs were terribly distracting; Quinn fought to keep her eyes fixed above her shoulders. "Are you going to stab me with that?" she joked, gesturing to the screwdriver. "Because I deserve that."

Riley chuckled and lowered it. "No. I was just trying to fix one of the doors upstairs. It won't fall into the lock properly." She pointed to the flowers Quinn was holding. "Are those for me? Because I deserve them," she shot back at her.

"Yeah, you do. I came to apologize for last night." Quinn winced. "I'm so, so sorry. I never get angry, and it wasn't personal. Well, it was personal," she corrected herself. "Personal to me. Will you please let me explain?"

Riley hesitated for a moment, then nodded and opened the door farther. "Would you like a coffee?"

"I'd love a coffee if I'm not interrupting. I could repair

the door for you?"

At that, Riley smiled. "Why don't you teach me about locks? I need to get better at this stuff, and so far, YouTube has been of no use." She swapped the screwdriver for the flowers and took them into the kitchen. "Thank you. They're beautiful." At the lack of another vase, she used a jug and put them next to the other two bunches on the dining table. "Coffee first?"

"Let's get that door out of the way. I'm sure it won't take long." Quinn was relieved Riley didn't seem angry. "Which one?"

"Upstairs." Riley walked ahead of her up the stairs and Quinn stared at her behind. It was impossible not to look; Riley had a fantastic figure. Feminine, with modest curves in all the right places. Quinn was a sucker for a nice ass and could have happily walked up ten flights of stairs behind her. "It's this one."

"Okay." Quinn swallowed hard as she stared at the open door to her old bedroom, then took a deep breath and told herself not to get sentimental. She checked the handle and poked the lock. "The latch isn't falling into the hole."

"I already established that," Riley said humorously.

Quinn arched a brow as she turned to her. "Don't get cheeky with me now. Watch and learn."

"Sure, boss. You have my full attention." Riley's eyes lingered on hers for a long moment before she averted her gaze with a subtle flinch. Was Quinn mistaken or was there a hint of flirtation there?

"That's what I like to hear," she said, shaking off that thought. There was no way Riley would flirt with her; it made no sense. She opened and closed the door a few times. "The latch is too low. See how it doesn't fall into the middle of the strike plate but slightly below?" She held her breath when Riley leaned in so close that their cheeks almost touched.

"Yes."

"We need to reposition the strike plate, so the latch falls into the middle. Solutions are often simple. It's all about analyzing the problem."

Riley looked a little flustered as she straightened herself. "Does that mean someone did a bad job at installing it?"

"Exactly. They didn't measure it properly." Quinn tapped the handle. "See this system? It looks brand new. My guess is the previous owners did it themselves as a quick fix before they put the house on the market." She handed Riley the screwdriver. "If you screw off the latch and measure how much higher it needs to go, I'll go get my electric screwdriver from the truck to put it back on."

By the time Quinn returned, Riley had already done what she'd asked her to do and carved a line a quarter of an inch higher. "Perfect. Have you ever used one of these?" She held up the small, wireless screwdriver.

"No. Is it dangerous?"

Quinn laughed and shook her head. "Far from. I'll hold the latch while you screw it on. Just position it on the screw and press the button, that's all there is to it."

Riley didn't look too sure of herself as she did so, and it was kind of adorable how she seemed terrified of a user-friendly household screwdriver even kids would be fine with. When the screw went in, her eyes widened, and she gasped. "It works!"

"Of course it works." Quinn stepped back. "You can do the others yourself now, as long as you hold it in place."

"I love this thing," Riley said as she fixed the last screw. "It's so quick and easy. I must get one."

"You did great. Now try to close the door."

Riley pumped her fist when the door fell into the lock, and to Quinn's surprise, she hugged her. "Thank you! This was so much fun."

"Fun?" Quinn's heart did a little jump when she felt Riley's breasts pressed against her chest. Yes, it was most certainly fun, especially this part.

Riley opened and closed the door again a few times, observing the basic mechanism that was clearly a miracle to her. Then she ran her hand over the doorframe, pointing out the carved ridges. "Now that you're here, I might as well take advantage of your expertise. Can I use wood filler for this?" she asked. "Or should I sand it down and repaint it? It doesn't look terrible, but I like things to be smooth."

Quinn smiled sadly as she caressed the ridges. *Happy birthday, Quinnie. Let's see how much you've grown in a year.* Her grandfather's voice echoed through her mind. It was their birthday tradition, as she was always with her grandparents on August first. He'd made it so much fun for her that she didn't even care that her parents were hardly ever there on her special day.

"Quinn? Are you okay?"

Riley's voice pulled Quinn out of her memory. "Yeah." She sighed and bent down to scrape off some of the paint with the screwdriver. "They're not deep, so sanding would be best." There it was; her name.

Riley followed her gaze and bent down to read it. "Quinn, August first, 1999." She looked from Quinn to the doorframe and back and frowned. "You?" she asked.

"Yeah." Quinn pointed to the top ridge. "This was my last birthday here. I was fourteen."

A long silence followed as Riley studied her with intense curiosity. Then she frowned and cleared her throat. "I think we should have that coffee now."

17

RILEY

"Your great-grandfather built this house?" Riley sat back and blew out her cheeks. "Wow. No wonder you were a bit touchy about my clumsy home improvements."

"No. I had no right to be precious about it. It's your house."

Riley nodded. "Still, it must be difficult to see someone else move in here."

"You're not the first to move into Aster House after my grandfather lost it. I got used to it over the years. The only difference is that you're the first new owner to invite me in, so it all came back."

"Where were your parents?" Riley asked as she handed Quinn her second coffee.

"They ran a big, popular restaurant in town, and they were so busy over the summer months and didn't have much time for us, so Rob and I moved in with our grandparents. We saw Mom and Dad, of course, but our life was here from early April until late September."

"And are they still in the restaurant business?" Riley bit

her lip and waved a hand. "Please tell me if I'm being too nosey."

"No, it's fine." Quinn paused, wondering how much to share. But what did it really matter? It was in the past. "The restaurant was called The Harbor House. It's still in business, just under new ownership. My grandfather owned the building, so when he lost Aster House in his bankruptcy, my parents lost the restaurant too. They eventually got a loan to start a new, much smaller restaurant, and they're retired now, but times were really tough for a while."

"Are they here, in Mystic?" Riley asked.

"They moved to Groton, as the rent was cheaper there, but they're not far and I see them regularly. My grandmother is there too, in a home."

"And your grandfather?"

"He went downhill after the truth about his gambling came out. He drank too much and isolated himself, even from my grandmother, and he died of a heart attack a few years later."

"I'm so sorry to hear that. From what you've told me, you were very close to him." Riley reached over the table and squeezed her hand. Quinn's story was a shocking revelation and her reaction last night made so much sense now. "And then some stranger from New York bought Aster House and complained about how terrible it looked."

"Something like that." Quinn looked around the kitchen. "But you're right. It does need updating." She reached into her back pocket and handed Riley a business card. "Here's my number. Call me if you need help or advice, anytime. I know I said I was busy, but we can always squeeze in a few jobs here and there, and my people are excellent."

"Thanks, but I won't bother you. If it's hard for you to be here, then—"

"Please. I mean it. Change is good, and the more I come here and see things change, the better." Realizing she'd been here longer than she planned, Quinn got up. "I need to get to work but I'd love to cook for you in my humble abode.

"I'd love that."

"Great. How about Sunday? If you're okay with small spaces," Quin added with a wink.

"Unless you live in a coffin or an elevator, I don't see how I could get claustrophobic in your home," Riley said with a chuckle as she followed her to the front door. "Message me the address, I'll be there." She closed the door, then sighed as she leaned back against it, relieved that she and Quinn were okay again. For some reason, it mattered what Quinn thought of her. Riley liked her very much, and she felt a strange kind of attraction to her that left her almost as shaken as Quinn's story had.

It was a sensation she hadn't felt in years, a tingle low in her belly. Was it because she had too much time on her hands to think? Had her mind been with her new friend simply because there wasn't much else going on in her life, or did she really feel a hint of attraction there? Was it because she'd noticed Quinn checking her out a few times and she liked the idea of being desired again? It was probably a combination of all those factors, and she had to be careful not to stare at her again, like she had today when they were repairing the door. Quinn was attractive in every sense. Her eyes were mesmerizing, and her messy hair and the way she carried herself held a charming carelessness. She was kind, funny, strong, and capable, and Riley imagined she had a way with women. Her thoughts drifted to Quinn wearing a tool belt and checked flannels over those tight jeans before a vision of her in nothing but a tool belt manifested.

God, what am I doing? She'd never felt attraction toward a woman, but truthfully, she hadn't been all that attracted to men either. After years of mediocre dates and equally mediocre sex, she'd given up on it altogether and decided her vibrator and her job were enough to keep her satisfied. Maybe she just hadn't met the right man. Maybe she should try one of those dating apps everyone was on. It wouldn't harm her to see what the area had to offer, and at worst, she might end up with some new friends.

Not yet, she told herself. First things first. She wouldn't be able to focus on anything until those awful living room walls were white and spotless, and she was itching to get it out of the way. Heading there, she opened the large tub of white paint, poured some into a tray, then rolled her paint roller through it. She hated the carpet, so she didn't bother covering anything up. Ripping it out would be the next big job.

Carefully rolling the paint onto the wall, she marveled at how satisfying it was to see the now brown and patchy wall turn spotless, and as she continued until the white area was large enough to give her an idea of the finished effect, she found herself rather enjoying the job. Quinn would hate the white, but this wasn't her house, and the only way of making living here bearable was to erase anything that could possibly scare her.

18

QUINN

"I told her everything." Quinn took her grandmother's frail hand in her own and kissed it. "Well, not everything, off course, but the general story. The new owner's called Riley, and she's nice. I invited her over for dinner on Sunday."

Her grandmother smiled at her, and for a moment Quinn was convinced she understood what she was telling her. "What was her name again?"

"Riley," Quinn said, returning her smile.

"No, I don't think that's right." Her grandmother turned to the window and narrowed her eyes as she dug through her memory. "Her name was Dorothy. That was her name," she said triumphantly.

"No, Grandma. That's *your* name. You're Dorothy." Quinn stroked her hand. It was difficult when she got her hopes up because her grandmother still had the occasional bright moments in which she recognized Quinn and remembered things.

"Oh. I suppose you're right." From the way her smile

73

dropped, the confusion was clearly causing her stress, so Quinn tried to distract her.

"How about we go outside to get some fresh air? It's a beautiful day. Would you like that?" Without waiting for an answer, she grabbed a blanket from the couch and put it over her grandmother's lap, then steered the wheelchair toward the exit. "See? Sunshine. Isn't that nice?" she asked, steering her over the path that ran through the yard. It was a decent home, with plenty of outside space and a communal living area where the staff organized music, movie, and game nights, and Quinn felt comfortable with her living there. "Not long until summer now. I can't wait to swim in the river again."

"Yes, it's a lovely day." Her grandmother raised her face toward the sky and closed her eyes. When she opened them again, Quinn knew she was lost in the past. She recognized that faraway look, but more often than not, they were good memories that drew her back decades. "Where are we?" she asked. "I need to get home to prepare dinner. My husband will be home soon. He's been away for business."

"You must miss him when he's away," Quinn said, playing along while avoiding the question. "What does he do?"

"He's an investor," her grandmother said proudly. "He owns hotels and restaurants, both in Mystic and in Nevada." She hesitated. "Are we in Mystic? I don't recognize this park and I need to get home. I live in Aster House—you might have heard of it. Can you take me there?"

"Yes, we're in Mystic," Quinn lied. "And I can take you home to Aster House, but it's still early, so we don't need to go back just yet. We could feed the ducks. I have some old bread with me."

"All right. Let's feed the birds," her grandmother said.

She turned to look at Quinn. "You're a nice young lady. What's your name?"

"Quinn."

"Quinn..." she repeated. "That sounds familiar." It was somewhere in the back of her subconscious, but she was currently stuck in a time before Quinn was born. Quinn had learned the hard way that it was a bad idea to try to bring her back to the present. It rarely worked and only caused unnecessary confusion.

"We may have met before," she said, handing her grandmother the paper bag with bread. She parked her by the fountain and sat on the edge while she watched the old woman tear off chunks for the ducks and throw them in their direction. "What are you cooking tonight?"

"I'm cooking Arnold's favorite. Golden pork chops and cherry pie. He loves my cherry pie, but he's got to watch his waistline, so nowadays, I only make it on the weekend." Her grandmother looked at her. "You should come too. What was your name again?"

"Quinn." Quinn smiled. "Thank you for the offer. That's very kind of you, but I have to go back to work." She checked her watch and noted she still had a good twenty minutes left before her team would be back on site. She, her brother, and their parents took turns visiting her grandmother, so she had company three days a week. It never felt like a chore, but sometimes it was difficult when she was having a bad day. Today, though, was pleasant, and she was enjoying small talk with the lovely lady who currently had no idea who she was.

"Nonsense. It's Sunday. No one works on a Sunday."

Quinn didn't have the heart to tell her it was Friday, so she nodded. "You're right. I guess I was confused."

"That's okay, sweetheart. We all get confused sometimes. Did you go to church this morning?"

"No, I didn't because I forgot it was Sunday," Quinn said and chuckled when her grandmother burst out in laughter. "Did *you*?"

"Of course. Can't you see I'm wearing my Sunday best?"

"You look beautiful."

Her grandmother looked Quinn up and down, and her eyes settled on her hair. "Why is your hair short? Did you have lice? You know, there are remedies for that nowadays."

Now it was Quinn's time to laugh. "No," she said, shaking her head. "I just like it like this."

"Forgive me for saying this, but it's not very ladylike, and there's only a certain type of women who wear their hair like that. What does your husband think of it?" Her grandmother threw the last piece of bread into the fountain.

"I don't have a husband." Quinn wondered if her grandmother ever knew she was gay. She'd never told her, but she must have suspected she had no interest in men, as she'd stopped asking about boyfriends when Quinn was around seventeen. She certainly couldn't tell her now; the woman was stuck in the sixties and wouldn't understand. "Perhaps you know of some handsome, single men?"

"I sure do, but you'll have to grow that hair out before I introduce you." Her grandmother winked, and she had a wonderful, humorous twinkle in her eyes.

"That sounds like a plan." Quinn tucked the blanket tighter around her when she saw her shiver. "Are you cold? Shall we get you inside?"

"Yes, I'm a little chilly."

Waiting for the usual protest, Quinn was surprised to see her nod off as she wheeled her back to the home. That was nice for a change, as she didn't have to hand her grandmother over to the staff in a state of distress. Today had been a good day, and she was grateful for that.

19

RILEY

*S*itting at the kitchen table with a glass of red wine, Riley downloaded the first dating app that showed up in the long list of options on her phone. Still not used to her huge living room, she preferred the smallest space in the house where she felt comfortable and safe. She'd managed to make a pot of chicken soup that was bubbling away on the stove and was feeling rather smug with her accomplishments of the day. The living room walls were covered in a fresh lick of paint—she could apply the second coat tomorrow—and the door was repaired, so that was another win.

And now she was about to create an online profile after making chicken soup. What a change from her former life. Did she enjoy it? Not really. Not yet at least, but all in all, she felt a little more optimistic than she had when she'd arrived last week.

Riley thought about her profile name, and the first thing that sprang to mind was *Aster*. It was taken, so she changed it to *Aster1*, which included her house number, then searched through her photographs of a picture of herself.

Sadly, she didn't have any recent pictures of herself as she hadn't been social at all. Her only one was from years ago, and it was one of her and her sister together. She stared at the photograph, suddenly missing Lynn, and she made a mental note to call her soon. The picture was taken on one of Lynn's rare trips to New York, in a restaurant. She remembered that day well; she'd been stuck in her office until seven p.m. and had been an hour late for dinner. That was incredibly rude, she realized now. As Riley never came to Florida, Lynn visited her every so often, and when she was there, they always had fun together. It scared her to contact Lynn after being silent for so long. She'd never made much of an effort with her niece, who was six now, and she felt ashamed for not even remembering to send anything other than Christmas and birthday presents that her assistant chose.

Giving up on her search, Riley took the first selfie ever. Well, she snapped about fifty because it took a while to figure out what her best angle was and how to smile without looking weird and uncomfortable, like someone was holding a gun to her head. Was it a bad idea to put her real picture on there? What if someone she knew recognized her? Did people in Mystic use the app? Unlikely. It was such a small community that it would be embarrassing for them to see each other on there, right? Hoping she wasn't wrong, Riley chose one of her selfies and uploaded it, ignoring the request for three others.

"Age and profession," she mumbled when she skipped to the next section. *Forty and unemployed.* That didn't sound good. Could she say she was retired? That wasn't entirely true; she still needed to do some kind of work, even if it was investment based, and that didn't sound remotely interesting enough. *Renovations,* she typed, as again, it was the first thing that sprang to mind. The next page was about interests, but she didn't really have any. Her company had always been her life and her passion, and she couldn't think of a single thing that made her happy apart from that. Staring at the pot of chicken soup, she typed *cooking* and felt like a charlatan when she added *home improvement* and *family*.

Hoping she was done, Riley sighed when another question popped up. *What kind of music do you like?* She groaned and wanted to throw her phone across the kitchen. They were mean questions that didn't do people like her any good. They made her feel inadequate and robotic, like she wasn't a real person if she couldn't answer them. Randomly selecting a few genres, she was relieved to see the message, *Congratulations! You've now set up your profile. Just a few more steps.*

"Thank God," she muttered under her breath. The only thing left to do was to choose her radius, which she set to within twenty miles of Mystic, and her sexual preference. She selected "men," then hovered over the "women" and "both" options. *What am I doing?* She frowned as she felt a hint of excitement. The subtle tingle in her belly made her pause, and she put her phone down and topped up her wine. Taking long sips, she stared at her screen while she tried to analyze what was going on. Why was she even considering women? Was it because of Quinn? Was she suddenly feeling adventurous in her new life stage? The answer had been straightforward before, but she wasn't so sure anymore. *Men. Women. Both. Come on, Riley. It's a simple question.*

What if she checked the "both" box? That meant she could look at female profiles and get an idea of what kind of women were on there. If she browsed tonight, she could change the setting back tomorrow and no one would know. There was nothing wrong with a little snooping to pass the time. Right?

After downing her glass of wine, Riley bit the bullet and ticked "both." There. She'd done it. Feeling a little tipsy, she went to the profile section, and the first seven profiles were men. Two of them seemed okay, but she wasn't that interested. Truthfully, all she really wanted to do was look at women while she had the chance. When she swiped to the next profile and saw a pretty, dark-haired woman, she tapped her screen to look at the other pictures. A picture of *Empress2000,* as she called herself, in revealing lingerie put her off, so she continued browsing the five hundred and thirty profiles left. There were far less potential female matches, and that made sense, as most of the population was straight. Many clearly had a fake profile picture, which made Riley think they might be married, or perhaps they were men pretending to be women.

Getting bored as she didn't see anyone who spiked her interest, Riley was about to give up when a picture of Quinn appeared, with the profile name *Mystic84.* She slammed a hand in front of her mouth and sat there, frozen. It wasn't strange that she showed up; Quinn was single, gay, and lived nearby, but Riley was still shocked to see her. It was a great picture of her face against a blue sky that was almost the exact same color as her eyes. She smiled into the camera and Riley goofily smiled back at her screen while she poured herself more wine. Then she tapped the other pictures and indulged. There was one of Quinn with a beer on the roof of a barge, and one of her and Lindsey on a beach, which especially caught Riley's attention, as Quinn was wearing bikini shorts and a flimsy white tank top. She had a great body, toned and tanned, and her wet hair was slicked back.

Riley felt it again: the tingle. It was stronger this time, followed by a flash of heat that shot between her thighs. She hadn't felt anything like that in years, certainly not as intense. Quinn turned her on, and now that she had the chance to really look at her, she couldn't stop. The profile told her that Quinn loved to swim, spend time with her family and friends, and eat Italian food, but she didn't give much else away apart from that she was looking for "something casual." Riley squeezed her legs together at the latter, and her mind filled with fantasies. Quinn was looking for sex, and for some reason, that fired her up.

Then another thought made her stomach drop. If she could see Quinn's profile, Quinn would be able to see her too. Riley had been so busy staring at her pictures she hadn't noticed the green light above them that indicated Quinn was online. "Fuck," she hissed, then quickly went into her own profile to change her settings. In her panic, she couldn't find where to untick her preference for "both," and terrified she'd show up on Quinn's feed, she deleted her profile altogether.

When the termination of her profile was confirmed, Riley leaned back and let out the breath she'd been holding. Her pulse was racing, her hands were shaking, and as she got up from her chair, she realized she'd had too much wine.

20

QUINN

"Anything interesting?" Lindsey asked, scrolling through dating profiles on her phone. She propped her feet up on the coffee table, grabbed a cookie from the box on her lap, and broke half off for Quinn.

"Not really. Same old, same old. You?" Quinn was sitting next to her, equally slouched.

"I have a match with someone called Nick. He's a lawyer, and he lives nearby." Lindsey held up her phone to show Quinn a picture of a man sitting on a beach with his dog. "He's cute, right?"

"Don't ask me if he's cute." Quinn scrolled through his profile and nodded. "But he seems nice. He's got a dog, so he likes animals. I see a wine bottle on the table, so that's one thing you have in common..." She smirked as she read up on him. "But his passions are running, climbing, and he's a clean eater, so you may not be the best match."

"I can be a clean eater," Lindsey protested.

Quinn laughed and pointed to the cookies. "You're addicted to sweet stuff. You could never be a clean eater."

"Hey, I only eat half of everything."

"Sure. You give me half, and then when I start declining the other halves, you still end up eating the rest, which is eighty percent of the box." Quinn handed the phone back to her. "But go ahead and message him. He's probably got great stamina after all that running and clean eating, so if you're looking for a one-night stand, he's perfect."

Lindsey rolled her eyes and chuckled. "You know what? Fuck it. I'm going to message him. It's been a while and I could do with some action."

While Lindsey typed a message—Quinn suspected she was lying about her slouchy lifestyle and telling him she was a marathon runner—she continued to scroll through the profiles. A notification appeared, telling her there was a potential new match in close proximity, so she clicked on it and frowned as she stared at a picture of Riley. Instinctively, she gasped, and her initial reaction was to show Lindsey, but something told her that was a bad idea, so she kept quiet. With her friend distracted, she shifted on the couch so Lindsey couldn't see her screen and read the profile of *Aster1*. Apparently, Riley's job was in renovations now, and that amused her. No one was ever entirely honest on these apps, and she occasionally told a little white lie herself.

"What's going on?" Lindsey looked up from her screen but only for a moment.

"Nothing. Already swiped past her. You know what it's like." Quinn hoped Lindsey was too busy with Nick to notice the tremble in her voice, as she was utterly shocked to see Riley in her pool of potential matches.

"Yeah, tell me about it," Lindsey mumbled, engrossed in her message.

Quinn studied Riley's picture and felt that old familiar stir again. She was simply beautiful, and apparently, she had an interest in women. *I knew I was right.* She'd felt it when they were repairing Riley's door; she had an instinct for women checking her out. Should she give her a "like"? Sipping her tea, Quinn thought about that, but just as she decided to do so, Riley's profile disappeared. She went back, trying to find it and even used the search option, but there was no sign of *Aster1* on the dating site, and the only conclusion she could draw from that was that Riley had deleted her profile. *How strange.*

"How about this?" Lindsey asked, showing her the message she'd typed to Nick.

Having trouble concentrating after what she'd just seen, Quinn glanced over it and nodded. "Go for it."

"What? You're not even going to tell me I'm a liar?" Lindsey's eyes widened. "What's up with you?"

"Nothing. It's a great message." She glanced over it again and vaguely registered Lindsey had announced she was an ex-professional athlete. "Lying is okay as long as it's only for a one-night stand."

"Good." Lindsey propped her feet underneath her and helped herself to another half cookie. "I hope he gets back to me tonight. He's not online right now." Then she slammed a hand in front of her mouth and turned to Quinn. "What if he wants to meet up tonight? I'm not even decent. I haven't shaved in weeks."

Quinn laughed. "It's not like he'll expect you to be up for sex on the first date, let alone rock up straight after he's messaged you back." She rolled her eyes. "You're always so invested. Just chill out. If it happens, it happens."

"That's easy for you to say," Lindsey said with a huff. "It always happens for you."

"It does not." Quinn got up to make more tea. She held up the kettle, and Lindsey nodded.

"Yes, please. Do you have any of that tea left I got you from New York? The Japanese one?"

"I do." Quinn searched for the pack Lindsey had bought her on her latest shopping trip. "Speaking of New York, do you think there's a possibility Riley might be bisexual or gay?" she asked, hoping she sounded casual.

"Okay, interesting change of subject." Lindsey eyed her suspiciously. "No chance. I know I teased you with her, but I was only joking. She screams straight. Why?" She frowned. "Was she flirting with you when you went over to apologize?"

"No, not at all." Quinn held up a hand when Lindsey continued to stare at her. "I promise, she didn't." Already regretting bringing it up, she sighed. "I just got this really subtle vibe from her, that's all. I invited her over for dinner," she added, aware she might as well tell her that, as Lindsey would find out one way or another.

"Here? And you're hoping to get lucky?" Lindsey burst into laughter. "Riley hardly strikes me as someone who'd be impressed by this." She spread her arms, gesturing to the crammed space.

"I'm not hoping to get lucky." Quinn gave her a warning look. "I was just asking you a simple question because I think she might be hiding something."

"Dream on. She's straight, but I'm not claiming she isn't hiding anything. Who tells the whole truth nowadays?" Lindsey waved her phone in front of Quinn and grinned. "I certainly don't." She leaned in and put an arm around Quinn. "But all joking aside, it's blatantly obvious that you like her, so don't get your hopes up."

"I felt something," Quinn admitted. "She's sweet and intelligent and beautiful, and she showed this adorable sense of enthusiasm when I taught her how to fix a door handle."

"Well, you are pretty hot with a hammer in your hands," Lindsey said. "So you went up there to say you were sorry and ended up fixing her door?"

"Yes."

"And then you got a 'vibe' as you just called it?" Lindsey fell silent as she pondered over that. "Although it seems unlikely that she's into women, you've proven to me over and over that your vibe generally has roots..." She grinned mischievously. "So, dinner in your lair, huh? Are you going to make a pass at her?"

"No." Quinn fixed her eyes back on the screen, where Riley's profile had been only minutes ago, and she shook her head. "Of course not. I may find her attractive, but she doesn't have to know that."

21

RILEY

"*W*elcome." Quinn took Riley's coat and hung it over the back of a chair. "Please, sit down. Would you like a glass of white wine?"

"Thank you, that would be lovely." Riley looked around the narrowboat and took in its charming interior and the intricate woodwork. It was fascinating to see how Quinn lived; Riley had speculated whether the barge in the picture on Quinn's dating profile was her home. It was interesting and quirky, and even though it was small, it had lots of character and felt like a warm hug. She'd happily trade homes for a while so she wouldn't have to lay awake at night, tensing at every strange sound. "This is stunning. Is it yours?"

"Yep. All mine. My brother keeps telling me I need to get something bigger, but I like it. It's not great for entertaining, though. The table doesn't allow for more than two. I use the roof in summer when I have people over, but it's still a bit too chilly to sit outside at night."

"That must be amazing, with this view." Riley glanced out of the window and kept her gaze fixed on the river. Aster

House lay on the opposite bank, and it looked pretty impressive from here. She worked out which window was the one to her bedroom and that Quinn would have been able to see that her light was on every night. Riley was afraid to look at her after the reaction she'd had to her pictures last night, and she'd thought about her all day.

"Yeah." Quinn handed her a glass of wine, and realizing she couldn't avoid the inevitable any longer, Riley finally looked up at her. "I love being near the water," Quinn continued. "I think it's the reason I never left Mystic." She frowned as she studied Riley. "Are you okay?"

"Uh-huh." Riley swallowed hard and nodded. "Yes, I'm fine." She tugged at the collar of her blouse; she felt hot and her mind was spinning as she searched for something to fill the silence. "What are you cooking?"

"Spaghetti vongole." Quinn put a bowl of olives and a small plate of tomato bruschetta on the table and joined her.

"Yum. Your sister-in-law's recipe?"

"Yes. I make it at least once a week. So, what have you been up to since I last saw you?"

"A lot of scraping, sanding, and painting." Riley's breath caught when Quinn's foot brushed hers by accident. "The living room looks okay now, but I need stuff to fill up the vast space, so I might take a day off and go shopping." Her eyes met Quinn's, and she felt herself blush. "What about you? Did you finish the job?"

"Yes. Right on time. I have a few days off before we start on the next one, which is in Groton. I'll honk the horn when I drive past Aster House in the morning. Give you a wake-up call."

Riley chuckled and took a sip of her wine. She felt self-conscious, even though she had no reason to. "I'm an early riser. You're welcome to stop by for a morning coffee anytime."

"Thank you. I might take you up on that." A small smile played around Quinn's lips as she stared at her with those piercing, dark eyes. "Talking about our week, I also went back on my dating app. I tend to do that between jobs because then I have more time to meet women." She added, "Just for a bit of casual fun."

"Oh?" Riley hated the way her nervous, high-pitched voice went up another notch. "And? How did that go? I imagine it's hard meeting women in a small town." Her hands were clammy, and her heart was pounding. Had Quinn seen her profile?

"It's surprisingly easy in summer actually, with all the tourists around. But outside the season, it can be challenging, so I have a notification that alerts me to new members." Quinn's eyes narrowed, and she shot her an amused look. "And guess what?"

Fuck. Fuck, fuck, fuck. Riley knew she was busted, so she focused on her wine. "What?" she asked, avoiding her gaze.

"There was this superhot new woman on there who apparently lives close by. Quinn regarded her curiously and gave Riley a smile that caused a flash of arousal to shoot through her. "So obviously, I wanted to give her a like, right?"

Riley's heart pounded. *She just called me superhot.* "Right." She wasn't sure if Quinn was flirting with her or making fun of her, but she decided to play along. "And then what?"

"Then she disappeared. She was gone, just like that." Quinn snapped her fingers. "And I couldn't find her anymore."

"That's a shame." Riley's cheeks were burning while her body thrummed with so many contradicting messages. Part of her wanted to escape, to just run out of there and avoid Quinn forever. But another part of her was immensely turned on by this silly game and the way Quinn looked at her.

"Yeah. It was a shame. Her name was *Aster1*." Quinn dropped a dramatic pause. "Aster is an unusual name. In fact, I'm not even sure if it's a real name, and the only association I have with it is Aster House, which happens to be located at one Aster Drive." She tilted her head and grinned. "Also, her resemblance to you was astounding."

"Okay, okay." Riley leaned back, creating some distance between them, and she held up her hands. "Let's cut the crap, you know it's me."

"I'm sorry, I couldn't resist." Quinn's smirk dropped, and she shot her an apologetic look. "I won't tell anyone, I promise."

"I don't care who you tell. I'm not gay. It was a mistake," Riley lied. "I had too much to drink when I set up my profile. It was an accident."

"Then why did you delete it? Why not just change your sexual preference in the settings?"

"Because I panicked, okay? I panicked because all these women's profiles appeared, and I didn't know what to do." Riley wasn't going to admit she'd been snooping around Quinn's profile.

Quinn chuckled. "Okay, fair enough. You still don't strike me as someone who would panic at something like that, but I'll give you the benefit of the doubt."

"Thank you. Now can we please talk about something other than my failed attempt at online dating?"

"Sure." Quinn got up to check on her pasta, then added a slug of olive oil and chopped garlic into a pan. Looking over her shoulder, she gave Riley a teasing look. "But before we skip to the next subject, I need some advice from *Asteri*, kitchen queen and renovator. Tell me, what's the best way to cook these clams?"

Riley rolled her eyes and laughed along. "I have no idea. I had to put something on there, and I couldn't think of anything else. I don't even know who I am these days and I have literally no hobbies."

At that, Quinn stopped stirring the pan. "I apologize. I shouldn't have made fun of you. It must be hard to start over and leave everything you're comfortable with behind."

"I'll be fine. I just need some time to get used to my new life." Riley didn't want her embarrassing confession to dampen their night, so she painted on a smile and pointed to the pan. "How about *you* teach me how to cook those clams? Then I can add another dish to my kitchen-queen repertoire and I won't be a total liar if I ever sign up again."

22

QUINN

*Q*uinn wasn't convinced Riley was telling the truth about her online dating disaster. She'd clearly detected some kind of mutual attraction, but if Riley wasn't ready to admit that, she wasn't going to push her. There were so many hints pointing in that direction, and Quinn was rarely mistaken about chemistry. There was the way Riley looked at her, her body language, and her nervous demeanor. But most importantly, she felt this zinging sensation every time their eyes locked.

"Tell me about your dating history," she said. "If you were on that app, you must have an idea of what kind of man you're looking for. Lindsey told me you'd been married before."

"Yes, I was married for five years, and I got divorced when I was twenty-nine." Riley's gaze focused on the ceiling as she sighed. "Adam was a nice guy, and on paper, we were very suited, but I guess we both realized there wasn't much else than that."

"Did you love him?"

"I did. But I wasn't *in* love with him."

"Then who was your one, big love?" Quinn asked and added, "If that's not too personal."

"I don't think I've had a big love," Riley said with a shrug. "If I did, I would have known, right? I haven't dated very much. I guess I never made time for it, and hookups were always disappointing and felt like a waste of time, so I stopped dating altogether. Now that I have time, I figured I might as well try, but honestly, I have no idea what I'm looking for." She looked up at Quinn. "What about you?"

"I can't say I've had a big love either." Quinn passed Riley the bowl of pasta, and Riley helped herself to more. Quinn was pleased that she liked her food, and she loved how Riley moaned in pleasure while she ate. "I've been in relationships, but it never got serious enough to move in together or plan a future. As I said, the women I hook up with are often just staying here over the season or they're tourists passing through."

"So you're not a commitment-phobe?"

"No. I'm open to something serious. I just haven't found The One yet." Quinn had so many questions for Riley, but none of them were appropriate to ask tonight. Was she closeted? And if she was, how long had she been living like that? New York wasn't exactly a closed-minded city, and she didn't seem like a closed-minded person either.

"My turn now," Riley said, interrupting her thoughts. "What's your type? Do you have one?"

Quinn mulled over that as she nibbled on an olive. She wasn't sure how far she could go with her subtle flirtations, but she decided to take a chance. "Physically speaking, I like feminine women, and I'm a sucker for a pretty brunette." She leaned in closer and locked her eyes with Riley's. *Yep. She definitely looks flustered.* "But there has to be chemistry, of course. That's important."

Riley bit her lip and nodded. "Yes," she whispered. "Chemistry is important."

"And I like intelligent and independent women," Quinn added. "I guess someone like you would be my type."

At that, Riley moved back even more. She opened her mouth to say something, then closed it again and frowned through a long silence. "Are you flirting with me?" she finally asked.

"No," Quinn said casually. "I was just answering your question. I wouldn't dare flirt with you. You're straight. You've made that very clear, so you wouldn't be interested in me anyway, right?"

"Right."

Quinn gave her a small smile as she looked her over. "Sorry, but I have to ask again because none of this adds up. Are you sure you didn't go on that app because you wanted to meet women?" She rested her chin in the palm of her hand. "It's okay. I really won't tell anyone."

"Not even Lindsey?"

"Especially not Lindsey."

Riley twirled the wine around in her glass and looked up at the ceiling again as if all the answers to difficult questions were plastered over the intricate woodwork. "I was curious," she finally said. "I wanted to..." She stopped herself with a subtle shake of her head. "I just had a few drinks, and I was curious."

"There's nothing wrong with being curious."

"I know that."

Quinn nodded, relieved to learn she hadn't imagined the pull between them. She was unsure if she could push any further with her questions, but Riley's confession felt like an invitation to discuss it. "Have you been curious for long?"

she asked, aware this conversation could change their new friendship for the worse or for the better.

"No," Riley said matter-of-factly. "I never had time to think about these things." She paused, then repeated her previous statement. "I was just curious."

"Did you find what you were looking for?"

"I wasn't looking for anything." Riley's eyes darted to the door now, seeking an escape.

"Okay. But if you're curious, there's no harm in talking about it." Quinn shrugged. "You might as well. I'm gay. It might help to talk, and we're friends, right?"

Riley braced herself with a deep breath, then met Quinn's eyes. "I was filling in the profile," she said. "It asked me for my sexual preference, and for the first time in my life, I actually started to doubt myself."

"Like a hunch?"

"Maybe."

"Any reason you suddenly started to doubt your sexuality?" Quinn asked, her core tightening as she considered the possibility that she might have ignited something in Riley.

Riley pursed her lips and hesitated. "No. It was probably the wine. I had too much." She shook her head. "So no, I don't feel the need to talk about it."

"Sure." Quinn held up the bottle. "Would you like another glass?" She winked. "Or would that turn you gay?"

Finally, Riley's shoulders dropped, and she laughed, visibly relaxing a little. "It might."

"In that case, I'll keep topping you up," Quinn said humorously, pouring them both a generous amount. The night had been interesting to say the least, but Riley was no less of a mystery.

23

RILEY

*R*iley couldn't sleep, but for once, the house wasn't the reason. There were still the constant creaking and howling noises and the occasional slamming doors, but her mind was elsewhere. She'd been tossing and turning for hours, her thoughts consumed by Quinn and the way she'd regarded her while she shamefully crawled back from her lie. And then there were the looks between them that quite frankly set her on fire. She had a feeling it was mutual, especially after Quinn's teasing comments and the flirty glimmer in her eyes.

A tightness spread between her thighs, and she lowered her hand between the sheets and under her T-shirt. She gasped, shocked at how sensitive her nipples were when she caressed her breasts. Her body was reacting to the vision of Quinn in ways she'd never experienced, and Quinn wasn't even here. She imagined Quinn's hands stroking her, Quinn's lips on her mouth and neck, those intense eyes locked with hers while she gave her that lazy smile. *What would it be like?*

Riley shivered as she ran her fingers over her ribcage

and her belly, then slipped them into her panties. She knew she was wet, but she hadn't expected the pool of desire she found when she lowered them farther. It was astounding how much fantasizing about Quinn aroused her; she felt a need for release she hadn't experienced in years.

Quinn's face appeared in her mind's eye, and she stroked herself as she held on to the image. She was so sensitive that she buckled under the touch and moaned through the eerie silence. Her voice filled the room, and even though there was no one around, she covered her mouth with her hand to stifle the sound. In this house, she always felt like someone or something was watching her; she felt lonely, but never alone. While her rational mind told her ghosts didn't exist, she still imagined Quinn's ancestors watching her, knowing she was fantasizing about Quinn. Because the dead, in the unlikely event that they were still around in some form, surely knew everything.

Riley squeezed her eyes tight shut, banning those thoughts from her mind, and moved her fingers faster, circling her clit until a surge of warmth started building, teasing her with the promise of something explosive. She entered herself while she imagined Quinn's fingers inside her and threw her head back as her walls started squeezing around them. A groan came from deep down, strangled, almost alarming as she came with a force that left her limp and breathless.

She breathed fast, withdrew, and covered her damp face with her hands. The night was cool, but the room felt broody, and heat radiated from her as she turned on her side and sighed. At the age of forty, she'd just masturbated while thinking of a woman for the first time, and she felt more satisfied than ever. That was something to think about. Did this happen to others? Did people suddenly develop a lesbian crush out of nowhere after being straight their whole lives? Riley had always been convinced stuff like that only happened in movies, but she wasn't so sure anymore.

She needed distraction and she needed it bad because it was looking like it would be another long, sleepless night full of questions she had no answers to and feelings she didn't know what to do with. With that thought, she got up, put on her robe, headed downstairs, and turned on the TV and all the lights. She put another coat of paint on the living room walls, then sat on the couch for a while, watching it dry before she wandered through the big house, aimlessly, restlessly, contemplating what to do with the kitchen, the laundry room, the downstairs restroom, and the hallway. Her eyes fell on the office adjacent to the hallway. She'd only entered it twice; the space confused her, and with no need for an office anymore, she wondered if it could serve as an extra bedroom if she ever decided to go ahead with the idea of a guesthouse.

There was little light in the office; some of the bulbs were broken, and it felt eerie. It was damper than the other spaces too, and she'd noticed the edges of the wallpaper were curling in the corners. There were deep marks in the thick carpet where a heavy desk had once been, and the only piece of furniture still standing was a large, built-in bookcase against the back wall.

Riley pulled at the wallpaper, and it came off much easier in here. Tearing off a significant piece without much effort made her smile and gave her immense satisfaction. She suspected the dampness had caused it to loosen over the years, and at the lack of something better to do, she brought in the ladder and started stripping the walls. It was addictive; she'd been fighting the house since she arrived, and finally she was winning.

"I'm going to beat you, you fucker," she mumbled to herself. "And when I've beaten you, I'm going to sell you and you'll be someone else's problem."

She imagined Quinn's great-grandfather sitting there behind a mahogany desk, cursing and pointing at her with his fancy pen. She looked at the spot where the desk had been and grinned at her imaginary ghost.

"All of this is coming off, do you hear me? All of it. Because it's my house now, and I'm going to do with it as I please, no matter how much you try to scare me."

As she said it, she wondered if she might be going crazy, talking to herself while she violently tore at the floral wallpaper in the middle of the night.

"Quinn is okay with it. She told me herself, and you'll just have to live with my changes. Well, you're not alive, so I suppose that's not a correct statement," she continued, unsure if she was actually saying it out loud. She'd read about insomnia and how it could affect one's mind, and that was the point she decided it was time to finally get some sleep, one way or another.

With a sigh, she dropped her scraper and headed for the kitchen where she poured herself a generous glass of Scotch and downed it in one go. She didn't even like Scotch; she'd only bought it with this specific goal in mind, and as she climbed the stairs with a refill in hand, she was hopeful her strategy would work.

24

QUINN

Quinn was on her way to work when she'd turned off the main road and found herself in front of the gates of Aster House. It wasn't the house that drew her in this time, but rather the attractive new owner she hadn't stopped thinking about since their dinner last week. Apart from a message from Riley thanking her for dinner and a polite reply from her side, they hadn't been in contact, and she felt an urge to see her.

"Sorry about the wait. I was looking for my robe when you buzzed the gate." Riley came out with a beaming smile, holding two mugs. "I'm glad you decided to take me up on my coffee offer. I just made some," she said, handing Quinn a mug. "Shall we sit outside? I bought a new bench. It's in the backyard, facing the river."

"Perfect. I hope it's not too early?" Quinn followed Riley, who looked incredible in the cream-colored satin robe that draped around her curves and showed off an enticing hint of cleavage. Her hair fell in wild waves around her shoulders, and without makeup, she was even more beautiful.

"No, not at all. But I was up later than usual, which is why I'm not dressed yet. I've been having trouble sleeping."

"I'm sorry to hear that." Quinn tore her eyes away from Riley's behind and focused on the view. The river looked still this morning, as if it had just woken up along with Riley. "Anything bothering you? Or is it the house?"

"The house, mainly." Riley led them to a white, cast-iron bench positioned under one of the big willows and touched one of the light-blue cushions to check if it was dry, then sat down and crossed her legs. "There are so many strange noises, it freaks me out."

"Are you afraid?" Quinn sat next to her.

"Honestly, yes. I don't believe in the paranormal and I'm not easily spooked, but there's something about Aster House that frightens me at night." Riley paused and sipped her coffee. "Were you never afraid when you lived there?"

"Never. But there were always people around." Quinn shot her a reassuring smile. "I know the noises you're referring to, though. I always imagined the house was sleeping at night—the steady creaking a deep inhalation, causing it to expand like a chest, then exhaling when the soft whistling of the wind followed."

"That's poetic," Riley said, meeting her eyes with a smile. "I'll keep that in mind next time I'm lying awake."

"I hope it helps." Quinn realized she was staring, so she focused on the bench and changed the subject. "This is great. Very Victorian. And you found the perfect spot for it."

"Yes, I like this tree, and it shelters it from rain." Riley closed her eyes and took a deep breath. "It smells wonderful when it's been raining overnight. There's no pure freshness like this in New York." She draped her arm over the backrest and turned to Quinn. "So, what are you up to today?"

"Nothing much, just work. The start of a new job is always a bit hectic, so it might be a late one. You?"

"I'm ripping out the carpet in the living room and the office, and Lindsey's nephew Gareth is coming today. He's starting on the yard."

"Gareth? I've met him, he's a nice guy." Quinn inspected the backyard as she sipped her coffee. It was just as overgrown as the front, if not more. "It might take him a week. It's been neglected for quite a while. Are you planning to change anything?"

"Not for now. I just want it to be tidy, and it would be nice if we could get the fountains and the lights to work again."

"Yes, they're quite magical at night when they're lit up."

"Hmm…" The corners of Riley's lips curled up. "Are you a romantic?"

Quinn had a feeling Riley was flirting with her. "I can be." She felt that tingle again, and when Riley's eyes lowered to her lips for a brief moment, she knew it was mutual. "Are you?"

"I don't know. There's a lot I'm yet to learn about myself."

"You bought this house, so there must be a romantic in you somewhere," Quinn said, wondering if Riley was referring to something entirely different. "It doesn't get more romantic than an old mansion on the river. Just wait until late summer when the asters start to bloom. The whole yard turns into a sea of lilac."

"So that's why it's called Aster House. Funny. I never thought about the name."

"It was built on an aster field. That was the very reason my great-grandfather chose the spot—his wife loved them. The view over the river was only a bonus."

"The romantic side runs in the family, then," Riley said. "Should I tell Gareth about it, so he doesn't pull them out?"

"No need. They're wildflowers, so they're resilient. When late summer comes, I suggest you hold off on mowing the lawn for two months and let it grow and bloom. It'll be absolutely stunning."

"I can't wait to see that." Riley was so intently fixed on Quinn, that Quinn didn't know what to do with herself in the long silence that followed. Then, suddenly, Riley averted her gaze and focused on the waterfront. "I was thinking of building a dock," she said. "It will add value to the house, right?"

"Definitely," Quinn agreed. "There used to be a dock, actually, so there might still be a base construction under the surface. That will save you a lot of work if it's still in good condition."

"That's useful to know. I'm lucky to have you as the Aster House expert." Riley paused and turned back to her. "Is it still difficult for you? Being here?"

"It's easier now that I'm getting used to it." Quinn shivered as their eyes locked. Her friends didn't look at her that way. Not like they wanted to kiss her. "And your company is pleasantly distracting."

"Good." A blush settled over Riley's cheeks, and she hesitated. "Look...I want you to know that I'll respect the house when I renovate it. I'll make it my own, of course, but I'll respect its layout and history, and I won't remove any of the built-in features."

"Thank you. I appreciate that, but you should do whatever you want."

"What I want is to make it feel like a warm home again, and I'd like your help." Riley put her hand on Quinn's arm, and the light touch caused Quinn's breath to hitch.

"I don't think it's a good idea for me to get involved…"

"Please. You don't need to do anything. I just want your opinion. I'm not good at the homemaking thing, I've always hired others to do the interior for me."

With the pleading look Riley gave her, Quinn cracked, because how could she ever say no to her? "What did you have in mind?"

"I'd like you to look at some color and fabric swatches next time you're here. I've started painting everything white, but it doesn't suit the style of the house, and this morning when the light poured in, it felt wrong. You're welcome to tell me you were right, by the way," Riley added humorously.

Quinn laughed as she got up. "I'm no interior designer, but sure, I'll take a look. I can drop by sometime at the end of the week if that suits you?" She handed Riley the empty mug. "Thanks for this."

"Anytime. There will always be coffee waiting for you."

Quinn smiled. "I'll take you up on that. And good luck with the carpet today."

25

RILEY

*R*iley pushed and pulled, but the huge bookcase that was standing in an alcove in the office wouldn't budge. Moving it was the only way to remove the last bit of carpet and the wallpaper behind it, but she had no idea how to get the damn thing out. Figuring it must have been screwed into the wall, she took out the decorative items Wendy had placed on the shelves and studied the back of it. She found four big screws in the corners of one half of the unit, so she went to get a screwdriver and a ladder and balanced on her tiptoes to take them out.

Riley tried again after removing the screws, wedging her fingers behind it and tugging, but to no avail. What was going on here? Was the thing glued to the wall, or was she just not strong enough? She knocked on the back of the bookcase, hoping she could work out where the majority of the glue was by the sound, then found that the left side where the screws had been sounded completely different. She tapped both sides again and focused on the left half, which had a hollower sound to it, like there was nothing behind it. Contemplating taking a hammer to it, she thought of Quinn and how much it would upset her if she tore it to pieces, and decided against it. Maybe she should wait and ask her for her opinion. It had been Riley's idea, after all, to involve her in her renovations.

Stepping back, she looked over the bookcase and noticed the alcove was in a strange, seemingly random position. Why would they put it there of all places, on the right side of the main wall? Why not center it so it looked tidier? Knocking again, she wondered if there could be a dead space behind, then she started taking out the shelves at the lack of a better idea. The top two shelves came out without effort, but when she pulled at the third shelf, it seemed stuck to the back of the case. Instead of coming out, the whole bookcase turned inward like a door, hitting her ladder and causing her to tumble off.

"Ouch!" Landing on the floor, Riley winced and rubbed her sore thigh. Still confused as to what had happened, her eyes widened as she stared at the bookcase that was now divided in two. There was only a small gap between the left and the right side, but it was enough to see that it was an entrance of some sort. She picked herself up and moved the ladder so she could pull at one of the bottom shelves; the bookcase easily opened outward.

Her heart raced as she peeked inside and saw stone steps going down. She'd been wondering if there was a basement below the house but hadn't found any evidence of one in her paperwork. Grabbing her phone, she turned on her torch and pushed the bookcase back farther, wedging the ladder between it and the wall so it wouldn't fall back into the lock. She carefully went down the narrow, damp staircase, which led to a large, open space. Feeling up the walls in search of a light switch, she found one and narrowed her eyes as the bright light almost blinded her.

It looked like a file room, and it smelled of damp paper and moldy carpet. Filing cabinets and boxes were lined up in long rows on the right side of the basement, and on the left side were wine racks with hundreds of bottles. There was a desk with a lamp and some stationery, and other furniture was piled up in the far section. She saw cabinets, chairs, an old sofa, a handful of bedframes, and antique lamps and vases, surrounded by more boxes.

Riley ran her hand over a cabinet and brushed off a thick layer of dust. It was still in good condition, even after what might have been decades in a basement. She picked up a heavy vase and put it on top to examine it. It was made of porcelain with a beautiful, intricate Chinese-style floral pattern. What was all this stuff doing down here? Some of it looked valuable—she suspected the storage units alone would be worth quite some money—and there was so much of it scattered around as if it had been placed here in a rush.

Crossing the basement to the section with the wines, she brushed off more dust and studied the labels. They were old, but some would have improved over time, like the Bordeaux, the Cabernet Sauvignon, and the vintage port. There were whiskeys, too, and a couple of clear bottles she thought might be home brew. Even if the previous owners had considered the furniture clutter, it made no sense for them to leave a whole wine collection behind, and Riley wondered if they'd even known this basement was here. She'd only found out by coincidence, after all.

The lights flickered off and back on for a beat, and Riley froze to the spot. She'd been so fascinated by what she'd found she'd almost forgotten she was generally terrified when it came to Aster House. She put the bottle back on the rack, then grabbed one of the boxes before she rushed upstairs. Her heart was still thumping hard in her throat when she reached the daylight-flooded living room, where she put the box on the coffee table and held her chest as she half collapsed onto the couch.

Riley felt like she'd jumped time. The bookcase was a portal to the past, perfectly preserved over decades. She'd left it open in case it fell back into the lock, hoping she'd be brave enough to explore further at some point. For now, she focused on the box in front of her. It was made of hard leather, like a high-end hatbox but square instead of round. Inside were beautiful baby memorabilia: a little white dress, an embroidered baby blanket, a silver rattle, and a silver photo frame with a color photograph that looked like it dated from the eighties of a woman holding an adorable baby. There was also a children's bible, an embroidered bib, a stuffed teddy bear, a jeweler's case holding a tiny silver bracelet, and finally, a small leather case that held a silver spoon.

This baby had been born into money, Riley thought. She'd had quite the opposite childhood herself; her parents could barely afford to buy her a stuffed animal when she was younger. It was the very reason she'd always worked so hard, to prove that she could make something out of herself, even though all the odds were against her. She took the spoon out of the case and smiled as she read the inscription engraved on the handle.

Quinn, 01-08-1985.

26

QUINN

"What was it you wanted to talk to me about?" Quinn stepped inside Aster House only twenty minutes after Riley had messaged her. She was a sucker for a beautiful woman, and it was worrying how fast she'd made her way over here. Riley's hair was messier than usual, and she had dust stains on her jeans and shirt.

"Thanks for coming. I want to show you something." Riley seemed elated as she beckoned Quinn to follow her into the office, then gestured to the old bookcase that had come away from the wall. "Did you know there was a basement?"

Quinn approached the bookshelf and was mesmerized to see a staircase behind it. "No, I didn't." She glanced down the steps and turned to Riley. "I honestly had no idea."

"Then you should take a look. There's a lot of stuff down there, and it belongs to your family. I only opened one box. When I saw it contained your baby stuff, I thought it would be best to leave the rest to you."

"Mine?"

"Yes." She gestured to the box on the floor. "Take a look. I didn't want to open more, as it felt private."

Quinn frowned as she rooted through the delicate garments and toys. "Mom wondered where all of this had gone. My parents used to store their stuff here, and she assumed it had been taken away by the bailiffs."

"There's more," Riley said. "A lot more." She handed her a flashlight. "Take this. The light bulbs are old and need replacing."

Quinn felt sick with nerves as she went down. How could she not have known there was a basement? And why was the entrance hidden behind a bookcase? The answer soon became clear when she saw the vast variety of furniture and other treasures from her childhood. She recognized the dining chairs, the art-deco console, and marble tiger statue that used to be in the hallway. There was the collection of Chinese vases that once graced the living room and her old bed among other furniture, all buried under a layer of dust. They'd been hidden here all those years ago so they couldn't be sold off. Unable to get an untraceable storage unit, she supposed her grandfather didn't have much choice but to store it underneath the house to save it from being auctioned off. Did her grandmother know? And if she did, why had she never told anyone? Had they planned to come back for their belongings? Maybe they'd hoped they could buy the house back one day, and this was a desperate attempt to hold on to any valuables still left.

Overwhelmed with questions and emotions, she pointed the flashlight over the rows of files and boxes containing her family's legacy. Everything that had been dear to them, all their memories, were still here. Everything was marked and dated, she noticed as she studied them, but the furniture was randomly placed, which made her think that moving it down here had been a last-minute job. The big, round table with eight chairs next to the file cabinets was a mystery; she'd never seen those before, and they had no place here as it looked like somewhere meetings had taken place. By now, she knew her grandfather had never been an open book, but this was a whole new level of secrecy, and that table intrigued her more than anything else.

"It must be a lot to take in." Riley's voice was sweet and soft as she came down behind her and stroked her back. "Are you okay?"

"Yes. I'm just shocked. I thought it was gone—we all did."

Riley wrapped her arm around her waist, and Quinn inched closer. It was comforting, and they stood there for a while, simply staring at the new space Riley had discovered.

"I'm surprised no one found the entrance before me."

"Apparently, no one bothered to rip out the carpet or take off the wallpaper. Most of it was original when you moved in." Quinn smiled as she turned to Riley. "Lucky for me, some flashy New Yorker decided the interior wasn't good enough for her."

"I never thought you'd thank me for stripping walls." Riley chuckled. "You should take your time with this. I'll give you a key so you can let yourself in when it suits you."

"Thank you, but you don't need to do that, and technically, all of this is yours, as is anything else found on your property. I'd like to have the pictures, though, and some other personal items."

"No. This belongs to your family. I know a thing or two about wine, and that collection has to be worth a fortune, but the memorabilia are priceless." Riley lowered her voice to a whisper as if she was worried she'd wake something. "It's here for a reason. It was here for *you* to find."

Quinn nodded. Perhaps it was here because her grandfather had hoped *she'd* be able to buy the house back one day. And yes, it was here for her to find, but she'd failed him. Instead, the new owner of Aster House had found it; the fifth owner since the estate was taken from her family, and she had no place to store any of it. She was grateful, though, to have it back or to even lay her eyes on all the old memories that warmed her heart.

Keeping her thoughts to herself, she let out a deep sigh. "I don't even know where to start."

"Then how about we start with dinner?" Riley suggested. "I was just about to order. This stuff isn't going anywhere, and you can take a few boxes upstairs while we wait for the food to arrive." She hesitated. "Unless you'd rather stay down here?"

"No, dinner would be nice." It was good to be with Riley right now, to have someone to talk to. Quinn had thought about her a lot today, and despite the shocking discovery, their chemistry was still as palpable as this morning. From the way Riley's eyes lingered on her, she had a feeling Riley was as aware of it as she was. "But let me order it, please," she said. Tearing her gaze away from her, she randomly selected two boxes; Riley carried one of them upstairs, Quinn the other. "Are you up for pizza?"

"Only if it's Mystic pizza," Riley said with a smile as she put the box on the coffee table in the living room.

"A margherita with a small salad and chili oil on the side?"

"You remember." Riley chuckled. "How on earth do you remember that?"

"How could I not?" Quinn placed her box on top of the other one and fell back on the couch. "I don't think I've ever heard anyone order so fast in my life. You clearly knew what you wanted, and you wasted no time. It made me laugh."

"Hmm..." Riley slumped down next to her, and pulled a leg underneath her. "Are you making fun of my ordering style?"

"No. I'm making fun of how adorably straightforward you are. It's cute and—" Quinn stopped herself as she realized she was flirting again. Even now, after finding out her legacy lay below the house in the basement, she still couldn't stop flirting. *Jesus, Quinn.*

"What? What were you going to say?" Riley asked.

"Nothing." Quinn gave her a playful look and shook her head. "It's not important."

27

RILEY

"*W*ould you like a beer?" Riley placed the pizzas on the table along with salad, chili oil, and two bottles of beer that she'd already opened.

"Yes, please. I could do with one." Quinn leaned back on the couch and stared into space like she'd done for the past hour in between going through memorabilia. Riley imagined seeing the house through her eyes; it must be a surreal experience for her.

"Do you hate it?" she asked.

Quinn looked at her quizzically as she sipped her beer. "Hate what?"

"The living room."

"As I said, my opinion doesn't matter, but no, I don't hate it. It actually looks quite fresh and clean. I'll admit I had reservations about what you were doing, but the wooden floor will be lovely once it's sanded and oiled, and it's much brighter without the dark wallpaper." She tapped her foot on the floor. "I get why there was such thick carpet now. Since there's a basement underneath, it sounds hollow without it.

LISE GOLD

"I thought the floor had a strange sound to it, but it didn't click." Riley took a sip of her beer and winced, still unsure if she liked it or not. Although she didn't normally drink beer, she'd bought a few in case Quinn came around. She'd done a lot of "just in cases" lately, like shaving her legs every day, blow-drying her hair in the morning, and making sure she looked at least semi-presentable throughout the day.

"You might need some insulation," Quinn continued. "I can hook you up with someone who can help you with the floor."

"Thank you, I appreciate that. I'm still surprised the previous owners never discovered the basement. Maybe they decided to keep the bookcase there, as it's fixed to the walls. I only tried to move it because I'm a perfectionist and it bothered me that I could still see a tiny bit of wallpaper behind it. Anyway, I'll just paint over it now. I don't want to break the entrance." She smiled. "Pretty cool, though, right? A secret room in the house. Do you think your parents knew about it?"

"No chance. My mother grew up here, and she would have mentioned it." Quinn turned to Riley. "I should probably tell my family. Mom will be delighted to have the photographs back. Thank you for calling me."

"You can leave everything there if you have nowhere to store it. It'll take a while before I even think about starting on the basement I never knew I had. Or you can bring everything up to one of the bedrooms and go through it there. There's more than enough space, and it'll be much more comfortable."

"As long as I'm not in your way."

"You won't be. I like your company." Riley shrugged. "It can get lonely here by myself." She felt excited about the

116

prospect of having Quinn around, and the discovery of the basement had given her a new sense of positivity.

"I'm always happy to keep you company." Quinn shot her a lazy smile that made her shiver. "I'm really glad I met you."

"Yeah." Riley's core swarmed with butterflies as she held her gaze, and without thinking, she reached out to touch Quinn's face. "You have some dust here," she whispered. Quinn's eyes fluttered closed, and she leaned into Riley's touch. It was in that moment that Riley knew for sure; Quinn wanted her too. She kept her hand there and stroked Quinn's cheek with her thumb, and Quinn placed a hand over hers. Her touch was warm and comforting but also immensely arousing.

Quinn opened her eyes and shook her head before she let go and inched back. She looked as if she were about to say something, but instead, she took another sip of her beer and studied the label that was nothing out of the ordinary.

"I'm sorry. I..." Riley's voice trailed away. She wasn't sure what she was apologizing for because the moment had felt so perfect, it couldn't possibly be wrong.

"Don't be." Quinn met her eyes again. "But I can't be around you if it's going to be like this. I like you and I'm only human." She paused. "Do you understand what I'm saying?"

Riley nodded slowly and braced herself to confess. If she wanted to tell Quinn the truth, now was the time. "That night when you saw me on the dating app..." She took a deep breath and a long sip of her beer before she continued. "As I said, I was curious."

"I know."

"The reason I became curious...is because I met you."

Quinn's breath visibly hitched, and her eyes darkened. "You must have met gay women before."

"Of course. But I've never met a gay woman I felt attracted to." Riley swallowed hard. "I'm very, very attracted to you, Quinn."

"Oh." Quinn parted her lips as she glanced at Riley's mouth, and for a second, Riley was convinced Quinn was going to kiss her. "So it's mutual."

"Uh-huh." Riley waited for her to come closer, to make a move. Because if Quinn kissed her now, she would kiss her back like she'd never kissed anyone before. She held her breath in the long silence that followed, then muttered, "Please say something."

Quinn bit her lip and frowned as she studied her intently. "Are you sure about this? Because we're friends, and—"

"Yes," she interrupted her. She felt much braver now that the truth was out. "I'm sure."

A flash of desire passed over Quinn's features, but still, she didn't move. "I want you too," she whispered. "But I need you to think about this." She took Riley's hand and squeezed it. "Because I don't want to ruin what we have over a one-night stand."

"Isn't that your thing, though? Casual?" Riley realized she'd just given herself away. "I read your dating profile," she admitted.

"I knew it." Quinn smiled teasingly. "But casual is not what I want with you. Is it what *you* want?"

Riley thought about that. What *did* she want? Quinn was right; they were friends, and she didn't want a meaningless fling to ruin their friendship either. What she felt was far from meaningless, though; it was a yearning that kept her awake at night, a longing for something unknown that already felt familiar. She had a burning desire for a woman she barely knew, yet this woman understood her like no one else.

"No. I don't want casual," she said, meeting Quinn's eyes. They were beautiful, sincere, and seductive, those eyes, and they made her lose her train of thought each time she looked into them.

"Then you need to give yourself some time because these feelings are very new to you." Quinn paused. "I'm not going anywhere."

Riley nodded, but starving for a taste of Quinn, her hungry body protested. "Okay," she whispered. "I'll think about it."

28

QUINN

*T*here was so much to go through, and unsure where to start, Quinn had randomly picked five more boxes to take upstairs to her old bedroom. The first three she'd gone through last night had contained her baby memorabilia, her brother's baby photos, and trinkets that held little value but were hugely sentimental, such as souvenirs from her grandparents' travels and their favorite coffee mugs. There was a story behind every item, and she knew them all. Her grandfather had bored her to tears when she was younger, but now she cherished the silly trinkets, and she'd shared the stories with Riley.

She'd chosen her old bedroom because she felt most comfortable here, and she loved the view from the window over the yard and the river. She'd brought one of her decorator's folding tables over, borrowed a chair from the kitchen, and screwed a brighter light bulb into the ceiling fixture. All in all, she was prepared for a long week of sorting through her family history after work.

Opening the first box of the day, she jumped back when a big spider crawled out of it, and she carefully opened it farther to make sure there wasn't a spider's nest inside. What she found was old paperwork from the seventies. Title deeds to land in Nevada, which she assumed had been sold at the time of her grandfather's bankruptcy, real estate certificates, and contracts with hotel chains, some in her great-grandfather's name. She divided them into piles, then moved on to the next box.

This one was filled with photo albums dating all the way back to 1940. Her great-grandparents' wedding photos, photos of the land on which Aster House was built, then some more that were taken during the build. She took her time and smiled as she looked through them. There were baby photos of her great-grandparents on holiday and of their little family of three posing in front of a Christmas tree. The first picture of them in front of Aster House was dated 01/08/1943, and they looked so young and happy. Her great-grandmother was wearing a floral dress, and her husband was in his Sunday best, holding his son—Quinn's grandfather—who was two years old.

"I thought you could use a coffee." Riley came in and put a mug of steaming brew on the folding table.

"Thank you. But you don't need to cater for me."

"I want to, and besides, I'm curious." Riley leaned in over her shoulder to look at the photo album. "Who are these people?"

Quinn shivered at her nearness. After their confessions last night, something had changed between them. Casual touches were no longer casual, and harmless flirting had taken on a new meaning.

"That's my great-grandmother, Simone Kendall, and that's my great-grandfather, Frank Kendall. The baby is my grandfather, Arthur Kendall." Quinn pointed them out. Although the colors in the photograph were faded, the lilac of the asters surrounding the house stood out in the picture. "It's sweet, isn't it?"

"It's a beautiful picture," Riley agreed. "I see what you meant about the asters now. But why did they hide the albums down there? Surely, the bailiffs would have allowed them to keep them as they have no value other than of the sentimental kind."

"I don't know. It doesn't make any sense." Quinn had asked herself that question already. Even if her grandparents didn't have the storage space in the small apartment they moved to after being evicted, she'd expected them to at least take their photo albums. "We all wondered what had happened to these after my grandfather passed away. My grandmother already suffered from dementia by the time my grandfather died, so we couldn't ask her. She still has her few bright moments, but it's not enough to ask detailed questions. Things just come to her randomly."

"She might remember something if you show her the pictures," Riley said. "You said she was in a home, right?"

"Yes, I visit her once or twice a week, but it's very rare that she even recognizes me. I'll try, though." Quinn closed the album and retrieved a pile of postcards from the same box. They were cards that her grandfather had sent while he was on his business trips. Most contained short and sweet messages, telling her grandmother he missed her, but some were longer with updates on business deals and things he'd seen or experienced.

"It must be pretty special to be so close to your family."

Hearing the hint of regret in Riley's voice, Quinn turned and looked up at her. "It is," she said. "Can I ask you why you're not?"

Riley shrugged. "It's me. It's all my fault. I've only ever focused on work, and now I feel like it's too late to rekindle.

They probably hate me because I haven't been in touch much."

"Who are 'they'?"

"My sister, my niece, and my father. I have uncles and aunts too—I've never been close to them—but the people I grew up with and love..." She paused. "I've neglected them. I've only ever thought about myself."

"You don't strike me as a selfish person."

"I am." Riley shook her head. "At least, I was," she corrected herself. "Maybe I still am. I don't seem to know myself these days."

"It's never too late to make up for lost time," Quinn said, detecting a hidden message behind her statement. She regarded Riley, resisting the urge to reach out and run a hand through her hair. "It's never too late."

"Hmm..." Riley stared at her, then turned her gaze to the window. "I've been thinking about calling my sister. I might do that tomorrow." She gave Quinn a small smile and straightened herself. "Anyway, I'll leave you to it. I hope you find the answers you're looking for."

29

RILEY

*I*t was scary after not speaking to her sister for months, but the call was long overdue. Riley held her breath as the phone rang and sighed in relief when she heard Jane's voice.

"Riley?"

"Hi, yes, it's me." Riley hesitated. "I'm sorry it's been so long. How are you?"

"How am I?" Jane sounded even sharper than Riley had expected. "I've been trying to speak to you for God knows how long and you keep fobbing me off. What happened? Are you on vacation and suddenly bored or something?"

Something like that. Riley sighed. "You're right," she said. "I've been a bad sister and an even worse aunt." She hesitated. "I've been selfish, and it took me some time to gather the courage to tell you that I'm very, very sorry." There was an uncomfortable silence, and Jane made no effort to make conversation, so she continued. "How's little Mindy?"

"She's fine. She's been asking about you." Jane's voice was still cold.

"I'd love to see you both." Riley cleared her throat. "Any chance we could meet up?"

"Just so you can leave me waiting at a restaurant for an hour or be on your phone the whole time we're together?"

"No." Riley swallowed hard as a ball of guilt formed in her core. "My life is different now. I've moved away from New York, and I sold my company."

Another long silence followed, and this time, Riley didn't fill it.

"Are you okay?" Jane finally asked.

"Yes. I just needed a change of lifestyle, that's all. For good,' she added, not wanting to go into detail. "I live in Mystic now. It's a small town in Connecticut along the river. I bought a house here—an estate, actually—and I have more bedrooms than I know what to do with, so you're both welcome to come and stay here anytime, for as long as you want."

Jane laughed. "You're kidding me, right?"

"I'm serious. It's a nice place for a vacation, and I'll pay for your flights. Or I could come and see you, whatever you prefer."

"Wow." Jane paused. "So, what caused you to suddenly move out of the city and become interested in family? You're not dying, are you?" Although she sounded sarcastic, there was definitely a worried undertone in her voice.

"I would if I'd carried on the way I did," Riley retorted in a joking manner. It wasn't that far from the truth, but Jane didn't need to know that. "I needed to slow down."

"I never thought you'd even consider that. What are you doing in Mystic? Workwise, I mean."

"Workwise, nothing, but I'm doing up the house I bought."

Jane laughed even harder now. "You and home improvements?"

"It's not my strong point, but I'm learning." Riley smiled, relieved that her sister had thawed a little. "I'm also trying my hand at this strange new concept of friendships. It's scary but refreshing."

"Who are you and what have you done to my sister? What's next? Dating?"

Riley's smile widened as she thought of Quinn and their moment on the couch. They'd almost kissed. Almost. "No, I'm not dating," she said, wondering what Jane would say if she told her she had a crush on a woman. "What about you? Do you have a new man in your life?"

"No. I tried the whole internet dating thing, but being a single mom, it's not easy. Men run for the hills as soon as I tell them I have a child."

"Typical," Riley said with a huff. "Well, maybe you'll meet a nice man when you visit me in Mystic. People are really friendly here. Or, as I said, I could come to Orlando. I miss you, Jane."

"Sentimental too now, huh?" Jane hesitated, clearly puzzled by Riley's revelations. Riley had never taken the time to talk to her on the phone like this. Their interaction usually consisted of short messages to confirm a meet-up or a quick call on birthdays and holidays. "Okay, sis. We'll come and visit. I miss you too, believe it or not, and I want to check if you're okay because you don't sound like yourself at all."

"I'm okay, I promise." Riley's shoulders dropped as she sank back on the sofa and propped her feet up on a pillow. "And you? How's work?"

"Busy, busy, but I shouldn't complain, as I only work

part-time," Jane said with a chuckle. "They offered me a full-time contract as a resident nurse in a home, but I prefer to spend more time with Mindy. Paul has been paying alimony, so all in all, it's not too bad."

"Are you on speaking terms again?" Riley asked. "It's been four years since you got divorced, right?" That was another thing she felt guilty about; she hadn't been there for Jane when she went through her divorce. She hadn't understood what loneliness meant until now, and it hurt to think that Jane must have been so lonely during that period.

"We're civil, but that's about it. He's moved on, I've moved on. At least we have Mindy, so it wasn't all wasted time."

"I can't wait to see her again." Riley genuinely missed her niece, and she imagined she'd grown a lot since last time. "I'll make sure she has her own big-girl bedroom." She paused, anticipating asking the dreaded question. "And Dad? How is he?"

"Not too bad," Jane said to her surprise. "He's living a healthier life now. I've practically forced him to eat better, he goes out for walks every day, and he's got help at home twice a week. The doctor thinks he can still live a normal life as long as he takes care of himself. You should call him. He's been asking about you."

"I will." Riley cleared her throat. "I should have called him sooner."

"True. But better late than never. He's not going to be around forever, you know. Especially with his heart condition, it's tricky, so you need to make an effort or you'll regret it one day."

"Yeah." Riley sighed. "I'll call him."

"Good. Anyway, Mindy is calling for me, I've got to go.

I'll call you back to discuss our visit." Jane yelled something at Mindy, and before Riley could get another word in, the line was cut off. She blew out her cheeks and braced herself for the next phone call, then dialed her father's number.

30

QUINN

*U*nder the stacked-up furniture was a small safe. It was wedged under a bedframe, right at the back of the basement, and Quinn's name was written on top with a black marker. It was heavy, but Quinn had managed to move it upstairs, and she'd tried several combinations that included birthdays and other memorable dates, but none of them worked. She'd called her brother and her parents to update them on the situation, and at Riley's invitation, they were coming over to inspect the contents of the basement tomorrow. They couldn't give her any clues as to what the safe combination might be, but they'd been terribly excited to hear the news, especially her mother, who still felt bad about the fallout with her father—Quinn's grandfather—after they'd lost her beloved restaurant as a result of his bankruptcy. It wasn't about money anymore, though; Quinn suspected her mom was hoping for something to remember him by now that he was no longer with them. At a loss for ideas, she tried another code—a random one this time, of course to no avail.

"Any luck?" Riley asked. She placed a bowl of soup and some bread on the desk.

"No." Quinn's mouth watered at the sight of the fresh baguette. "Wow. Thank you. I haven't had one of those in a while."

"Why not?" Riley asked. "It's from the bakery in town. It's nice to have one nearby—one of the perks of small towns, I suppose."

"It's a fantastic bakery, but I can't go there anymore. I had some beef with the owner." Quinn already regretted mentioning it, but it was too late now, and Riley would find out at some point, as people still wouldn't seem to stop talking about it. "I had an affair with his wife," she said, wincing as she saw Riley's smile drop. "It was years ago, but needless to say, he never forgave me."

Riley arched a brow at her. "You had an affair with his wife? Do you make a habit of having affairs with other people's wives?"

"No, I don't." Quinn met her eyes. "And I promise, it's long over."

"I didn't mean that. I don't care if it's over. I..."

Quinn regarded her and detected a hint of jealousy in her voice. "Are you sure you don't care?" Riley didn't answer, so she continued. "It ended four years ago, and she moved away. Rebecca lives in New Orleans now, with her new partner, but as you can probably imagine, I avoid the bakery like the plague."

"Right. Understandably." Riley met her eyes. "Well, you can ask me to get bread for you anytime."

"Thank you, that's very sweet." Quinn scooped a piece of baguette through the creamy broccoli soup and smiled as she tasted it. "It's delicious. Did you make it?"

"I did. I've been experimenting with cooking a little, and I find it rather relaxing now."

"The flashy New Yorker is becoming domestic," Quinn teased.

Riley laughed. "You sound like my sister. I finally summoned the courage to call her yesterday."

"Oh? How did it go?"

"Better than expected. Jane was totally shocked to hear about my change of lifestyle, and she and my niece, Mindy, are coming to visit me." Riley paused. "And I called my father. He was a little short with me at first, but toward the end of the conversation, he mellowed, so I'm hopeful I can repair our relationship. I invited him over too, but he doesn't like to fly, so I'll go and see him soon."

"That's fantastic news." Quinn rubbed Riley's arm. "You must be relieved."

"Yeah." Riley rested her hand on Quinn's shoulder. "Thank you for being so supportive."

"I'm very grateful for you too." Quinn held her breath at Riley's touch, wondering if she could feel her temperature rising. Riley's lips looked insanely kissable—even the findings in the basement couldn't stop her from constantly imagining what it would feel like to kiss her.

She'd been here every night after work, fighting their attraction. Their silent exchanges were long and searing, but Quinn refrained from acting on impulse. Diving into bed with someone without thinking it through had hurt many women and even caused a marriage to fall apart, and she wasn't going to repeat her mistakes. Not anymore, and certainly not with Riley, who was way too good for a one-night stand.

Riley's cheeks flushed, and she let go of Quinn and folded her hands in front of her, focusing on the safe. "Have you tried your birthday?" Talking about the combination of the safe seemed contrived, as the tension between them was palpable, but Riley, too, kept playing the role of a friend.

"Yes. And everyone else's."

"There must be a way. Wouldn't the manufacturer have a reset code?"

"I already looked them up. They went out of business ten years ago, but I could probably drill it open." Quinn narrowed her eyes at the metal box. "If my grandfather wanted me to find it, the answer must be obvious."

"Maybe leave it for a while. I'm sure ideas will come to you." Riley paused. "What about the dates on the backs of the photographs?"

"Hmm...there's an idea." Quinn searched for one of the first albums she'd gone through and took out the photograph of her great-grandparents in front of Aster House. It was just a hunch, the first one she'd gravitated toward, as it was a significant one. *01/08/1943*, it said on the back. Quinn didn't hold much hope, but she tried it anyway. She put in the combination *0108*. Nothing happened, so she tried *1943*, and her breath caught when she heard a clicking sound.

"Did it work?" Riley leaned in and gasped, then jumped up and down in excitement. "Oh my God, you've cracked it!" She wrapped her arms around Quinn's neck from behind. "I can't believe it."

Quinn's hand was trembling as she retrieved a small jeweler's box and an envelope from inside the safe.

"Do you want me to leave?" Riley asked.

"No, please stay." Quinn opened the box and found a ring. It looked like an engagement ring; gold, with one single diamond.

"It's beautiful. Is it your grandmother's?" Riley asked.

"No, it can't be. She's still wearing hers, but it must be a family heirloom." Quinn focused on the envelope and found a letter inside, addressed to her. Seeing her grandfather's handwriting again made her eyes well up, and she swallowed away her tears to read the letter out loud.

Dear Quinnie,

I sincerely hope it is you who finds this letter. I'm writing this in the idle optimism that one day you will move into Aster House and discover the basement. As the eldest grandchild in my bloodline, Aster House was always meant to be yours, and I know how much you loved it. I cannot express how much I regret wasting away our family fortune, but most of all, your and your brother's future.

This letter is for your mother too, my only daughter, whom I love dearly. She will not talk to me after what I did, and I don't blame her. She lost her life, her restaurant that she poured her heart and soul into. Your mother and brother never felt a connection to the house the way you did, and I doubt she'd read this letter to the end. Therefore you, my dear, are my only hope of some form of redemption.

I'll admit, I haven't lived my life like the good Christian that your grandmother was, and I didn't always follow the law. The basement was originally built as a wine cellar, but my father also used it to store cash and host illegal gambling nights. When I took over the house, I followed in his footsteps and continued to host small events for men of high standing in our circles. This in complete discretion, of course. Your grandmother never went into my office. She was aware there was a secret passageway and a basement, and perhaps she even had an idea of what went on down there on Saturday nights, but if she did, she turned a blind eye and told herself we were in a business meeting. Your grandmother is an angel, and I never deserved her.

Gambling is the devil's game. I followed him like a fool and fell into darkness. During my private events, the stakes were reasonable. It was simply a fun pastime that felt exciting and special. We were a secret society that only few were lucky enough to join. When I started traveling to Reno for business on a regular basis, I spent my nights in casinos and lost control. It all went downhill from there. I kept going, hoping to earn back what I'd lost, but of course, I kept losing because that's the nature of the game.

And then, one day, it was too late. I'd accumulated so much debt, borrowing against my properties, land, hotels, restaurants, and even Aster House, that I couldn't keep up with my payments anymore. It was then that I realized I'd failed everyone I loved and there was no coming back from it.

When I knew I was going to lose the house, I saw no other option than to save what I could. Aster House was my legacy, after all. It was, in a way, what defined me. It gave me a sense of pride and a feeling of belonging. That week, I sent your grandmother to a friend's house, as I didn't want her to witness the bailiffs taking away her things, and I hid as much as I could in the basement, hoping no one would find the passageway behind the bookcase in my office.

I have not told anyone about the basement. Only after my passing will my debts be cleared, and if the new owners find it, they will claim ownership. If they don't and Aster House becomes yours, you will be in charge of our legacy that is buried under the house. Apart from some good wines and antiques that I desperately tried to save from being confiscated, most of what I've hidden is of sentimental value. Perhaps that was a mistake on my behalf, but I felt it belonged there. Your great-grandmother's engagement ring is yours too. Please keep it in the family.

You're in college now, and I'm so proud of you. I have no doubt you will have a very successful career, and I know you will find a way to make this your home again, my dearest Quinnie, because Aster House is where you belong. Your roots lie between the thick walls of a home that was lovingly built in a very special place.

Please take care of it and continue to flood it with love.

I hope you can forgive me,

Your grandfather, Arthur Kendall

31

RILEY

"*H*e clearly loved you very much," Riley said as they went outside for a break.

"Yeah. I loved him too." Quinn followed her around the house, but instead of the bench, they headed to the riverbank and sat down on the grass. "It's both sad and exciting at the same time. I love seeing all the old pictures, but it won't bring him back, and the fact that he went through all that trouble because he assumed I'd get the house back makes me feel like a bit of a failure, to be honest."

"How can you say that? The loss was his and only his. It was never your responsibility to get the house back. You're not a failure. You're a beautiful, loving, caring woman with a successful business, and you're doing something that you love." Riley took Quinn's hand, and Quinn leaned into her. She smelled so good that Riley wanted to inhale against her neck, but instead, she took a deep breath and cherished the closeness. This wasn't something friends did, sitting hand in hand, shoulder to shoulder, and she was highly aware of that. "Just because you weren't able to buy the biggest and most expensive estate for miles around doesn't make you a failure."

"I know," Quinn whispered. "He may have been a gambler, but he wasn't a bad man. He just made bad choices."

"And he regretted those choices. He wanted to make it right, for you and the family. You've found something that is irreplaceable. Your family history. It's pretty special, and no one can take that away from you."

Quinn nodded as she silently stared across the river. "The last time I saw him, he begged me to do everything in my power to get it back," she said. "I was in college and visiting him during my summer break. He was drunk, slurring his words, and I think he was trying to tell me about the basement, but I couldn't make much sense of what he was saying apart from that I had to get the house back. He kept repeating that year too—*1943*. I had no idea what it meant until now. And you're right. That wasn't fair on me, but I didn't see it back then. His words impacted me more than I realized. I think that's why I've always been so obsessed with the house. Everyone else moved on—my parents, my brother—but I somehow felt like it was my responsibility." She sighed. "In a way, I even think I felt entitled to it. So, I tried, and I tried, but the market kept booming. The price went up after each new owner, and in the end, I wasn't even close to making the down payment."

"I had no idea you wanted to buy it," Riley said softly. "I knew you had an emotional connection with the house, but..." She winced. "I'm sorry."

"For what?"

"That it's mine now." Riley pulled her knees up and hugged them. It was a mild night, and the sound of the river and the rustling of the trees was soothing. The lights of

Mystic town sparkled in the distance, and people walked back and forth over the pier where Quinn's narrowboat was moored.

"Don't be silly. It was a ridiculous dream," Quinn said with a sweet smile.

"Still, I'm living your dream..." Riley regarded Quinn, who was staring into space. "You never told me you went to college."

"I studied business management at UConn—Connecticut," Quinn said. "My mother never wanted to study. She was more interested in running a restaurant because she loved the hospitality industry. Besides, when she was younger, she lived with the blissful assumption she would come into a lot of money one day, so she never worried too much about building a stable career."

"That makes sense. She came from a very wealthy family."

"Exactly. But by the time I was that age, I knew being successful was the only way to get the house back, and that meant going away to college."

Riley nodded. "So, what happened?"

"I worked as a financial manager for a building firm for a few years, but I found myself more interested in the building process than in the day-to-day operations. I was bored behind a desk, and I wanted to be out there and be part of the hands-on team, so I quit and took on an internship with a local building firm. That meant I had to push my dream of owning the house to the background, but at least I wasn't miserable in my work," Quinn said. "I learned everything I know on that internship, and my business background helped a lot when I eventually started my own company, so in the end, I'm glad I got my degree."

"But you still couldn't buy Aster House."

"No. But as I said, it was just a silly dream. I'm very happy with my life, and my brother is right. I should probably find somewhere more sensible to live."

"Are you sure about that? I like your barge."

Quinn smiled. "You know what? Me too." She looked down at their entwined hands and squeezed Riley's before she let go.

Riley wanted to take it back; she missed the contact already. "I'm looking forward to meeting your family on Saturday," she said. "Do you think they'd like to stay for dinner? I'd love to cook for them."

"That's very sweet of you, but you've done so much for me already."

"No, I want to. I mean that." Riley hoped Quinn could see how sincere she was. She'd been imagining the dining table in the kitchen filled with people, and she longed to hear noise in the house. "They can bring the kids too. I'll get them ice cream." She hesitated. "Unless you think that would be a weird situation. I don't want your mother to feel uncomfortable since she grew up here."

"My mother will be fine," Quinn said. "And if you're sure, I'll ask them. I think they would love that. Thank you."

"Great. I'll make sure to steer away from Italian food because from what I've heard, I can't possibly compete with your sister-in-law," Riley joked. She was already excited about the prospect of throwing her first dinner party. It was an alien concept to her, a room filled with people eating, talking, and having a good time. Her parents never threw dinner parties; they couldn't afford to feed anyone other than their own family, and in New York, Riley hadn't used her kitchen once. "Would you like to have a drink out here?" she asked. "Or would you prefer to continue going through the basement?"

Quinn turned to her, and her eyes lowered to Riley's lips. Licking her own, she shook her head and smiled. "It's late. I should probably get going."

Riley nodded. She hated it when Quinn went home at night. Her absence left a palpable sense of emptiness in the house, and she felt restless on her own. "I'll see you tomorrow."

Quinn leaned in and placed a soft kiss on Riley's cheek. "See you tomorrow," she whispered, lingering against her before she inched back and got up.

Riley touched her cheek where Quinn's lips had been and stared after her as she disappeared around the house. She couldn't ignore what was growing between them much longer. The innocent kiss was doing sensational things to her body, and her cheek was glowing. She sat there, thinking about what could have been. Fantasies filled her mind, as they did every night, and it wasn't until the lights in Quinn's narrowboat went on and pulled her out of her thoughts that she realized she was cold. In the distance, she saw a figure passing through the boat, and she wondered if Quinn could see her sitting here in the dark and regretted going home as much as Riley regretted not asking her to stay. It would happen eventually, she told herself. It was as inevitable as the changing of the seasons.

32

QUINN

It felt surreal to see her family in Aster House. Quinn watched her parents and her brother carry the photo albums to her pickup and their cars, going back and forth with boxes. She'd shown them the letter, and they'd talked for hours while they went through the stuff in the basement. Her mother, who rarely talked about Quinn's grandfather, had opened up for the first time in years and told them stories about when she was younger. Rob couldn't remember very much, and he loved hearing them.

"There used to be a swing right here," her mother said, pointing to the big willow that arched over Quinn's pickup.

"I know. I remember it." Quinn gave her a smile as she placed a box into the trunk of her parents' car. "Do you miss it?"

Her mother looked up at the house as if she'd find an answer there, then shook her head. "Not really. Your grandfather and I never saw eye to eye, but that was mainly because I was the rebellious type. I dreamed of a life in the city when I was younger and wanted to get away from nosey, small-town people. I thought if I could prove myself by getting a

Michelin-star rating for The Harbor Place, he'd let me open a restaurant in New York City and I'd be out of here." She shrugged. "But then I met your father, and I never left."

"Do you still dream about a life in the city?" Quinn asked.

Her mother chuckled. "No, sweetheart. That desire left me a long time ago. When we had you, actually. I figured Mystic was a pretty great place for a kid to grow up. Looking back, it was great for me too. I just didn't see it at the time." She glanced over the yard that was now pristine. "I was very lucky, and I should have appreciated it more."

"Everyone is entitled to their dreams, no matter what age."

"That's true." Her mother smiled. "Riley seems like a lovely lady, and it's so sweet of her to cook us dinner. Are you two close?"

"Yeah, we've become close." Quinn didn't dare look her mother in the eyes, so she pretended to rearrange the stuff in the trunk.

"How close?"

"We're good friends, that's all."

Her mother nodded. "I was asking because you seem so natural around each other. It's almost like you've known each other for years." She paused and narrowed her eyes as she regarded Quinn. "She's very pretty."

"Don't you get any ideas, Mom," Quinn said, wiping her hands on her jeans. Her brother joined them with a teasing grin, and she gave him a warning look. "Or you." She didn't want any of them to know she had feelings for Riley or that there was chemistry between them.

"I just think it would be nice if you met someone special, that's all."

"I'm happy, Mom. I've told you that a million times." Quinn patted her back. "Come on, there's more. Or do you need a rest? Rob, Dad, and I can take care of it."

"No, I'm fine, honey." Her mother sighed. "I'll try to stay out of your business."

"Thank you." Quinn pulled her mother into a tight hug and kissed her cheek. "Let's just focus on what you want to take home. What do you want to do about the furniture? Riley said it can stay here for a while, as we don't have anywhere to store it."

Her mother thought about that as they walked back to the house. "It's yours, Quinn, and it's your decision. All I want is some trinkets and the photographs, which will be passed on to you and Rob eventually. Other than that, you decide." She waved a hand when Quinn opened her mouth to protest. "I don't want to hear another word about it. It's up to you. Well, technically, it's up to Riley, as it's her house now."

"Riley wants everything to stay in our family," Quinn said. "We've talked about it, and she's been very clear about that."

"Then she's not only pretty but a woman of honor. And I noticed Mary has taken a liking to her."

"Yeah. She's helping Riley with dinner. They seem to have hit it off."

Mary, who was keen to stay out of the family business, had offered to help Riley with cooking, and Quinn heard them chatting nonstop each time she passed the kitchen. The kids were in there too, after examining every inch of the house and running up and down the basement through the passageway.

"Mary is a good judge of character," her mother mused

with a teasing gleam in her eye. "So, tell me more about your new friend. Why have we not heard of her before?"

"We've only known each other for a month. She just moved in."

"But we've spoken to each other many times in the past weeks, and you haven't mentioned her once."

"Seriously, Mom, I don't have to tell you everything, and besides, there was nothing worth reporting." Quinn noted her mother had become one of those nosey small-town people she once tried to escape from. "You promised me you'd stop going on about it." She slammed the trunk shut on her parents' car and had a look in Rob's. "There's still some space in here, and we can use your backseat too, so between us, we should be able to fit everything in one drive."

"All right, Grouch." Her mother chuckled. "If you're not talking, I'll just have to interrogate Riley."

33

___

RILEY

*R*iley was experiencing pleasant nerves when Quinn and her family entered the kitchen. She'd done everything to make it as homey as possible, with candles, flowers, and snacks waiting on the dining table. She wanted them to feel welcome. No, she wanted to impress them because impressing Quinn's family meant impressing Quinn.

Quinn's mother was short with shoulder-length gray hair. She had a friendly, open face and an approachable manner, typical of someone who came from a hospitality background. Quinn's father was tall, like Quinn, with a shaggy beard and a good head of hair. His rolled-up sleeves showed scars and burn marks from many years of being a chef, and there was a certain rugged handsomeness about him.

Rob was shorter than Quinn but handsome too, like his father. He was chatty and fun and didn't seem to take himself too seriously. Riley liked him and his wife, Mary, very much, and she'd enjoyed getting to know Mary while they cooked together.

"Please sit and make yourselves at home." She bit her lip and winced at the misplaced comment that had slipped her tongue. "I mean... I didn't mean to..."

"It's okay, sweetheart," Quinn's mother said. "Please don't feel like you have to walk on eggshells around us. Although it's strange to be here again, it was a long time ago that we called this home, so it's not a touchy subject anymore. We're very grateful for your generosity and hospitality." She smiled. "What are we having? Do you need help with anything?"

"It's all under control, thank you. Mary saved me tonight. I was struggling with the batter for the fish, but she showed me how to do it." Riley put an arm around Mary. "I was a little apprehensive about having two chefs over for dinner, so I've kept it simple. Anyway, we're having fish tacos, salads, and lots of little side dishes, so I hope you like Mexican food." At that, her guests started cheering, and Riley laughed. "You sound like you haven't had Mexican in a while."

"There is no good Mexican in Mystic," Rob said.

"None whatsoever," Mary agreed. "And I'm by no means an expert on Mexican food, but I love it, and Riley has cooked an amazing meal."

"And we're having ice cream!" Lila yelled, repeatedly slamming her little fist on the table.

"Yes, you can have ice cream for dessert," Riley said with a chuckle as she ruffled a hand through Lila's hair. "So, what would you like to drink? You must be gasping after a day like this."

"Coca-Cola!" Lila and Tommy screamed in unison.

"Okay, Coca-Cola. I can make that happen." Riley took a big bottle of Coke out of the fridge and placed it in between them. "For the adults, I have the ingredients to make you a margarita, or alternatively, I have both red and white wine, and beer."

"That sounds lovely," Quinn's mother said, "and I can't wait to have one of your margaritas later, but why don't we open one of those bottles from the basement? It seems fitting for the occasion, and my father would have wanted us to have a drink on him."

"Great idea, Mom," Quinn said. "You should pick one. You're good with wines."

Her mother laughed. "Only with new-age wines, honey. I know very few of those old vineyards down there in the basement, but I'll use my intuition. It rarely lets me down." She grabbed the flashlight from the kitchen counter, and when she left the kitchen, Quinn lowered her voice to a whisper.

"Is it just me or is Mom in a really good mood today?"

"I think the letter and the photographs gave her some form of relief," her father said. "The fact that she and your grandfather fell out has bugged her since his passing, and she never spoke about it much until today, not even with me. She seems lighter."

"Yeah." Quinn turned to look at Riley and instinctively reached for her hand. "Thank you," she said, then quickly let go when she saw her brother staring at their hands. "Are you sure I can't do anything?"

"You can help me put everything on the table if you want." Riley grinned as their eyes lingered. Quinn made her smile each time she looked at her. She opened the fridge, took out various salads, and handed them to Quinn, then retrieved the spiced fish from the oven, along with corn tacos, refried beans, and freshly grilled corn on the cob.

"Oh my, this looks fantastic!" Quinn's mother said, glancing over the spread on the table when she returned with a bottle. "I know it's unusual to have red wine with Mexican food, but my curiosity got the better of me and I really want to try this one." She carefully pulled out the brittle cork, sniffed it, poured a little into her glass, and took her time to smell and taste it. "Mmm."

"Approved?" Quinn's father took her glass and nodded as he tasted it. "Excellent. What is it?"

"It's a vintage Bordeaux—a Liber Pater from Graves." She poured everyone a glass and sipped it as she scrolled through her phone. "Mmm...it's really good. Let's find out more—I have an app for this. The bottle doesn't have a barcode, but I can put it in manually." She entered the information from the bottle, then her eyes widened, and she almost choked on her wine.

"Are you okay, Mom?" Quinn asked, patting her mother, who couldn't stop coughing, on her back.

"Yes, I'm fine," she said, looking a little pale. "It's just that the wine I've opened..." She stared at the now empty bottle. "It's worth almost four thousand dollars."

34

QUINN

Quinn had rarely laughed so much as she had tonight. Her mother, who considered herself a wine connoisseur was teased relentlessly for opening one of the most expensive wines in the world to go with fish tacos. After the initial shock had settled, her mother had been able to laugh about it too, and they'd joked about how slowly they were drinking it to savor the experience as much as they possibly could.

"That was a great last two-hundred-and-fifty-dollar sip," Rob said with a grin as he finished his glass. Well chosen, Mom."

Quinn's mother rolled her eyes and chuckled. "I'll never hear the end of this, will I?"

"Never. And the food was delicious. Thank you so much, Riley." Rob picked up the last piece of fish with his fingers and laughed when Mary slapped his hand.

"Rob! The kids will copy you. You know that."

"Daddy's eating with his fingers." Lila laughed loudly, and Mary shook her head and glared at Rob.

"Can we have ice cream in front of the TV?" Tommy asked.

"Yes! Ice cream! Ice cream!" Lila got up from her chair and bounced up and down.

"If your mom and dad are okay with it," Riley said.

Mary nodded, and Riley filled two bowls with a generous amount of vanilla ice cream.

"Here you go. Do you know how to work the remote?"

"Of course!" Lila giggled. "I'm five."

"I'm sorry, I forgot what a big girl you were." Riley turned to Mary and Rob once the kids had left the kitchen. "They're so sweet."

"They are, but you might change your mind when they get their sugar rush from the ice cream," Mary joked. She looked around the table and arched a brow. "Now that the kids are gone and it's all calm, are we going to discuss the elephant in the room?"

"The elephant? You mean the wine in the basement?" Quinn laughed. "Yes, I imagine we're all thinking the same. If that bottle was worth four thousand..." She paused and shook her head. "It's crazy. There are at least three hundred bottles down there."

"If not more," her mother said. "Goodness, I had no idea my father was such a wine collector. I knew he appreciated a good bottle, but I hadn't expected *that*."

"What are you going to do with it?" Mary asked.

"That's up to Riley," Quinn said. "It's her house and her wine, so—"

"No," Riley interrupted her. "It's *your* wine. He left that for you and your family. I already told you that. You should have it valued. It will undoubtedly do great in an auction." From the looks on everyone's faces, it seemed they were surprised to hear her say that.

Quinn's mother waved a hand. "We can't accept that. The personal items and photographs are one thing, but as Quinn said—"

"And as *I* said, absolutely not. It's yours and I don't want to hear another word about it. Now, as we're already on the red, would you like another glass? It won't be as good as the one we've just had, but I think you should leave your basement wine alone for now." Riley opened a bottle of red without waiting for an answer.

"Thank you." Quinn's mother smiled as Riley poured her a glass, and Quinn knew she wasn't just referring to the wine. Her parents didn't struggle financially anymore, not like they had after they lost their restaurant, but they were far from wealthy, and any extra income would give them some relief. "So, tell me, how did you and Quinn meet?"

"The first time we met was at the pizza restaurant in town, actually. Quinn was there with the kids. And then, a few days later, she kindly helped me bring a ladder back from the hardware store."

"She was going to take it home in her Mercedes," Quinn said with a chuckle, remembering how adorably helpless Riley had looked on her high heels. "I couldn't let her drive like that." She shrugged. "And we've seen a lot of each other since." When her mother looked from her to Riley and back, Quinn knew exactly what was coming.

"How sweet. And are you single, Riley?"

"Mom, I told you not to get nosey," Quinn warned her.

"That's okay, I don't mind personal questions." Riley poured a final glass of wine for herself and crossed her legs as she sat back. "Yes, I'm single. I've been single since my divorce many, many years ago."

"You haven't dated at all?" Mary asked incredulously.

"I dated a little bit here and there, but I haven't been in a serious relationship at any point. I guess I've never met someone who made me feel..." Riley's eyes darted to Quinn for a split second, and she stopped herself. "I just never met the right person."

Quinn noted Riley didn't use terms such as "the right man," or "husband material," and suspecting her mother might have noticed their connection, she didn't dare look in her direction.

"You will one day. Maybe now is the time?" Mary said. "A fresh start. A new home—have you tried a dating app?"

"Mary!" Quinn widened her eyes at her sister-in-law.

"What?" Mary spread her arms. "It's a perfectly normal question."

Seeing Riley's cheeks burn, Quinn wished she could make them all stop interrogating her. It was awkward for both of them, and all she wanted was to be alone with her.

"I...ehm...I have," Riley stammered. "I mean, I've tried it, but it wasn't for me. I prefer meeting people in real life, I suppose. But you're right. A fresh start is the perfect time to meet new people and make new friends." She painted on a smile and glanced at Quinn again. "And I'm so happy I've met Quinn. She's been such a support in a scary time for me. Starting over is hard, but she's made it easier."

"Likewise." Quinn returned her smile and thought it was incredibly sweet that Riley was being so open with her family. "I don't think you have any idea what you've done for us. We're so happy to have things to remember our grandfather by."

35

RILEY

"*I*t was lovely to meet you." Riley walked Quinn's family to the door. She'd had a wonderful night and she was pretty sure they had too. Rob was carrying Lila, who was sleeping in his arms, and Tommy had just woken up after falling asleep during a movie.

"And you, Riley. Thank you so much, I hope to see you again soon." Quinn's mother gave her a long hug, then looked at Quinn as she stepped back. "Are you following us?"

"I'll drop off the stuff in my pickup tomorrow," she said. "You go. I'll help Riley clear up the kitchen."

When Riley closed the door behind them, Quinn let out a long sigh.

"What's wrong? Are you okay?"

"Yes. I'm just sorry for my mother and Mary. They wouldn't stop asking questions, even though I warned them upfront."

"I didn't mind. I had a great night." Riley lingered by the door and looked up at her. "I sensed you were mildly uncomfortable, though, perhaps because of our..." She hesitated. "Our situation."

"Our situation." Quinn tilted her head and shot her an amused smile. "Yes, it's quite a situation, isn't it? I can't seem to stop thinking about kissing you, not even for a second and—" She closed her eyes and shook her head. "I'm sorry. I shouldn't be flirting with you. We're friends and I don't want to mess things up unless you've really thought this through."

Riley stared at her and finally allowed herself to indulge. God, Quinn was attractive, and she didn't even know it. The way she was standing there with her hands in her back pockets as if she were trying to restrain herself made Riley weak in the knees. "I don't want you to stop flirting with me," she whispered, and Quinn glanced up. Riley could drown in those eyes. "There's not enough thinking in the world that could make me change my mind."

Quinn's gaze darkened, and Riley's heart pounded so hard she could feel her pulse at the base of her neck. Quinn moved her hands out of her pockets for a split second but then tucked them back in as she looked Riley up and down. Her eyes went to Riley's hips, framed by the tight jeans she was wearing, then up to her cleavage where they lingered before settling on Riley's face, darting from her mouth to her eyes and back and swallowing her with her gaze.

Riley closed the distance between them until they were so close she could feel the tickle of Quinn's breath against her nose. It carried a hint of red wine, and Riley had never craved the taste more. She wanted to savor her like she'd savored the vintage Bordeaux tonight and work her way through Quinn's complex layers until she found the very essence of her. The part of her still buried.

Quinn's chest heaved fast as she licked her lips, but she

still didn't move. Waiting patiently like a predator luring in prey with its beauty, the corners of her mouth tugged up into a small smile. She knew Riley would come to her, and she was ready to devour her. The tension between them was electric as they stood there, neither of them acting on their raging desires. Was this a game of seduction, or was it fear holding them back? Both, Riley suspected. It was thrilling and terrifying at the same time. What she felt was so intense that, once they kissed, nothing would be the same again.

Unable to restrain herself any longer, Riley leaned in and brushed her lips over Quinn's as lightly as a drifting feather. It caused whimpers and soft moans to escape them both, and stunned with surprise at how her body reacted, Riley took in a quick breath as she inched back a little. She grabbed hold of Quinn's arm to steady herself; blood rushed to her head, and she swayed on her feet. She vaguely registered her ragged breathing and the tremble of her hand as she held on to Quinn. No words could describe how her body felt in that moment, other than it needed more or she might die. Giving in to her desire, she leaned in again and tilted her head to meet Quinn's mouth. She brushed Quinn's cheek with her fingertips, then parted her lips to softly tug at Quinn's, exploring her delicious, pillowy mouth.

Quinn moaned and finally released her hands from her pockets. She cupped Riley's face with both palms, pulled her in, and pressed their lips firmer together. From there, the kiss felt like a whirlwind, and Riley was swept away. Quinn kissed her, hard and demanding, her fingers lacing through Riley's hair as she pressed their bodies together. Parting her lips and finding Riley's tongue, she claimed her fully, drawing something out of her that had always been there, hidden, dormant, waiting for this moment to reveal itself. Heat blossomed in Riley's chest, and she twitched with longing as she surrendered to Quinn's wandering hands, her lips now on Riley's neck and her thigh wedged between Riley's. She felt it everywhere. A million thoughts and emotions in one moment, a thousand butterflies and a rush of endorphins overpowering her senses as Quinn pushed her against the wall and ground into her, finding her mouth again in a hungry kiss.

Riley slid her hands under Quinn's shirt to find her warm, smooth skin. It felt right, and in that realization, it almost became too much, too overwhelming, too intense. She couldn't stop, though, and it was Quinn who finally stepped back and brought a hand to her lips as she stared at her.

"What was that?" she whispered.

"Yeah." Riley leaned back against the wall because her limbs felt like ice cream. She was melting, and if she didn't steady herself, she'd turn into a pool at Quinn's feet. "That was…" Her voice trailed away as she met Quinn's eyes.

Quinn nodded, then took another few steps back. "I should probably go."

"You don't have to go. You can—"

"It's a lot," Quinn interrupted her. "I don't regret anything, I just…" She shook her head and smiled. "I want to do this the right way. Can I take you out on a date?"

"A date?" Riley swallowed hard as she studied Quinn. She seemed just as fired up as she felt, only clearly, she had more restraint. Riley's lips burned from the heated make-out session, and she had trouble thinking clearly. Yes, of course, a date. That was what people did when they liked each other; they went on a date. Obviously, the same counted for two women. "Yes," she said. "I'd love to go on a date with you. Just know that you're torturing me by leaving."

"Trust me, this isn't easy for me either." Quinn held up both hands as she backed up toward the door. "And thank you for today." She hesitated and bit her lip as if she were dying to say something else, then quickly slipped out before Riley had a chance to protest.

36

QUINN

"And?" Lindsey picked at the piece of carrot cake in between them as she glanced at Quinn from across the table in the ice cream parlor. "How was it, being with your family in Aster House? That must have been awkward. And how was Riley with them?"

"We actually had a really nice day." Quinn absently sipped her coffee. It was hard to hold a conversation when all she could think of was that kiss. "It was cathartic for my mother, I think, and Riley cooked us a lovely dinner." She checked her watch, looking for an escape. "And it was a late one, so I need to catch up on sleep before I get back to work tomorrow. I should probably go soon."

"Oh, come on, it's only four p.m., so don't give me excuses." Lindsey cocked her head. "You look like you've got something on your mind. Spill it." She narrowed her eyes, and her lips pulled into a teasing grin. "Does it have something to do with Riley?"

Quinn hated that Lindsey knew her so well. "I asked her out on a date," she admitted, leaving out the kiss that had impacted her like no kiss ever had.

Lindsey's eyes widened as she leaned back and stared at her in utter disbelief. "You did not."

"Yes, I did. And she agreed. I messaged her this morning. I'm taking her out on Saturday."

"And she knows it's a date-date?"

"Yup." Quinn shrugged. "So that's what's on my mind."

"I'll be damned. I didn't think she'd go there, no matter how persuasive you are." Lindsey slammed a hand on the table. "What is this mysterious hold you have over straight women? What is it that I don't see?"

"We're friends. I'd never flirt with you." Quinn grinned. "But if I did, I promise you'd be turned in seconds and never go back to men," she joked.

"Gross, Quinn. I don't even want to think about that." Lindsey grimaced. "Seriously, eww…"

Quinn laughed. "Thanks for the compliment, and to answer your question, there's nothing mysterious about Riley and me. We like each other and there's attraction."

"Huh. Well, that's great, and I like Riley very much, but you said you'd never date close to home again."

"Yeah, I said that." After Rebecca, Quinn had sworn never to date someone who lived in Mystic again. If it went wrong, it was hard to avoid the other person, and she had no energy to deal with more gossip. "But I've changed my mind."

Lindsey nodded. "So, Saturday… I get it. You're hoping to get lucky so you can stay over when you don't have work in the morning."

"No," Quinn lied again. "Saturday is just a good night for a date."

"Hmm. Where are you taking her? Somewhere in Mystic? I bet she has expensive taste. Has she been with a woman before? Are you sure she doesn't think it's just a friendly dinner?"

"Okay, enough with the questions." Quinn laughed. "Yes, I'll take her somewhere local, no, she does not make a habit of dating women and yes, I'm sure she's aware of my intentions."

"So you've been flirting?"

"Yes. For a little while."

"That's why you were asking about her the other night when we were on our dating apps." Lindsey broke the last bit of carrot cake in half and gave a piece to Quinn. "It's the first time I've heard you talk about a woman this way. It doesn't feel impulsive either. It's like you really want to get to know her, like you're serious about her."

"I don't want to mess it up," Quinn said. "And before you ask, yes, I'm worried it will affect our friendship, and yes, there's certainly a chance she'll change her mind, but I'll deal with that if the time comes." Nerves swirled through her as she sipped her coffee. Anticipation was a new experience; she usually acted on her impulses. Well, she *had* acted upon them, she supposed. But leaving after that kiss had been one of the hardest things she'd done. "She's worth the risk."

"Wow. Those are big, grown-up words." Lindsey pointed at her. "Typical. Out of all the women in the world you could have, you fall for the straight woman who stole your house."

"She didn't steal my house."

"You never said as much, but I know you were thinking it."

Quinn didn't reply because Lindsey had a point. She'd been ready to dislike Riley from the beginning, but seeing her so adorably helpless at the hardware store, she hadn't had the heart to ignore her. If she'd driven away, they wouldn't have become friends, and she wouldn't be in the position she was now—nervous, like a teenager, and unable to function until Saturday, which seemed like light-years away. Eager to take her mind off their upcoming date, she asked, "What happened to Nick the health freak? Did you ever get a reply?"

Lindsey jutted out her bottom lip. "We chatted for a while that night, but then he started asking me all these complicated questions about sports and nutrition since I'd told him I used to be an athlete, and things got too complicated because I had to Google everything before I could answer. Anyway, he left the following day, so that was that. I'm currently talking to a new guy. His name's Marcellus, and he lives in a five-mile radius, but he didn't specify where. He seems really nice."

"Oh? Can I see a picture?"

Lindsey scrolled through her phone and showed Quinn the profile.

"Lindsey, you do realize this isn't a real person, right?' She studied the picture that looked like it came straight out of a nineties hair catalogue she used to flip through at the salon.

"No, he said that was him," Lindsey said in defense. "He sent me another picture, it's just not on his profile. Wait..." She scrolled through the long conversation between them and finally found the picture Marcellus had sent her. "This was taken on his vacation, in Barbados. He's still there."

"It's a picture of his back. You can't even see his face." Marcellus was standing on a beach, facing the ocean. His body was ripped and tanned, and Quinn felt even more skeptical now.

"It's him, okay?"

"Okay, whatever you say." Quinn was convinced it was wishful thinking on Lindsey's part, but she was pretty sure that deep down, Lindsey was aware of that too. "So, are you meeting the stud anytime soon?"

"When he comes back from his vacation, yes, we're going to meet up. He just extended it for a week because he also had some business to take care of there. He's a lawyer."

"A lawyer?" Quinn suddenly felt protective of her friend. Lindsey was clearly being lied to. There was no way a handsome, single lawyer lived nearby without it being public knowledge; their community was too small for that. "Just be careful with him," she said. "And let me know when you're meeting him and where you're going."

37

RILEY

*T*he days and nights were dragging by, and Riley was restless like never before. To take her mind off her upcoming date, she'd finished the living room and the office, and she'd started on the hallway. Working her way up seemed like the logical thing to do. As long as the main part of the house was livable, there was no particular rush to finish any of the bedrooms until her sister had confirmed when she and Mindy were visiting.

The hallway looked even more bare now that she'd removed the wallpaper and painted it white. She'd stripped the old-fashioned carpet from the grand staircase and sanded the steps, and although it was clean like she'd intended, it also reminded her of the entrance to a fancy clinic. It needed stuff—paintings, fixtures, rugs—anything to make it resemble a home and take away the echoes of her lonely footsteps.

Riley was planning on ordering furniture, but she had no idea where to start. Anything modern would look misplaced, and finding the right pieces took time. She'd wondered how the space would look filled with the furniture from the basement. It used to be here, after all, and they would probably suit the space very well. Did she have to ask Quinn for permission to do that? She didn't think so. Whether she kept them in the basement or here made no difference; Quinn could pick them up anytime she wanted.

There was a knock on the door, and she opened it to find Gareth there. He'd been around twice a week since she'd hired him, and he'd done great work.

"Hey," she said. "Do you need anything? A coffee? Water?"

"No, thank you, I'm good." The young man smiled widely. "I just need to know what you want to do with the roses."

"Roses? I didn't know I had them," Riley said with a chuckle.

"Yeah, they're by the waterfront. They're climbers, so they need something to hold on to. I suspect there used to be a fence there leading to the water. Climbing roses have sturdy roots and grow beautifully, so it would be a shame to remove them."

"Okay, sure, I'll come and have a look." Riley followed him outside barefoot. She often didn't bother with shoes anymore, as she was mostly on her own property, and she liked the feel of the thick grass underneath her feet. "Do you think I should get a fence with a trellis for the climbers?"

"No need for a fence if you don't have kids. It would only obstruct your view, but you might want to consider getting a wooden pergola. A shaded space on the riverside would be nice, in my opinion."

Riley thought about that as Gareth pointed to the rose stems coming out of the lawn.

"Yeah, I like that idea," she said. "Do you know where I can buy one?"

"If you give me the cash, I can pick one up on my way next time I come over. I pass by the plant nursery daily, so it's no bother." He ran a hand through his shoulder-length, blond hair and scratched the stubble on his chin.

"Thank you, that's so kind of you." Riley imagined herself sitting there under the roses, and in her new, romantic fantasies, Quinn was beside her. Realizing she was grinning, she looked away. "I'm happy to go along with whatever you suggest. What else do you think we should do?"

"I can probably get your fountains up and running today if you want me to," Gareth said. "I know a thing or two about fountains." He turned to the house. "And I could lead some climbers up the back of the house. They're high in upkeep, but with this huge yard, you'll need regular maintenance anyway, whether that's with me or another company, so you might as well go the extra mile."

"Perfect, let's do that, then. I'd like to keep you on if you can find the time," Riley said. "Do what you want, it's your blank canvas. I know nothing about yard work, so I trust your opinion."

Gareth seemed delighted by her comment. "Thank you, Miss Moore. I'll gladly take you up on that."

"Riley. Please call me Riley." She rubbed his shoulder. "Do you happen to know a strong guy who could help me move some stuff up from the basement this week? I'd like to bring some furniture up, but it's a two-person job, and I can't do it on my own."

Gareth shrugged. "I could help you with that. I've got enough to get on with today, but I could come back tomorrow if that suits you."

Riley shot him a look of surprise. "Are you sure? You don't mind doing other stuff than yard work?"

"No, I like keeping busy. You're only my third client—and my biggest, I should add—so while I have the time, I'm always happy to help out with anything. I need the business since I'm a new starter and all that." He smiled gratefully. "I've placed adverts left, right, and center, but getting new clients has been hard. If it wasn't for Aunt Lindsey recommending me, I'd still be working at the retail park."

"Well, you've got yourself a new, long-term client now. Your aunt's right. You're very good at what you do." Hearing a car approach the gates, Riley looked behind her. "Wait a minute. That'll be Tammy. I'm interviewing for a cleaner."

"I know Tammy," Gareth said. "She used to date my friend." He waved at Tammy. "She's a nice girl."

"Is she any good?"

"I have no idea about the cleaning, but she's certainly reliable."

"Thanks. That's very helpful." Riley smiled. "Well, I'll go meet Tammy and let you get on with things."

38

QUINN

"Hi." Quinn grinned sheepishly as she handed Riley the flowers. "I owe you another apology. I completely forgot I was supposed to help you clear up before I left last week. I wasn't exactly with it after..." She paused. "You know."

"That's okay. It wasn't much."

Riley blushed and stared at the flowers that had taken on a whole different meaning since the last time Quinn had brought flowers. There had to be a lot of things going through Riley's mind in that moment.

"Let me put these in water and I'll be back in a minute." She hesitated as her eyes met Quinn's. "Or would you like to come in?"

"It's okay. I'll wait," Quinn said, knowing there was no chance they wouldn't fall into another kiss as soon as she stepped into that hallway. "You look beautiful, by the way."

"Thank you. So do you." Riley chuckled nervously as she looked Quinn over. "Can I say that? Or should I say attractive? I have no idea how this works."

"You can say anything you want." Quinn's heart swelled

at Riley's innocent stammer. She clearly didn't know how to handle the situation, and from what Riley had told her, she hadn't dated that much at all, even when it came to men. Glancing into the hallway, she noticed the walls were stripped. "How on earth did you do that?" she asked, pointing to them when Riley returned.

"I used the ladder," Riley said as if it was nothing. She looked stunning in a tight, black dress, high heels, and a black trench coat, and her lips were coated in a layer of red gloss that made Quinn's core tighten. "I pulled it all the way out and could just about reach the top of the wall on my tiptoes."

"Okay...that's dangerous. You know that, right? The ceiling is way too high in the hallway to do yourself."

"I put two mattresses underneath in case I tumbled off. It seemed excessive to hire scaffolding." Riley shrugged cheerfully. "I managed, and I'm quite proud of myself."

"You should be. But please don't go up there again when you're painting. I'm really not comfortable with that."

"Are you worried about me?" Riley asked, closing the door behind her and crossing her arms as she walked. It wasn't a cold night, but she didn't seem to know what to do with her hands. Or maybe she wasn't sure how to greet Quinn.

"Of course I'm worried when you pull stunts like that. I don't want anything to happen to you." Quinn kissed her cheek and put a hand on Riley's back as she led them to her car.

"You're sweet." Riley blushed and smiled as she looked up at her. "Is that yours?" she asked, pointing to the Chevrolet.

"Yeah. I don't use it very often." Quinn chuckled as she

opened the door for her. "I wouldn't let you climb into a pickup wearing a dress like that. It would be sinful."

Riley laughed and straightened her dress as she settled in the passenger's seat. "My first date in years... This is quite the night."

Quinn slid into the driver's seat. "Because you're going on a date with a woman?" she asked as she started the engine.

"Yes..." Riley began. Quinn headed down the long drive and onto the main road, then took a left toward the drawbridge. "But mostly because I'm going with you," Riley eventually continued. "I'm excited. Where are we going?" She shook her head. "Not that it matters. I would happily have dinner on your barge or in my kitchen."

"I wanted to take you somewhere nice. There's a fish restaurant at the end of the pier by the harbor—The Harbor House. It's the one my parents used to run." Quinn smiled as she glanced sideways at Riley. "It's still very good. My mother claims they've gone downhill since it was taken away from them, but I disagree. Don't tell them we've been there, though, when you see them again. She's practically banned me from setting a foot in there. It would be a betrayal."

"I won't say a word." Riley met her eyes with an amused look. "*When* I see them again? You mean when the auditor comes to value the wine collection?"

"Not just that. They really liked you. Both my mother and my brother have been telling me to bring you to their homes for dinner. They want to return the favor." As she crossed the bridge, Quinn took her hand off the steering wheel for a moment and placed it on Riley's arm. "It's nothing official, I promise. They don't know we're going out tonight, so no pressure. They just thought you were a lovely woman, that's all, and they want to thank you for your kindness."

Riley smiled. "I thought they were absolutely wonderful. I had such a great night. I really clicked with Mary, by the way."

"Yeah, Mary loves you too. She's a close friend of mine, actually. I knew her before she got together with my brother."

"And that never caused any friction?"

"Not really. We've always remained very close, and she tends to pick my side when I have a spat with my brother." Quinn steered the car into a side street parallel to the pier and parked in front of a beautiful, large, stately building. "Here we are." She walked around the car to open the door for Riley, who giggled as she got out.

"You're holding the door open for me," she said, stating the obvious.

"Does it bother you?" Quinn asked.

"No. Like it." Riley smiled flirtatiously and glanced up at the restaurant. "This looks fancy. I've seen the building from my backyard, but I assumed it was a house."

"Nope. Best fish restaurant in the wide vicinity."

Quinn had reserved a table in the corner by the window, and instead of sitting opposite her, Riley took a seat beside her on the bench. The lights were dimmed, and candles were burning on their table. The Harbor House had always been a romantic establishment, but the new owners had really gone out of their way to make it special. A pianist was playing classical tunes behind a grand piano, and they had implemented silver service, with waiters in white suits and a sommelier who looked like he'd jumped straight out of an Agatha Christie novel.

"Would you like to start off with a glass of Champagne?"

he asked, handing her the wine list.

"Yes, please. And we'll have a bottle of Chablis with dinner." Quinn turned to Riley. "If that's okay with you?"

Riley nodded. "Sounds good. I appreciate it when someone makes the decisions for me. I'm not used to that," she whispered when the sommelier had left. "You're more gallant than any man I've ever dated."

"You've clearly been dating the wrong men."

"Clearly." Riley scooted closer until she was right next to Quinn and crossed her legs. "I've always been the one in charge, but I like this arrangement. It makes me feel... desired, I suppose. Taken care of."

Quinn felt her core tighten, and she was unable to keep her eyes off Riley's legs. They were long and elegant in those killer heels, and she imagined Riley wearing those heels in bed. "You're not uncomfortable, being on a public date with me?" she asked.

"No..." Riley paused as her gaze shifted to Quinn's mouth.

Tonight couldn't come fast enough.

The evening had been intimate, filled with delicious food, flirty conversations, and deliberate touches that would have seemed casual to anyone around them, but to Quinn, they were loaded with a promise of more to come. She took the last bite of her lobster before the waiter cleared their table, and she noticed Riley was lost in thought as she gazed out over the river.

"What's on your mind?" she asked, placing a hand on Riley's thigh.

Riley met her eyes as she fiddled with her napkin. She

looked apprehensive, nervous even. "What's it like? Being with a woman?"

"The same as with a man, I would imagine," Quinn said. "Although I can't be sure, as I've never tried that." She shrugged. "I guess it depends on the person you're with. Some people work in bed, and some don't. If there's chemistry, it can be spectacular." She held Riley's gaze and smiled when she saw Riley take in a quick breath. "Have you never had great sex with someone you had chemistry with?

"I can't say I have." Riley swallowed hard, her eyes fixated on Quinn's hand resting on her thigh.

"Then you've been missing out." Quinn squeezed her softly. "For me, I like to be in charge," she continued, knowing the conversation was turning Riley on. "If my bed partner likes that too, then it's usually good." She smiled. "Really good."

"What do you mean by being in charge?" Riley's eyes darkened, and she shifted against her, moving her thighs apart when Quinn's fingers splayed wide and curled inward.

"It can mean a lot of things, but mostly it just means that I love to please."

Riley swallowed hard. "How?"

"I guess you'll have to find out...." Quinn saw Riley's breath hitch again, and she squeezed her thigh harder. "As I said, I aim to please. There's nothing to be nervous about."

"Hmm..." Riley's chest was heaving fast now, and Quinn felt her leg tremble. "I've never been with someone like that. Someone who doesn't put their own pleasure first. Men tend to do that."

"Are you curious to find out what it's like with a woman?" Quinn moved her arm to the backrest of the bench around Riley's shoulders and twirled a lock of hair around her finger. "Something tells me you are."

Riley didn't answer right away, but she leaned into the crook of Quinn's arm, seeking contact. "Of course," she finally said. "I'm curious about you. When I'm with you, my body gives off these intense signals. It excites me and frightens me."

"Is that happening right now?" Quinn asked, leaning in to whisper in her ear. "Because the thought of fucking you is making me incredibly wet." Her lips pulled into a smile when Riley shuddered against her. Realizing they looked like they were about to jump each other, she inched away a little and straightened herself. "Maybe we should save this conversation for another time. Would you like dessert?"

Riley stared at her, wide-eyed, and shook her head. "No," she whispered back. "I want to go home. With you," she added, meeting Quinn's gaze. "Do *you* want dessert?"

Quinn chuckled. "Only if you'll let me lick it off your body, but I don't think they'll appreciate that kind of behavior here."

"I'm sorry to interrupt." A waiter appeared at their table. "There will be a storm tonight, so I just need to warn you in case you're heading to the other side of the river. It may be tricky to cross the bridge later if the winds are too strong. The weather warning has just turned to amber."

"Of course, the storm..." Quinn had seen it on the news, but storms were rarely as serious as predicted, so she hadn't even given it a second thought. "Amber?" she frowned. "Okay, I guess it's best if we go, then."

"Very well, I'll get you the check."

Riley looked puzzled as she glanced out of the window. "It looks so calm outside."

"Yeah. It still is, but he's right. If there's an amber warning, we should probably get going. It can get pretty rough along the river."

39

RILEY

"*I* had fun," Riley said as Quinn stopped the car outside Aster House. "In fact, it was by far the best date I've ever had."

"Really? I'll take that." Quinn turned and draped her arm over the passenger's seat in a manner that bordered on cocky. Riley liked that Quinn was assertive; after years of being in charge herself, it was nice to let someone else take over. "I had fun too. The wind hasn't picked up yet, so I can get home safely."

Riley nodded as she focused on Quinn's mouth. The mouth that had been on hers and had caused fantasies to run through her mind all week. The mouth that had kissed her like she was all that mattered. Quinn licked her lips, and it made them shimmer in the moonlight. It was so quiet that Riley felt like she had to keep her voice down. *The silence before the storm.* "Are you coming in for a nightcap?" she asked.

Quinn chuckled and smiled. She was so attractive when she smiled; she radiated confidence and her dark eyes sparkled. "You're not making this easy for me." She paused, lingering close. "Maybe next time? I got a little carried away with my flirtations at the restaurant, but I think we should take our time. I want to do this the right way."

Riley leaned in and rested her forehead against Quinn's. Her body was on fire, and she needed Quinn now. "Everything about this feels right, though," she whispered, closing her eyes and cherishing Quinn's nearness. "You can't just turn me on by talking to me the way you have all night and then leave. It's not fair."

"Hmm…" Quinn didn't back away, and their combined breath quickened. *In. Out. In. Out.* It was the sound of pure desire. *In. Out. In. Out.*

Riley's lips parted and a moan escaped her. She was burning just being physically close to Quinn. "I want you." She swallowed hard and moved away to look at her. "I need you." Tilting her chin toward her, she met Quinn's lips, and Quinn crumpled, claiming her mouth. And then Quinn's hands were all over her again, tenderly combing through her hair and snaking around her neck.

Riley trailed her fingers over Quinn's shoulders, her arms, her back. She longed to feel that warm skin again. "Please come in," she murmured. "You know we can't stop this. Not now."

Riley's bedroom didn't feel daunting tonight. She wouldn't lie awake for hours, tensing at every noise and regretting her poor life decisions. She left the lights off as she closed the door behind her, shutting out the world. Tonight, this room was a safe space, and the house seemed friendlier, romantic even. Lighting the two candles on her bedside table, her heart pounded hard as shadows flickered over the ceiling, leaving a restless, golden glow in the darkness. She wasn't afraid, not in the literal sense, but she was aware her life was about to change. That everything was about to change.

She turned to face Quinn and took her in. Her gorgeous face, kissed by the candlelight, her thick hair that fell over one side of her forehead, her body that Riley craved with every fiber of her being, wrapped up like a present in tight jeans and a white shirt that showed a teasing hint of cleavage. She could hardly wait to unwrap that present because Quinn was everything she never knew she wanted, a gift from the universe that came into her life at the right time, when she was ready to feel and accept things that previously seemed unthinkable.

Quinn closed the distance between them and brushed a hand over Riley's cheek while she regarded her with an intense gaze like she wanted to swallow her whole. "You're so beautiful, Riley." Cupping her chin, she tilted it to kiss her, biting softly on Riley's bottom lip and tugging at it while she wrapped her arms around Riley and moved them down to her behind.

Riley held her breath as Quinn squeezed her and pulled her against her. The hold she had over her, the reaction she evoked, was otherworldly. It was another level of intimacy that Riley was yet to learn about, a sensation that brought her home to a place unknown.

"Take me," she murmured, clinging to Quinn's shirt. She wanted it to come off. She wanted to feel Quinn's heated skin against hers and melt together.

At that, Quinn pushed Riley back toward the bed and cupped her neck as she lowered her onto the mattress. She was a lot stronger than she looked and had no problem easing Riley down gently. "Are you sure about this?" Her expression changed as she steadied herself over Riley; she was in charge, all right, and it was sexy as hell. "Because we can wait."

"Yes. I'm sure." Riley inched back so she was lying in the middle of the bed, her pulse racing and her heart thumping.

"What do you like?" Quinn asked, trailing a finger from Riley's neck down to the dip of her cleavage. "Do you like soft?" Running it along the edge of Riley's bra, she looked down at her as she wedged her finger inside and teased Riley's nipple before pinching it firmly. "Or do you like hard?"

Riley's chest shot up at the delicious pain, and she shook her head. "Fuck! Anything... I don't know." With Quinn's hand on her breast, everything went blank apart from the way she felt.

"You don't know?" Quinn squeezed her breast, and Riley gasped in delight. "I guess I'll just have to find out, but something tells me you like a bit of pressure." She hiked up Riley's dress, wedged her thigh in between her legs, and when she pushed into her, Riley almost lost it. Yes, she loved pressure; she'd just come to realize that. She especially liked how assertive Quinn was, and in that moment, she'd take anything Quinn was willing to give her.

"Pressure is good," she finally said through moans, loving the weight of Quinn's body when she lowered herself on top of her.

"Okay..." Quinn lifted her head and smiled. "You like that? That's a start..." She took Riley's wrists and pinned them over her head, holding them down firmly with one hand while her other slipped into her bra again. "And do you like *this*?" Arching a brow, Quinn bit her lip as she studied Riley, who wriggled in her grip.

"Uh-huh." Riley couldn't speak through her arousal. She was throbbing and writhing, marveling at how Quinn had managed to figure out what she craved within a matter of seconds.

"Do you want me to let go of you?"

"No." If there was one thing Riley was sure of, it was that she loved being pinned down. The fact that she was at Quinn's mercy drove her wild, and somewhere in the back of her mind, she wondered why she'd never come to this conclusion before. Perhaps because the few lovers she'd had never made her feel this connected to them. She and Quinn were emotionally, physically, and spiritually in tune with each other, yet she felt raw and vulnerable.

Quinn brought her mouth to Riley's ear and inhaled deeply against her hair. "I think I've figured you out already," she whispered in a teasing tone.

Quinn's breath in her ear made Riley squirm. There was so much she wanted to say, so much she wanted to beg for, but she didn't know where to start.

"So, I'm going to give you what you need, and if you want me to stop, just tell me." Quinn hiked up Riley's dress farther, still holding her down with her other hand. "Will you do that?"

"Uh-huh." Riley was unable to form a sentence, so she held her breath while Quinn pulled her dress all the way up, revealing her black lingerie.

"God, you're gorgeous." For a moment, Quinn let go of her as she reached around Riley's back to unclip her bra and pull it away. "I've been fantasizing about doing so many things to you..." She paused as her eyes lowered to Riley's small breasts. "Many, many things."

In a reflex, Riley brought her hands to Quinn's face, but Quinn swiftly took her wrists again and pinned them back over her head. "Don't move, Riley. Give yourself to me. I promise you won't regret it."

40

QUINN

*R*iley tensed in Quinn's grip as she stared at her hungrily. Her eyes reflected immense arousal and a heightened sense of awareness but also a flash of nervousness and vulnerability. It drove Quinn wild when women looked at her like that; it was almost more satisfying than the act itself. She loved being in control; she ran her own company, she liked being single so she could live her life the way she wanted, and that same control extended to the bedroom.

Quinn had never asked herself why she felt the need to be in control, but now it crossed her mind for a brief moment. It was curious that she still wanted to have the upper hand, even though she trusted Riley with her life.

Riley's chest shot up again when Quinn skimmed her breasts, lazily tracing her fingers over Riley's nipples so softly she barely touched her, yet Riley was highly reactive, shaking at every touch. Priding herself on being a pleaser, Quinn wanted to give her a night she'd never forget.

"Can I take these off?" she asked, tugging at the thin elastic of Riley's panties that followed the curve of her hipbones. When she let go, it snapped back against Riley's skin, causing her to shudder.

Riley nodded and lifted her hips so Quinn could pull them down. Her legs were trembling and her chest heaving, but she kept her arms over her head while her eyes followed Quinn's every move. "I want to feel your skin," she murmured with a pleading look.

Quinn smiled and got up to undress, the premise of covering Riley's body with her own sending twitches between her legs. Lying there naked, Riley's beauty radiated from every pore, and Quinn absorbed her curves and her flesh with all her senses. Her small, perky breasts, her shapely legs and waist, the strip of hair between her thighs that Quinn was dying to trace with her tongue, her elegant neck, her lips the color of wild roses, her big, brown eyes full of longing, and her long, dark locks that were draped over the pillows like a crown.

Quinn took it slow, fixated on Riley as she peeled off her layers. Riley's eyes darkened and intensified as she looked Quinn over, and a soft moan came from her lips. She parted them as her gaze darted up and down, over Quinn's legs, hips, and torso, to her breasts and her face as she stood there in nothing but her boxers. Riley was drinking her in with her eyes, for the first time looking at a near-naked woman this way. Curiously, intently, hungrily, with a fascinated glimmer that told Quinn she hadn't changed her mind. Quinn was confident in her body. Doing physical labor five days a week was all she needed to stay in shape, and she could tell Riley appreciated what she saw.

"Are you still okay?" she asked, but only out of courtesy. It was clear that Riley had no intention of going back, and Quinn didn't want to stop either.

"Yes." Riley's ribcage rose, and she held her breath.

"Fuck, you're…" Her hands clawed at the fabric of the pillow above her head. "You look so…" Unable to find words, her voice trailed away.

Quinn crawled back onto the bed and steadied herself over her. "Riley, I'm so, so hungry to taste you, and I'm going to feast on you," she whispered, casting her gaze over Riley's hard nipples that rose and fell rapidly with the ragged sound of her breathing. She dipped her head to Riley's stomach and kissed it, then worked her way down while caressing her thighs, spreading them apart when Riley's hips bucked against her.

Slowly running her tongue over the length of her sex, Quinn moaned as she dug her fingers into Riley's thighs. She tasted delicious, familiar in a way, and although Quinn wanted to take it slow, Riley's reaction made it hard to hold back. Her body pushed into her, lifting, begging. Exhaling hot and damp air between Riley's legs, Quinn watched her tremble before she closed her warm mouth over Riley's clit and sucked. Riley tensed and cried out; a deep, strangled cry as if she was close to exploding already. Instinctively, her hands moved to Quinn's hair, fisting it while she pushed her tighter against her.

Quinn let her while she feasted on her, then came back up to meet her face with a teasing grin. "What did I tell you?" She enclosed Riley's wrists in her hand, restraining them over her head again.

"You…" A deep frown settled between Riley's brows. "You can't stop now."

"Who said anything about stopping?" Quinn smiled against her lips. "Have you ever tasted yourself?" Before Riley had the chance to answer, she kissed her hard and passionately, thrusting her tongue into Riley's mouth while her hand drifted down between Riley's thighs to stroke her.

She was wet, throbbing, and so responsive Quinn thought she might come instantly as she carefully entered her with two fingers. She sighed at Riley's tight wetness gripping at her fingers and her heated skin that felt so perfect against Quinn's.

Pushing into her with her body weight, Quinn penetrated her deeper, then pulled back and started fucking her, slowly at first, moving in sync with the rise and fall of Riley's hips as she kissed her. It was glorious to feel Riley's legs wrap around her as she gave herself, throwing her head back and moaning loudly. With her grip on Riley's wrists, their mouths pressed tightly together, and her fingers filling her up over and over, Quinn felt closer to Riley than she'd ever felt to anyone. Their movements turned wild and erratic as Riley pleaded for more with her body language, moaning, writhing, trembling, and nodding as she forced her eyes open to meet Quinn's when Quinn lifted her head to look at her.

"Oh my God. I'm..." Riley tensed as her fists clamped around Quinn's hand. Lightning struck outside, flashing across Riley's body and lighting up her angelic face that was bathed in ecstasy. Seconds later, the thunder rolled above them, and rain started clattering onto the roof in a rhythmic drip.

"Come for me, Riley," Quinn whispered, curling her fingers inside her. Her lips pulled into a smile when Riley shook in her arms, her body convulsing and her walls clamping around Quinn's fingers. She felt Riley's orgasm throughout her whole body, and it fed her with a sinful heat that made her throb. Never taking her eyes off Riley, she didn't stop until she relaxed entirely and her satisfied body became limp beneath her. Riley's fists loosened and her fingers stroked Quinn's hand. She lifted her head, her lips searching for Quinn's, and her feet softly brushing against Quinn's legs, like she wanted to caress all of her at once.

Quinn felt emotional as she watched Riley come back to her senses. She seemed confused, baffled, overwhelmed even. Tears trickled from the corners of her eyes, and Quinn kissed them away. "Are you okay?" she whispered.

"Yeah." Riley nodded and pulled her in, her lips lingering against Quinn's before she let out a soft breath. "But that was..." She paused, stroking Quinn's face. "That was crazy."

"Good crazy?" Quinn suggested.

Riley nodded, and Quinn kissed her forehead and the tip of her nose. The thunder rolled, and the rain clattered even harder, the noise nostalgic like a lyrical memory. For now, she was back home, but she wasn't the young girl anymore who had hidden under the covers, anxious about the storms. Tonight, it felt fitting, and she welcomed each clap of thunder and flash of lightning with open arms. The storm outside was as loud and clear as her feelings for Riley, who curled up against her and nuzzled her neck.

41

RILEY

*L*ying in Quinn's arms, Riley listened to the wind. It was picking up again, building after calming down for an hour. If she'd been here alone, she'd be scared, but tonight it felt dramatic, romantic, and even comforting as it filled the silence between them.

The branches of the willows blew against her bedroom window, tapping the glass as if pleading to let them in and shelter them from the storm. Their silhouettes danced underneath the dark sky, slowly at times, then violently as stronger gusts of wind came and went.

Riley felt at ease, lifted, as she snuggled into the crook of Quinn's arm, and she had a strange sense that maybe she was right where she was supposed to be, where she belonged. Living for her job, she'd never belonged to anyone, not even her ex-husband, who had tried so hard to make it work despite Riley never being around. Even if she had put in the effort, she doubted it would have worked out because he couldn't have made her feel like this. No man could make her feel like this; she knew that now. She'd never belonged to a place either; she'd only lived in the penthouse she rented for a year, and before that, she'd never stayed anywhere for longer than two years. Perhaps Aster House would grow on her and become a place that felt like home; the house seemed like a better place when Quinn was around.

Her thoughts were interrupted by the howling of the wind, and there was that familiar noise again, the slow creaking every few seconds. "I can hear it now," she whispered. "The house is breathing." She listened again, closing her eyes while Quinn stroked her face. "It sounds tired."

"It's old. But that's the charm of it, right?"

"Hmm..." Riley smiled, turned on her side to face Quinn, and scooted closer. She needed to be near her, to feel her heat, her softness that she would always crave from this night on. Now that she'd discovered the sensation of a woman—of Quinn—she couldn't go back, and she didn't want to. "What's it like for you to be here again, at night?"

"It's strange. Times have changed. *I've* changed. It's not my world anymore, but I love being here with you. It makes sense because of you." Quinn leaned in to place a trail of kisses down Riley's forehead to the tip of her nose and brushed a lock of hair behind her ear. "What's this like for you? Do you want me to leave? I won't be offended, I promise."

"No, I don't want you to leave. I haven't felt like this in... well, ever." Riley smiled shyly. "I'd love to wake up with you."

"No regrets?"

"None other than not trying this sooner. You're pretty amazing, Quinn."

"And you're...." Quinn rolled on top of her, and Riley sighed. The rush of Quinn's warmth against her skin and the feel of her weight ignited the fire in Riley again. "You're special," Quinn said. "I don't meet women like you here very often." She shook her head. "No, strike that. I've never met someone like you."

"I don't mean to sound negative, but I'm just a middle-aged woman with too much time on her hands and no idea who she is. I don't see how that can be special."

"That time can be put to good use now," Quinn joked, teasing Riley's nipple with the tip of her finger. Her mischievous expression dropped, and she kissed her softly. "You'll find your way, I promise."

"I know. This is a good start, for sure." Riley shivered at Quinn's touch and ran her hands down to Quinn's behind. The smoothness of her skin and the curved landscape of her body mesmerized her; she'd been apprehensive at first, but now she wanted to feel all of her. "I want to touch you," she whispered and pushed Quinn to the side before she steadied herself over her and kissed her neck. From her quiet moans, Riley could tell she liked it, but she still seemed apprehensive as Riley moved down to her breasts to fold her lips around a nipple. It hardened immediately, and Quinn's chest lifted, but she cupped Riley's face and pulled her back up. "Not yet," she said, then bit her lip regretfully.

"Why?"

"Because I'm not ready."

That statement seemed absurd to Riley after what Quinn had just done to her, but she nodded and ran her hands through Quinn's hair. "Okay."

"It's not you. I'm just not used to this kind of intimacy."

Riley nodded. "Do you mind if I ask why not?"

"It's just the way it's always been." Quinn shrugged. "I got used to playing a certain role in my life. I was always the pleaser, even with my first girlfriends in college. Most of them were only exploring their sexuality at the time. They all went back to men in the end, and I was reluctant to give myself to them, as it was never going to last.

"And you think I'm only gay for a day?" Riley joked.

"Possibly not." Quinn gave her a lopsided smile. "But I tend to go for straight women. It's a weakness. I just can't help myself. You're not just some straight-woman conquest if that's what you think," she quickly corrected herself. "You're very, very special to me. But until I'm sure we're on the same page, I'd rather spend my nights focusing on you, if that's okay."

Riley chuckled and laced her fingers through Quinn's. "Hey, I won't complain after what you just did to me, but I never thought you'd be the one to shy away." She regarded Quinn and noted how vulnerable she looked, so she dropped her smile and continued. "Take all the time you need. I've learned time is a gift, not a burden. That's what moving to the middle of nowhere and meeting a very special woman taught me."

42

QUINN

"What have you been up to, sis?"

Quinn looked up at her brother, who was laying the table for dinner. She was playing Jenga with Lila and Tommy, and they were both intensely fixated on the wobbly tower in the middle of the dining table. Lila's tongue was sticking out of her mouth while she decided which piece to pull out, and she went into a sulking fit when her brother blew on it.

"Nothing much," Quinn answered.

"Oh? You just seem to be in a good mood." Rob turned to the kids. "Tommy, stop winding her up."

"What do you mean?" Quinn smiled. "I'm always in a good mood!" She focused on the game and tried to hide her smirk. She'd been in a dreamy state after leaving Riley this morning, and she'd had trouble concentrating at work.

"I don't know. You've got this goofy look on your face, like you're feeling exceptionally smug or something."

"No, nothing to report. I just like playing Jenga with these two." Quinn had no intention of telling her brother about last night. It wasn't his business, and she had no idea where it would lead with Riley. They hadn't spoken or messaged today, and that made her restless. She'd never been one for actively chasing women, but right now, it wasn't easy to refrain from contacting her, and Quinn had put her phone in her coat pocket so she wouldn't check it every two minutes.

"Right." Rob regarded her for a moment before continuing with the task at hand. "I just want to say one thing. Riley's an angel. I can't believe she's letting us have all of Grandpa's stuff from the basement, including the wines. She didn't have to do that."

"Yeah, I love her," Mary, who was cooking, chipped in. "Can you please bring her over for dinner? I was going to ask for her number, but I forgot after all the wine we had." She rubbed her temple. "God, my head still hurts thinking about it. It's been a while since I've had a late night."

"I hope Rob drove back?"

"Yeah, it was his turn, so I thought I'd make the most of it. Anyway, don't forget to ask her along next time."

"Sure." Quinn attempted to sound indifferent, but she really liked the idea of coming here with Riley and having dinner with all of her favorite people.

Rob put cutlery next to the plates, then searched for napkins in a drawer. "To be honest, we could do with the wine money. It's been a squeeze these last few months, as the office hasn't been able to give me overtime."

"Why didn't you tell me?" Quinn asked. "I could always help you out. It's not like I have a mortgage or children to provide for."

"Nah. That's very sweet of you, but the wine auction will really help. I'm curious what the collection will be valued at."

"Mom found someone to come in on Friday to check it

out," Quinn said. "I have to work, but Riley's letting her in, and you can join them if you want."

"I have to work too." Rob paused. "Mom and Riley together. Imagine that. I bet Mom will enjoy her chance to have some alone time with her. As she said, you two seem pretty close."

"We are. We're good friends."

"Dad, be careful!" Lila yelled when her father's hand came a little too close to the tower for her liking. "You're going to ruin the game!"

"Sorry, sweetheart." Rob held up his hands and chuckled. "Dinner's almost ready, though, so you'll have to hurry up."

"But we're not finished yet," Tommy protested, carefully pulling out one of the wooden pieces. At that, the tower collapsed over the table, and Rob shrugged.

"You're finished *now*, son. Go wash your hands. You can play more later."

The sulking and protesting that followed made Quinn, Rob, and Mary laugh as Quinn helped plate the food.

"So...good friends, huh?" Mary said when Tommy and Lila had gone to the bathroom. "From what I witnessed, it seemed like you might be a bit more than that." She winked at Quinn and continued in a teasing tone, "Just the looks and the little casual touches—I was wondering how casual they were."

Quinn felt her cheeks heat, but she kept her cool. "I don't know what you're talking about," she mumbled.

"Oh, come on, Quinn. I've known you longer than I've known Rob, and I've never seen you like that around someone. You're so crushing on her." Mary drew out her words as she met Quinn's eyes. "And I have a feeling she's into you too. I mean, she told me she'd been married to a man and all, but you know my intuition never lets me down, and I got the same vibe from her. Also, I'm aware of your track record with straight women."

"I wish everyone would stop mentioning that."

Mary patted her arm and laughed. "Babe, in a small community like Mystic, there's no way you can escape from gossip after bad behavior."

"It wasn't that bad with Rebecca. It was all on *her* terms," Quinn said in her defense, even though she'd fully embraced the blame for it. She let out a deep sigh as she poured water for everyone. "Besides, there's nothing to gossip about."

"Of course." Mary sounded a little too cynical for Quinn's liking, but she let it slide. "You have my blessing, though. I like Riley, and I feel like we could be friends."

"That's what Lindsey said."

"Lindsey's a smart woman." Mary tasted her pasta, added fresh pepper, then scooped her homemade cacio e pepe into a big bowl. "So, what's the deal?" she asked, sprinkling some extra pecorino cheese on top. She lowered her voice when Rob left the kitchen. "Any flirtations?"

"There has been some flirting," Quinn finally admitted. She was more comfortable talking to Mary without her brother around.

"What's flirting?"

Quinn looked over her shoulder and shared an amused smile with Mary when she saw Lila behind her. "It's when you like someone, and then you say or do certain things because you want them to like you more," she said, wincing at her clumsy explanation.

"Flirting." Lila furrowed her brow, and Quinn scooped

her up, snuggling her, while Lila's little arms wrapped around her neck. "Like this?" Lila placed a peck on Quinn's cheek.

Quinn laughed and squeezed her. "That's not quite the right context, sweetheart, but I love your kisses."

43

RILEY

*R*iley waited for the baker to pack up her bread. Now that she knew about Quinn and his ex-wife's affair, it was hard not to think about it, especially since Quinn had been on her mind all day. Martin, the baker, was friendly, outgoing, and he'd already learned her name, which was charming. He was also handsome in an unconventional way, she supposed. Although a little on the short side, he was well built and had a nice smile as he handed her the paper bag.

"Here you go, Riley. Have a great day." His smile widened when Lindsey walked in. "Lindsey. Let me guess. One whole wheat and three chocolate-chip cookies?"

"Yes, please, Martin. You know me so well." Lindsey turned to Riley. "Hey, there. Nice to see you. How are you?"

"I'm great." Riley held up her baguette. "These are addictive."

"I know. You should try his cookies," Lindsey said with a wink. "I'm actually on my break. Do you want to have a coffee? Share a cookie?" She gestured to an empty table by the window.

LISE GOLD

"Sure. Why not?" Grateful for the distraction, Riley ordered a cappuccino, took a seat, and waited for Lindsey to join her with the coffees. She hoped it might stop her from obsessing over Quinn for a while because she'd been checking her phone every few minutes, hoping for a message.

A woman she recognized from the town meeting walked past the window and waved at her, and Riley waved back. She was getting used to living in a small community where people knew her, and there was something comforting about being able to have an impromptu coffee with a new friend.

"So..." Lindsey sat opposite her and lowered her voice as she leaned in. "How was your date?"

"It was..." Riley hid her grin behind her coffee cup. "It was really great. But I'm sure you've already heard all about it."

"I haven't, actually. Quinn was at her brother's house last night, so I haven't seen her or spoken to her. Anyway, she's been quite secretive in general when it comes to you." Lindsey shrugged cheerfully. "So I guess you'll have to fill me in."

Riley laughed. "Oh, no. You're not getting anything from me."

"Come on. At least tell me if you kissed." Lindsey waved a hand. "Actually, never mind. I can tell from that look on your face that something happened. Something more than a kiss, perhaps?"

Riley shook her head and pointed a finger at Lindsey. "Are you always this nosey?"

"Uh-huh. I don't have much of a love life myself, so I have to live vicariously through others. Although I have been messaging with this guy I met on a dating app. He

194

seems really nice, and he lives nearby, but Quinn is convinced his profile is fake."

"Let me see." Lindsey handed Riley her phone, and she scrolled through his profile. "I agree with Quinn, I'm afraid," she said, pointing to his picture. "This looks like it's been ripped from a catalogue and the picture on the beach could be anyone."

"Damn it." Lindsey let out a sigh of frustration. "We chatted all of last night and we agreed to meet up soon. But if he's not who he says he is…"

"Even if he's not who he says he is, you might still click. Just be careful and make sure you meet somewhere public, and needless to say, don't tell him where you live."

"Hmm…" Lindsey sipped her coffee as she contemplated that. "I suppose we could meet for a coffee in the daytime. I could ask Quinn to shadow me, just in case."

"I don't mind coming along either," Riley said. "I'll keep to myself, and your date won't know that we know each other."

"Or you could shadow me together," Lindsey suggested hopefully. "When are you seeing Quinn again?"

"You're not going to give up, are you?"

"Nope." Lindsey took one of the cookies out of the paper bag on the table, broke it, and gave half to Riley. "So you might as well tell me."

Riley chuckled, and a blush crept onto her cheeks. "I'm seeing her tomorrow," she said, her libido firing at the prospect. Yesterday had dragged by, and this morning was no better, even though she'd been busy grooming herself and getting groceries.

"Where?"

"My place. I'm cooking for her. Anything else you'd like to know? What color lingerie I'll be wearing?"

Lindsey grinned. "Feel free to tell me." She stared at Riley while she dipped her cookie into her coffee and sucked on it. "You've never been with a woman before, right?"

"No. Never."

"So why Quinn? I mean, she's my best friend and I love her dearly, so I can see why you like her, but it must be strange to have dated men all your life and then suddenly realize you're attracted to a woman." Lindsey's expression turned serious. "How did that happen and how do you feel about it?"

"I have no idea how it happened. It just did. It's unexpected, but it's also..." She hesitated, searching for words. She wasn't used to talking to a friend, or even having a friend, and she'd never opened up to her sister either, but deep down, she did want to talk about it, and even though Lindsey was nosey as hell, Riley liked her very much, and she trusted her. "I don't know. Better late than never, I suppose. I'm as surprised as you are, but it feels right. Like I was meant to meet her."

"Wow. So you're not just experimenting."

"Is that what you thought?"

Lindsey tilted her head from side to side. "I wasn't sure what to think, to be honest with you. Quinn is popular with straight women. She seems to have a way with them, and I thought you might have fallen for her charms just like all the other curious ladies looking for a one-night stand. Nothing wrong with that, of course," she added. "You're both adults."

"No, it's not curiosity." Riley sipped her coffee. "At least, I *was* curious, I won't deny that, but this has been ..." She paused. "It's been building for a few weeks. Looking back, I could feel there was something all along. I just didn't understand it, and maybe I was afraid or in denial."

"And now?"

Riley met Lindsey's eyes and smiled. "I'm scared, but I'm not scared of my feelings. I'm scared that it won't work out," she said honestly, her thoughts falling into place as she voiced them out loud. "And I'm not confused. If anything, it all makes sense now. My lack of interest in men, my failed marriage, my uninspiring dating history…"

Lindsey returned her smile and nodded. "Then I hope it works out, for both of you."

"Thank you. So I'm not getting the 'you better be good to my best friend' speech?"

"No, Quinn's a big girl. She can take care of herself," Lindsey said. "And besides, we're friends too now, right?"

"Yeah." Riley felt a lump form in her throat. Friendship was a beautiful new concept to her, having people she could talk to, people who really listened and even cared about her feelings. Why had she been so solitary? So anonymous? "And as we're friends and you're sharing your cookies with me," she continued with a smirk, "would you like to come over for dinner next week? It's getting warmer, and I've just ordered an outdoor dining table."

"Yes!" Lindsey clapped her hands together. "Count me in. I'll bring dessert." She got up and left some money on the table. "I have to get back to work. I'll see you soon."

44

QUINN

"Come in." Riley stepped back into the hallway. "What do you think?" Riley looked nervous as she waited for Quinn's reply. "If you'd prefer to keep everything in the basement, I can put it back. I just thought that until you decide what to do with the furniture, it would be better off polished and on display, right? It's a shame having them down there covered in dust when they look so perfect here. If you want, you could even have it valued and I'll buy it off you."

Quinn's lips parted as she glanced over the hallway. The furniture was back in its place like it had never left, and for a beat, it felt like home again. Like her grandfather would descend from the staircase any moment accompanied by the rhythmic click of his walking stick. "It's perfect," she whispered. "How did you know where to put everything?"

"I remembered what it used to look like from the pictures you showed me." Riley opened the door to the living room. "It's slightly different in here without the carpet and the wallpaper, but it still works, right? The rugs were a bit moldy, but I managed to get them back to a reasonable state with a carpet steamer. I'll buy new ones, but for now, it makes the space sound less hollow."

Quinn was too baffled to get a word out. Riley's modern, white corner sofa was covered in throws and pillows, and her glass coffee table had been replaced by Quinn's grand-parents' antique chest. The long, Chinese sideboard was placed along the side wall, topped with the collection of vases that were now filled with white lilies. Riley had brought up the dining table and chairs too, and on the table was a brocade runner and two silver candelabras with white candles she'd never seen before.

"I bought some antique decorative pieces online to spruce it up. Is it weird for you? Or uncomfortable? As I said, I can put everything back."

"A little weird, yes, but it's not uncomfortable. How did you manage all of this?"

"Gareth came in to help me this morning. I employed a cleaner too. She's been polishing for hours."

"It looks beautiful," Quinn said as she closed the distance between them and wrapped her arms around Riley's waist. She'd been wanting to do that since last time they parted. "Absolutely beautiful. Please leave it here for as long as you want. I'm not ready to say goodbye to it, so you might as well enjoy it."

Riley nodded as she met her eyes and smiled. "It's good to see you again."

"Yeah. I've been thinking about you." Quinn cupped Riley's cheek and ran her thumb over it, causing Riley's eyes to flutter closed. She was so incredibly gorgeous and gracious and elegant that it almost hurt to look at her. Her hair was silky smooth as Quinn ran her hand through it, and she was wearing a figure-hugging navy dress and her killer black heels. If Riley was trying to seduce her, she'd certainly succeeded. "I was planning on kissing you the moment I walked in, but you took me by surprise with all the work you've been doing."

"You can kiss me now," Riley whispered, tilting her head and inching closer to brush her lips over Quinn's. They both moaned quietly, and a gasp of breath escaped them at the electrifying touch.

Quinn pressed her body against Riley's, her core tightening at the contact. With every word or look exchanged, she felt the need to be all over her, and holding back was hard once they'd started. She ran her hands over Riley's behind and squeezed her, pulling their hips together. "You're killing me in that dress," she said in a breathy voice.

"I was hoping you'd like it." Riley smiled mischievously and ran a hand through Quinn's hair in return. "Are you hungry? I cooked, and the food will be ready in ten minutes."

Quinn chuckled. "I'd like to eat you first," she joked, nudging Riley against the couch until she fell onto her back. She pulled up Riley's dress in one, quick motion, and Riley gasped as Quinn traced the inside of her thigh. "And don't worry about the food getting cold," Quinn added. "I only need five minutes."

Riley's cheeks were rosy as they sat down at the dining table in the living room. Her eyes darted to the couch, clearly reliving what had just happened. She was flustered and a little out of sorts, forgetting the cutlery and their glasses, but she had a wonderful grin and a satisfied glow on her face. Quinn had made her scream, and she planned to do it again and again and again until Riley had no energy left to move or speak.

"This looks great," she said, helping herself to the fish pie Riley had made. "You're becoming quite the chef."

"Against all expectations, I enjoy cooking." Riley spooned a little onto her plate and poured the wine. "But I'm not sure if I can eat now. You've made me feel all funny inside."

"You should eat. You'll need your strength for later," Quinn retorted, licking her lips. She could still taste Riley and couldn't wait to have more of her.

Riley blushed even harder now, and she covered her face in her hands. "Oh God, what have you done to me? I can't eat, I can't sleep, I can't think. I'm a mess."

"If you're a mess, then you're the most beautiful mess in the whole world." Quinn's expression turned serious when Riley shook her head. "I mean it. I love everything about you. The way you talk and move and smile and laugh...and the way you frown when you're concentrating. I love how brave you are, how you've left everything you know behind to start over and tried to make the best of a difficult situation. I also love how kind you are and naïve in certain ways, even though you're highly intelligent. You're a beautiful person inside and out, and I adore you."

Riley dropped her fork and her eyes welled up as she stared at Quinn, who'd never seen her emotional before; she didn't seem like the vulnerable type. Quinn rarely opened up like this herself, but it was like a floodgate had opened and the words just kept coming.

"And for the record," she continued, "I can't eat or sleep or think either, so maybe we should talk about what's happening here."

"Yeah. We need to talk." Riley reached over the table and

took Quinn's hand. "I love how kind you are, how much you love your family, and how you make me smile inside every time I see you. I love how you make me feel, like I'm floating, and my emotions and dreams are entwined. This may sound cheesy, but you've lifted me and awoken my body. It's been asleep for so long and I'm alive again, perhaps only now really living for the first time." She smiled. "And on top of all that, I'm crazy attracted to you and I want you so, so much."

Quinn's soul warmed at Riley's words, and she squeezed her hand. "Do you think you're ready for something with me?" She hesitated. "I'm talking about being exclusive, maybe giving this a name. Because if you need more time, I'd understand, and I'd never rush you into anything."

"I've never been ready, but I am now," Riley whispered. "I've wasted the better half of my life doing something that had essentially no meaning, even though it seemed like it was everything at the time. I've been living on autopilot, working every minute of the day, avoiding emotional connections because they got in the way of my ridiculous goal of growing my company. I never want to do that again." She winced. "Ending up on intensive care the first time should have been a wake-up call, but it wasn't. I kept asking when I could get back to work, and when they told me I had to stop and take it easy, I didn't listen. It wasn't until the second time that I realized I wouldn't survive if I maintained my lifestyle, and that was devastating because I didn't think I had anything else to live for."

"And now you do?" Quinn asked.

"Yeah. I'm starting to learn what it's like to have friends and be part of a community, and I've come to realize that experiences are far more valuable than gross margin." Riley sighed as she met Quinn's eyes. "So yes, I would love to give this a name and see where it leads. I'm done wasting time."

"Then don't," Quinn said. "I've wasted time too. I've never settled because I was always working toward something I couldn't have, feeling like a failure every time this house changed owners. But I've found a sense of peace now. It's been cathartic coming here, so thank you."

"You're thanking me for stealing your dream?"

"I'm thanking you for opening my eyes. I wanted everything to be like it used to be, but change is good. I still love the house. I always will. But the walls are white now and the world hasn't collapsed around me. In fact, I feel happier and more content because I've been able to let it go. You're good for me, Riley." Quinn was aware that if it worked out with Riley, this could be a new chapter in their lives, but the house had no part in that. This was between her and Riley and their feelings for each other. It was a matter of the heart, not a place.

The corners of Riley's mouth tugged up as she nodded. "I'll remind you of that when I strip the bedrooms, girl-friend." She giggled. "Or should I say partner? This is new to me, so you'll have to help me out."

"You can call me anything you want. Whatever you're comfortable with." Quinn stood up and leaned in over the table to kiss her. "But I like the sound of girlfriend."

45

RILEY

"Tell me about your love life," Riley said, snuggling into the crook of Quinn's arm and wallowing in her warmth. Her bedroom window was open, and although the April night breeze was cool, she liked the sound of the river and the rustling of the big willows in the yard. What had scared her before was now romantic and soothing, and as she was making good memories here, she was starting to see the house in a different light.

"My love life?!"

"Yeah, I want to know everything. Or at least whatever you're comfortable with sharing."

"Okay, let's see." Quinn squinted her eyes and stroked Riley's shoulder as she looked up at the ceiling. "There was Jane when I was fourteen. She was my first love. Jane lived nearby on the farm by the T-junction, and she was mature for her age." "She chuckled. "By that, I mean she had breasts before any of the girls in my class did, and I couldn't stop staring at them."

Riley laughed. "Was she your girlfriend?"

"No. I never told her about my feelings and suffered in

silence each time she had a new boyfriend. We were sort of friends. Our parents were friends, so we saw each other regularly, but I think she knew I had a thing for her because she never suggested we did anything together without our parents around. I had a crush on her for years, until my attention shifted to Stephanie, who was here on holiday with her parents. She was a year older than me, the first 'out' girl I met, and I had my first kiss with her. She haunted me for a while after she left, but I never heard from her again." Quinn sighed. "Then I went to college and had a string of girlfriends, most of them closeted. I realized women liked me, and I suppose I was a bit of a playgirl when I was younger."

"I'm not surprised."

"Really? Why?"

Riley grinned. "You just seem like the type." She kissed Quinn softly and lingered against her lips as she continued. "You're all about confidence, and that's sexy."

"I'm not that confident," Quinn assured her. "Not when I really like someone."

"Are you sure about that?" Riley arched a brow. "Because you seemed pretty confident with me."

"It's just a front. I can assure you, I had sleepless nights over you."

"Okay…" Riley trailed a finger over Quinn's stomach and bit her lip as she watched her shiver. "So, who came after your closeted college girls?"

"Mainly tourists and seasonal renters," Quinn said. "Just women who happened to be around at the right time."

"Were they all straight?"

Quinn winced. "Who have you been talking to? I feel like you think I have a bad reputation or something. Was it Lindsey?"

"No..." Riley felt her cheeks go pink. "I mean, I may have spoken to her at the bakery, but she didn't mean it in a malicious way. We were just making conversation."

"Of course. Lindsey is never malicious, but she needs to learn to keep certain things to herself." Quinn rolled her eyes. "Anyway, to answer your question, yes, most of them were straight."

"Is that your thing? Converting straight women?"

"Not necessarily," Quinn said. "I just flirt with women in general and most women happen to be straight. You'd be surprised how many are bi-curious and looking for an opportunity to try it."

"And Rebecca was one of those women..." Riley knew it was silly to even mention the woman, but for some reason, she felt a little jealous of her in particular. "Do you still have feelings for her?"

"No," Quinn said resolutely. "I regret ever getting involved with her, but I suppose in a way, it made her life better because she's happy with someone now, and I want that for her. But I feel bad for Martin. He didn't deserve to be deceived, and I still feel guilty for breaking up their marriage, even though she would have eventually figured out her sexuality, with or without me. In a nutshell, we had fun, but I wish it hadn't been me."

Riley nodded. "Martin seems nice."

"He is. At least, he *was* nice to me before it happened." Quinn shrugged. "I still have to face the consequences regularly when our paths cross, and I guess I deserve that. He generally ignores me. Sometimes he gives me a polite nod, but it's that look in his eyes that stabs me through the heart every time."

"Judgment?"

"Yeah." Quinn smiled sadly. "Enough about me. It's my

turn now. Tell me about your heart condition." She met Riley's eyes, and Riley noticed there was a hint of worry in Quinn's expression. "Because that's what *I* really want to know. You don't talk about it much."

"My heart..." *My heart belongs to you*, Riley wanted to say, but she realized this was no time to crack a joke. "It's called stress cardiomyopathy, and it's rare. The condition causes severe heart muscle weakness under emotional or physical stress. It's likely to be genetic, as my father has it too. He was admitted to the hospital after my mother passed away. In my case, it's triggered by physical stress, and I've been admitted twice and spent weeks in ICU. I'm taking medication and I'm being monitored, so I'm hopeful it's under control now, as long as I don't take too much on."

"Like renovating a huge house?"

Riley chuckled. "The renovation isn't stressful. I find it relaxing, and I haven't had palpitations since I moved to Mystic.

"Okay. As long as you're careful. Have you talked to your father about it?" Quinn asked.

"No. He doesn't even know I have the same condition. I was only diagnosed a year ago. I don't want to worry him. It's my problem, and telling him may cause *him* stress, leading to heart failure, so I don't intend on telling him, ever."

"What about your sister?"

"She doesn't know either," Riley admitted. "I haven't told anyone in my family. It just seemed easier that way."

"Were you all alone in the hospital?"

"No. My assistant knew. She was there by my side going through day-to-day stuff with me." Riley rolled her eyes. "It seems crazy now, but we continued business as usual from my hospital bed."

"But no family? That's so sad. You shouldn't have gone through that alone."

"I wanted to. I've always done everything alone since I left home. I was independent from an early age. I wanted a successful career so I could help my parents out financially, but I guess in the process, I forgot that they would rather have *me* in their lives than my money." Riley sighed deeply. "When my mother passed away, I hadn't seen her in a while. I'd paid for her care home because she had trouble with her mobility, and I'd given her everything she needed, but I hadn't visited her, and that brought a lot of guilt along. I clearly didn't learn my lesson, as I've been doing the same with my father and my sister."

"You did what you thought was right," Quinn said. "Don't blame yourself. Your mother would have known you were only trying to make life better for her." She pulled Riley closer and took her into her arms. "Everyone has regrets but you need to try to let go of them. It's the only way to move on."

Riley inhaled deeply against Quinn's skin and ran her hand over her back. "I'll always have regrets," she whispered. "But one thing I'll never regret is this. No matter what happens."

46

QUINN

"I want to touch you." Riley's caress continued down to the triangle of dark hair between Quinn's thighs and teased it. "Will you please let me?" She hesitated. "I want to make you feel good too."

Quinn's core tightened at her touch, and she squeezed her thighs together. Yes, she wanted Riley to touch her; she wanted nothing more, but it had been so long since she'd given herself to someone.

"It's been a while," she finally said.

"Does it matter?" Riley kissed her neck and her jawline, then met her mouth in a searing kiss.

Quinn moaned as she sank into the kiss, meeting Riley's tongue and embracing her. Riley shifted on top of her, her warm skin coating her and sending her to higher places. "No...." She shuddered and gave in. "I guess it doesn't." Grabbing Riley's hand, Quinn guided it down between them, and she gasped at the sensational feeling of Riley's touch as her fingers stroked her sensitive lips. She hadn't expected her body to react this fiercely, and her hips lifted instinctively to meet her touch.

Riley's lips parted at feeling Quinn's wetness, and her eyes radiated desire as she seduced her with her fingers, exploring her and skimming her clit.

"Oh, God..." Quinn closed her eyes and covered her face with her hands. She'd only let her go there because Riley had begged her and she wanted Riley to experience what a woman felt like, but she'd been unprepared for the effect. Although Riley's touch was gentle and careful, it felt like lightning had struck her, and Quinn heard her own voice echoing through the room and bouncing off the walls.

"Let me see you," Riley whispered, moving Quinn's hands away from her face and kissing her while she started circling her most sensitive spot. "Is that good?" she asked when Quinn shuddered.

"Yes," Quinn said through short breaths, the surging tide inside of her building. "Perfect. That's—"

"What?" Riley looked at her in a whole new way, with curiosity and fascination, perhaps because she hadn't expected Quinn to let go so easily or for her to react so fiercely. "Like this?" She moved faster, and Quinn lost it. Her arms tightened around Riley, and she closed her eyes as she buried her face in her neck, shaking all over when she climaxed. Having an orgasm that was not self-inflicted was a whole new experience to her, and it was strange to surrender in such an intimate way. It felt beautiful and sacred, and when Riley kissed her and slowly pulled her hand away, all she wanted was to look her in the eyes and tell her how special she was.

"You slay me," she whispered, frowning while she took Riley in. "You do something to me that I can't..." Her voice trailed away. She couldn't find words because what she felt was unknown, and she had no idea how to describe it. "It's..."

"I know," Riley said when yet again Quinn failed to finish her sentence. "You don't need to say anything. Thank you for trusting me." Moving her hand to Quinn's cheek, she stroked her softly and smiled. "Isn't it bizarre? That feeling of euphoria when you're so crazy about someone?"

"Totally." Quinn wrapped her arms around Riley and squeezed her. "I'm falling for you, Riley." She sighed. "You've got me."

Riley lifted her head and smiled. "And you're not getting rid of me either. There's no way."

Quinn chuckled and noted that although her limbs were limp, she was wide awake. "Are you sleepy?" she asked.

"No, not really. Why?"

"I want to show you something." Quinn got up, put on her robe, and held out her hand for Riley to join her. "You won't need shoes," she said when Riley looked for her slippers. "We're not going outside. Well, not really."

"You got me curious now." Riley chuckled when Quinn led them to her old bedroom. "Any more hidden rooms I don't know about?"

"Not as far as I'm aware." Quinn opened the dormer window, placed a chair underneath it, and climbed out onto the slanted roof. "But this is a pretty special place." She helped Riley out and tapped the space next to her. "Be careful. Some of the tiles might be loose." She hadn't been here in years, not since she was fourteen and had trouble sleeping. This time, she wasn't mulling over cute girls who wouldn't give her the time of day, and she wasn't recovering from a teenage crush resulting in a broken heart. She was an adult, she knew who she was, and beside her was the most beautiful woman in the world.

"Wow! The view is amazing from up here." Riley scooted closer and rested her head on Quinn's shoulder. Before them was the backyard, Mystic River, and Mystic town, still and sleepy. The way its twinkling lights merged with the stars above, it was hard to tell where the town ended and the sky began. "Did you spend a lot of time up here?"

"For a while," Quinn said, remembering those nights when life had felt so dramatic to her teenage self. Sitting here with Riley was different. It felt peaceful. Perfect. "I only came here when I felt sad, and this is a good night."

"Your first good night on the roof of Aster House." Riley locked eyes with Quinn and smiled as she inched closer. "We should seal that with a kiss."

47

RILEY

"Oh my goodness, what a difference!" Lindsey's eyes widened as she got out of her car. "The yard looks beautiful, just like it used to."

"Thank you. Gareth has done a great job, I'm so happy with him." Riley smiled as they passed the fountains and walked toward the backyard. They were finally working, and she loved the gentle sound of the water and seeing birds drink from them. The lawn was pristine; the cobbled paths that spiraled through the yard had been cleared and cleaned, the hedges were tidy, and the flower beds along the surrounding walls were filled with daffodils. Her outdoor furniture had arrived this morning, and she'd set up a seating and dining area by the water's edge in the shade of the wooden pergola Gareth had brought back from the hardware store. Soon, climbing roses would spiral their way up over the trellis and cover the roof, but for now, she'd used white linen to create shade. On a sunny day like today, it was the perfect place to sit and enjoy the sunset over food and drinks.

"I love that I can see Quinn's barge from here," Lindsey

said, shading her eyes from the sun as she glanced over the river. "Do you think she's home?"

"I'm right here." Quinn turned the corner with a tray in her hands and laughed at Lindsey's baffled expression. "Do you mind if I join you guys?"

"Quinn!" Lindsey grinned as she looked from Riley to Quinn and back. "Wow...okay. No, of course not. Why would I mind?" She shook her head and stared at Quinn, who placed the wooden tray with bread and dips on the table before pouring them wine. "You're here."

"I finished work early," Quinn said, focusing on the food and rearranging everything like it was of huge importance. Behind her confident smile, Riley detected a hint of unease, and she suspected Quinn wasn't used to having Lindsey around when she was with women she dated.

"She offered to cook us food," Riley said. "Isn't that sweet?" She and Quinn had seen each other most nights since their second date, and it felt so natural to have her here.

Lindsey shot Quinn an incredulous look. "You never finish early, and you never cook for *me*."

"I do now." Quinn shrugged. "It's a beautiful evening and—"

"And I'm sure you'd prefer to spend it together," Lindsey finished her sentence in a teasing tone. "So...let me know if you'd rather have some privacy. I can come over anytime." She made herself comfortable in one of the chairs and propped her feet up on a bench. "Actually, no, I take that back. That ciabatta looks yummy, and I'm really craving a drink, so you'll just have to put up with me."

Riley laughed. "I wouldn't dream of sending you away. Wine?" Lindsey nodded eagerly, and Riley handed her a glass. "How was your day?"

"Busy. Thank God it's Friday." Lindsey stretched her arms over her head and yawned. "I've literally been on the go nonstop. The beginning of spring is our high season, and the bookings for long-term rentals especially are going mad right now."

"That's good for your commission though, right?" Quinn asked.

"True. I shouldn't complain, but I've hardly had time to chat to Marcellus."

"Marcellus the catfish?" Quinn shook her head. "Let it go, Lindsey."

"No." Lindsey sipped her wine, then helped herself to a piece of bread. "I like talking to him. He gets me. It's like we've known each other forever."

"He probably looked you up so he could pretend to have the same interests as you." Quinn frowned and looked at her intently. "I'm sorry. I don't mean to be negative, but I'm worried."

"Don't be. I trust him."

Riley didn't interfere but she wholeheartedly agreed with Quinn. From her short stint on a dating app, she'd seen more potential fake profiles than she could count, and she knew there was a good chance Marcellus wasn't who he said he was. She was about to change the subject to cut the tension when Lindsey beat her to it.

"Anyway, let's not talk about Marcellus. How are the renovations going, Riley? Have you decided what you're going to do with all those rooms in there?"

"I've done so much already, I've surprised myself," Riley said, scooping a piece of bread through the delicious tzatziki Quinn had made. "I'll show you my progress later. I'm curious to hear what you think of it. I'm currently busy getting two bedrooms ready because my sister and my niece are coming to visit in a few weeks."

"How lovely!" Lindsey smiled. "How old is your niece?"

"She's five. She's really cute."

"You should bring the kids over when they're here," Lindsey said to Quinn. "It would be nice for Riley's niece to have friends to play with."

"Yes, bring them over." Riley met Quinn's eyes, and Quinn gave her a shy smile. "I want you to meet my sister and Mindy, and it would be nice to get everyone together."

"Does your sister know about Quinn?" Lindsey asked.

"No, I haven't told her I'm dating a woman. I think she'll be shocked, and not just about Quinn." Riley shrugged. "My life is so different now, I don't think she'd get it if I tried to explain it." She winced against the lowering sun as she glanced over the river and realized she felt no more regrets over buying Aster House. She was in her backyard with her new lover and her new friend, and before her was a view so beautiful and serene; a view that was hers alone. She was able to relax without the constant thoughts of next steps in the back of her mind, and to simply take the days as they came.

Perhaps that was the biggest lesson she'd learned: the simple things were often the best things in life. Little moments, fleeting but meaningful ones like tonight, were the ones she'd cherish when she was older and looking back on her life. She wouldn't relive the global launch of a beauty brand or a commercial for a new sneaker, but she'd remember tonight, with the scent of spring in the air, her blooming yard, Quinn's hand around hers, Lindsey's sweet smile, and the sky that turned crimson over Mystic River. This, she thought, was what it felt like to really live.

48

QUINN

"*I*f you really want my opinion, I think this faded yellow will look good in the hallway," Quinn said, pointing to a bucket of paint in the hardware store. "It's a sunny shade, and it'll take away the clinical feel." She picked it up and studied the label. "You'll only need one coat, as you already have the white base."

"I can see how that could work." Riley smiled and kissed her cheek. "And yes, I do want your opinion." She lifted three buckets into her trolley. "Thank you. I've spent hours procrastinating over the past month, and you've just made it simple. Will this be enough?"

"That should be okay." Quinn glanced around to make sure no one was watching, then cupped Riley's face and kissed her lips. "You're cute when you're making decisions. You've got that little frown between your brows."

Riley laughed and ran a hand underneath Quinn's shirt to caress her back. "Oh, yeah? Well, you're pretty cute too. Are you sure I'm not taking up too much of your time?"

"Not at all. This is fun!" Quinn stepped back when a member of staff walked past. She was genuinely enjoying herself, and although the idea of helping Riley decorate her former home would have seemed absurd before, now it felt entirely natural. She loved doing things with Riley; normal, everyday things. "What else do you need? Paint for the bedrooms?"

"Yes, and nice bed linen and rugs and curtains. I probably need some extra furniture to spruce it up. I want the rooms to look pretty and romantic."

"Pretty and romantic. That sounds perfect." Quinn smiled. "We can get most of the stuff here, but there's a second-hand furniture store about a twenty-minute drive north. We could go there after? You might find some nice antiques and I can take everything back in the truck."

"Really? I'd love that!" Riley's eyes widened, and she nodded eagerly; her enthusiasm was adorable. She was a different person from the woman Quinn first met at the restaurant. Gone were the power suits and no-nonsense demeanor. Dressed in jeans, sneakers, and a simple, gray T-shirt, she had a girl-next-door vibe about her now, albeit a very beautiful girl-next-door. Her hair was pulled back into a ponytail, and she had a tan from enjoying her yard. She looked younger and healthier than when she arrived in Mystic, and certainly happier. "If you don't mind?"

"Of course not. It's Saturday and I have nowhere to be, so we can do whatever you want, beautiful." Quinn watched Riley turn back to the paint aisle with that cute frown on her face. She was really getting into home improvement and her skills had come on in leaps and bounds as her confidence with it had grown.

"Thank you." Riley gave her a grateful look. "How do you feel about light blue for the small bedroom? I think Mindy will like it, and this is a sweet shade that could work for both kids and adults. I don't want to make it too child-like, as I won't be having kids over that often."

"Go for it," Quinn said. "It's definitely a romantic color." She paused as she examined the shade cards hanging in front of the shelves. "I'd keep the windowsills white. It will look fresh." Although she was happy to help and advise with anything Riley needed, she also noted she was getting more invested than she should be, and she could already envision what the house would look like if it were up to her.

This wasn't the plan, going all the way with Riley and decorating Aster House as if it were her own. Was she getting carried away? She thoroughly enjoyed the process and seeing the transformation. The house was blossoming and entering a new era, fresh and bright with renewed energy. Quinn no longer begrudged the clean walls and stripped carpets. Since they'd discovered her family heirlooms in the basement, she had all the memories she needed, but there was one thing she really wanted to restore.

"Do you mind if I make a swing?" she asked.

"Of course not. Mindy would love that," Riley said.

"Great! I'll go get some wood. It's on the other side of the store."

"Can we do this first? We still need to decide on color for the other rooms." She blew out her cheeks and shook her head. "There are so many decisions to make and so much to do."

"I think you should focus on those two rooms first, and maybe your bedroom. I don't want you to get stressed."

"Aww." Riley smiled sweetly. "You don't need to worry about me."

"You're supposed to take it easy."

"I'm fine, I promise. I'm not having palpitations

anymore, and I certainly don't feel stressed." She took Quinn's hand. "But you're right. One thing at a time. The rest of the house can wait."

"Good girl." Quinn winked and put an arm around Riley's waist as she led her away from the paint aisle and headed for the wood section. "You know what's a great, relaxing activity?"

"Sex?" Riley smirked suggestively. "Or were you referring to antique shopping?"

Quinn laughed. "Yes, that too, but I actually meant sitting on a swing and enjoying the wind in your hair. I swear, it's therapeutic."

"Aren't we a bit old for that?"

"Never. I'll make a double swing so we can use it together."

"Okay, now we're talking. Where's the swing going? In the bedroom?" Riley slammed a hand in front of her mouth when an old lady suddenly turned the corner. She'd clearly overheard the conversation and stared at them, wide-eyed. "Oops!" She giggled and blushed as they quickly moved out of hearing distance.

Quinn couldn't stop laughing. "Riley Moore, you have a dirty mind and you're not afraid to share it with the world."

"It's all your fault. *You* gave me a dirty mind," Riley retorted, nudging her. "And now I'm embarrassing myself in front of old ladies. What's happening to me?"

49

RILEY

"The auditor is running a bit late, I'm afraid," Quinn's mother said as she checked her phone. "I hope I'm not taking up too much of your time."

"Not at all. It's nice to have you here, Mrs. Kendall." Riley pulled out a kitchen chair for her and made two coffees.

"Please, call me Audrey. I don't want to keep telling you."

"Of course...Audrey." Riley sliced the chocolate cake she'd bought and plated a piece for her. "Quinn told me you liked chocolate." She was a little apprehensive about being alone with Quinn's mother, as she didn't know Riley was dating her daughter. Quinn was going to tell her parents, but she'd spent so much time with Riley that she hadn't seen them since last time they were here.

"Sweetheart, you shouldn't have." Audrey took a bite and grinned through a mouthful. "But I'll take it. Is this from Martin's bakery? He does the best chocolate cake."

"Yes. It's addictive. I've been eating so much cake and bread since I moved here, and it's giving me indigestion."

Audrey chuckled. "Hey, it's worth it. Good food should be enjoyed."

"So true." Riley joined her and sipped her coffee. "Did you manage to store all the photographs and paperwork?"

"Just about. We had to get a small storage unit, and some boxes are in Rob and Mary's attic." Audrey smiled. "Did Quinn pass on the invitation for dinner? I only spoke to her on the phone for about ten minutes this week. She's been so busy with work."

Riley's cheeks turned pink as she nodded. "She did, thank you very much. I'd love to come over."

"So, you've spoken to her?" Audrey narrowed her eyes at Riley. "Or seen her?"

"Yes, I've seen her." Riley didn't want to lie to Audrey, but at the same time, it wasn't her place to tell her they were dating, so she left it with that.

"How nice." Audrey hesitated. "Have you seen each other a lot lately? It's a shame she couldn't be here today."

Riley bit her lip and focused on her coffee. Audrey was fishing, and she had no idea how to handle the situation. "She had an urgent job this morning," she said, avoiding the first question. "What about your husband?"

"He had a pickleball tournament," Audrey said humorously. "They're sacred. Nothing comes between him and his game. He's not exactly a pro, but he enjoys it." She shrugged. "But it's nice that it's just us two. It gives me a chance to get to know you better because something tells me I'll be seeing a lot more of you."

"I hope so." Riley's mind worked overtime as she tried to come up with a change of subject. "How did you and your husband meet?" she asked for lack of a better idea.

"Robert was a chef at a restaurant I was running at the time. I was very young, only twenty-one. It was a small place in the city center, with simple but good food and a great ambience. I hired him, actually." She raised a brow. "And looking back, I may have hired him because of his looks, as his CV wasn't exactly spectacular. I had a secret crush on him for a good year—I couldn't believe my luck when he finally asked me out on a date."

"That's so sweet," Riley said. "You seem so happy together."

"We still are, after forty-five years. We've been through a lot together. With the help of my father, we opened The Harbor House and made it incredibly successful. That restaurant was our pride and joy." Audrey shrugged, and a subtle flinch flashed across her face. "Then we had Quinn and, years later, Rob. We worked so hard that we didn't know how to balance our work and private lives, but thankfully, the children loved staying with their grandparents during high season. That's one regret I have, though. Not spending more time with them when they were younger. You can never get that time back."

"You shouldn't blame yourself. Quinn seems to have very fond childhood memories."

"Thanks to my parents. My father was so good with them, and Quinn was crazy about him. After we lost the restaurant, I was furious with my father. That restaurant was our life, a dream Robert and I built together. I didn't speak to my father for years, and then, suddenly, one day he was gone. That's another regret." She sighed and painted on a smile. "But hey, that's life. We all have regrets, right?"

"I have many," Riley said. "I haven't been in touch with my sister or my father much, but I intend to change that."

Audrey nodded. "Tell me about your parents. All I know is that you were born in Florida."

"My mother passed away two years ago. But my father and sister still live there."

"I'm sorry about your mother."

Riley smiled ruefully. "I guess I never really gave myself the time to process it. I've been thinking of her a lot lately. My father is eighty-five now—he was ten years older than my mother." She sank into memory, her mind going back to their small, two-bedroom bungalow. "We were far from wealthy. My father worked in a factory, and my mom was a stay-at home mom. When my sister and I were old enough to be home by ourselves, she worked as a night cleaner. Our parents both worked so hard, but they still struggled financially. Then the factory closed down, my father got laid off, and that really hit them hard. There was barely enough money to put food on the table. We often depended on the food bank, and my sister and I grew up wearing hand-me-downs from neighbors and relatives."

"That must have been hard." Audrey's gaze held compassion as she met Riley's eyes. "But look at you now."

"Yeah, I did okay. Luckily, I was smart," Riley said. "I managed to get a scholarship and studied business and marketing. I was determined to make something out of myself so I could give them a better life because they weren't getting any younger and they really needed a break. After I graduated, I got an internship in New York at a marketing agency. I worked my way up, saved every penny, and after five years, I started a small marketing firm that became the most successful firm in the city."

"All by yourself. That's admirable."

"I'm proud of what I built. I bought a nice house for my parents and supported them, but in the process, I lost track of what's really important in life because I hardly ever saw them."

"I'm sure they were very proud of you." Audrey leaned over the table and squeezed her hand. "Do you miss your job?"

"I do, but I'm also finding there's a lot more to life, and that's been a revelation. Do you miss working?"

"Sometimes." Audrey paused. "But hospitality is a tough business. It was time for retirement. Robert had no problem sliding into it. He's embraced new hobbies and he cooks at home all the time. It's been a little harder for me, but I've decided to look for a part-time job. I need to keep busy or I'll go mad," she said with a chuckle. "If you need help with the house, I'm pretty handy."

"Thank you. I might take you up on that offer." Riley liked Quinn's mother very much. She was such a warm, open woman and so easy to talk to.

The gate buzzer went, and Riley got up to press the intercom in the hallway. "That will be the auditor," she said. "Let's see how much that amazing wine collection of yours is worth."

50

QUINN

"Do you remember this, Mrs. Kendall?" Quinn helped her grandmother out of the car while Riley held the wheelchair so she could get in. The home had given Quinn permission to take her out for the day, and she'd been wanting to bring her to Aster House for a while. Perhaps it was a bad idea; her grandmother's flashbacks were unpredictable, and she may not even recognize the house or it may bring back bad memories. Quinn's other worry was that she might go straight back in time, settle into her past, and refuse to leave the house again. It was a risk worth taking, though, because she had a feeling it would make her grandmother happy to be back in her old home, even if it was only for a little while.

The old woman glanced around the yard, then stared up at the house. "It's beautiful, isn't it?" she said, her thin lips pulling into a faint smile.

"It certainly is. Shall we go to the backyard for a cup of tea?" Riley suggested.

"Yes. Why not? Or perhaps something stronger? I wouldn't mind a glass of port. It's been a long day."

Riley turned to Quinn, and she shrugged. It was only ten a.m., but if her grandmother wanted a glass of port, she couldn't think of a reason not to indulge her. If Quinn were ninety-six and craved a drink, she hoped someone would do the same for her. "Just a small one," she mouthed and gave Riley a sweet smile.

"One port coming up," Riley said. "What about you, Quinn?"

"I think I'll join Mrs. Kendall in a port."

"Very well, then I'll have one too." Riley disappeared inside, and Quinn took her grandmother to the backyard.

"I don't remember this thing," the old woman said, pointing to the pergola. "How did that get there?"

Quinn realized she hadn't thought this through. Every-thing looked different, especially inside, and that might be confusing. "It was installed this morning," she said for the lack of a better explanation. "It was a surprise from your husband. He sends his love. He'll be back tomorrow."

"My Arthur. That's so sweet of him." Her grandmother clapped her hands together, and her smile widened as Quinn parked the wheelchair at the table. "Such great woodwork, and it looks so modern." She narrowed her eyes as she studied the basic construction. "Goodness. I've never seen anything like it."

"Only the best of the best for you," Quinn said, relieved it was going well so far. "How was your day?"

Her grandmother cast her gaze over the river, and for a split second, she flinched, as if she wasn't sure how to answer. "I went to the market," she finally said. "Yes, that's it!" Her face pulled into a triumphant grin as if the random memory came to her clearly. "I went to the market, and I bought fresh cherries. I'm making cherry pie after church tomorrow before my Arthur gets home. He's in Nevada on a business trip."

"He must be an important man," Quinn said.

"Oh, yes. He's friends with all the men of high standing. They meet up on Saturday nights in our home."

"In the basement?" Quinn asked, her heart beating faster.

"Yes. How do you know about the basement? I thought it was the best kept secret of Mystic."

"Your husband showed it to me," Quinn said hesitantly. "He gave me a tour of the house, and he showed me the basement too."

"Oh." Her grandmother looked puzzled. "I don't believe he's ever taken a woman down there. It's a private gentlemen's club if you will. Then again, he might have mistaken you for a man with your short hair."

Quinn chuckled. "I think he might have. Do you know what the basement is used for when your husband has his friends over?" She'd been wondering if her grandmother was aware of her husband's gambling, and she wasn't able to let it go. If there was ever a time to ask questions, it was now.

"Who knows?" her grandmother said with a shrug. "They might be drinking or they might be gambling. Probably both, but a good wife never questions her husband, and whatever it is, I'm sure it's perfectly innocent. No women apart from me, and you too now," she added with an amused smile, "has ever set foot in there. All that matters is that Arthur loves me and takes care of me." She leaned in and lowered her voice to a whisper. "I'll tell you a secret, but you have to promise me it stays between us."

"I swear." Quinn crossed her heart.

"I'm pregnant." Her grandmother smiled widely.

"According to the doctor, I'm three months in, and I can't wait to tell my Arthur."

"That's fantastic! Congratulations." Quinn looked up when Riley arrived, carrying a tray with three small glasses of port and a bowl of cheese puffs. They were the most vintage snack she'd been able to find, and her grandmother happily attacked them with her frail hands.

"Thank you, dear. God has graced us, and we're finally having our little family."

"You're pregnant? Congratulations," Riley chipped in.

"You probably shouldn't be drinking if you're pregnant." Quinn glanced at the glasses on the table. She'd bought it in case her grandmother wanted one.

"Why?" Her grandmother seemed confused by this, and Quinn realized she was stuck in a time before anyone considered that smoking and drinking might be a bad idea while pregnant.

"You're right. I'm just being silly," she said, handing her a glass. "Now, shall we have a toast to your baby?"

"Yes, let's do that."

Riley took a glass too and held it up, then carefully clinked it against the old woman's glass that was unstable in her hands. "Cheers to you, Dorothy. I'm sure you'll have a beautiful family."

51

QUINN

Quinn was a little shaken after she'd hung up. The wine auctioneer had called her with an update on the auction, and she was shocked to learn that she, her brother, and her mother had made just over a hundred-and-fifty-thousand dollars between them from the sale of the rare wines from the Aster House basement. Although there had been a hefty reserve on the collection, she hadn't expected such a spectacular result, and it would make a huge difference to her financial situation. Combined with her savings, she'd have enough to purchase a house now, without a mortgage, which was a pleasing prospect.

She glanced through her window at Aster House and smiled when she saw a tiny speck moving in the distance. Riley was home, and she was sitting by the water. Living opposite, it was hard not to constantly look out for her, and on days she wasn't with her, Quinn found herself fixated on the house, hoping to catch a glimpse of her. She dialed Riley's number and went outside, onto the roof of her barge, to wave at her. "It's sold," she said and laughed when Riley pumped her fist. "It did well, way above our expectations."

"Amazing. I knew it! Do you want to come over to celebrate?" Riley asked, and Quinn saw her move toward the water's edge. "Wait..." she chuckled. "Does that narrowboat of yours sail? I mean, does it actually move if you want it to?"

"Sure. I don't normally move it, but there's no wind today, so I suppose I could." Quinn laughed. "Why? You want me to sail across?"

"It seems like a fun idea. There's an old mooring ring here, but if it's too much trouble, I could come—"

"No, I'll come over," Quinn said. "Give me twenty minutes. I just need to release the barge and get the engine up and running."

Riley was waving at her, waiting with a bottle of Champagne and two glasses. She was wearing paint-stained jeans and a tight tank top, and the blobs of paint on her arms and splatter on her left cheek made her look adorable. Her hair was pulled up into a top knot, with loose strands framing her face, and she was barefoot, her toenails painted a deep shade of red.

"Hey, beautiful. You look like you've been busy," Quinn said, hopping ashore once she'd secured her narrowboat.

"I have. I was working on Mindy's bedroom." Riley wrapped her arms around Quinn's waist and kissed her. "I'd just finished for the day when you called. Congratulations. You must be so happy."

"I am. Even more now that I get to kiss you."

"Mmm..." Riley parted her lips to deepen the kiss, and to Quinn, it felt like coming home. If it was up to her, she'd spend every free minute with Riley, but she didn't want her to think she was needy. "I've been thinking about you," Riley said. "Can't you just leave your boat here so we can be neighbors and I can see you all the time?" she joked as if reading her mind.

"I would love that, but I'll need electrics, I'm afraid." When Riley stepped back, Quinn took the bottle from her. "Want me to open this?"

"Yes, please. Are you free tonight?"

"I was actually going for dinner at my brother's house later. He just invited me." Quinn popped the cork and poured them both a glass. "Would you like to come along?"

"Tonight?" Riley blushed. "Are you sure?"

"Yeah. I haven't told them about us yet—and my parents don't know either—because I've been busy with…" Quinn smiled as she put the bottle on the table. "Well, with you."

"Yeah, we have been busy, haven't we?" The suggestive way Riley looked at her made Quinn all gooey inside. In the few nights they'd spent apart since their first night two weeks ago, she'd lain awake, missing Riley and fantasizing about her, and when she was with her, she tended to forget about everything else. "I'd love to come with you," Riley said, sipping her Champagne.

"Great. I'll message Rob to let them know." Quinn took her phone out of her back pocket and hesitated for a moment as she looked up from it. "I must warn you. I haven't brought a woman over there before, so they might make a fuss."

"You haven't? Why?"

"I don't make a habit of introducing women I date to my family. It's never been serious enough to do that."

"So why me?" Riley asked. "We haven't known each other long."

"No, but it feels right, don't you think?" Quinn paused. "It just feels right."

"Yeah." Riley's smile widened as she inched closer and cupped Quinn's cheek. Her long fingers curled around Quinn's neck, then softly grazed her hair, and it made Quinn shiver. "How long before we have to leave?"

"Two hours," she whispered when their lips brushed. "Does that work for you?" She took Riley's bottom lip between her teeth and tugged at it, then kissed her again, tasting the Champagne on her tongue.

"Hmm. I need to have a shower, but there are other things I'd rather do right now." She smirked mischievously as she inched back and ran a finger down Quinn's chest. "But I'm good at multitasking. Perhaps we could take a shower together?"

"I like that idea," Quinn said, shifting on the spot when a tightness spread between her thighs. "Have you ever had sex in a shower?" She bit her lip and paused. "Hot water, lots of soap, slippery skin…"

"No."

"No?" Quinn's voice went up a notch, and she drew out the word teasingly slow as she arched a brow at her. "Well, that's a sin. We'd better cross that one off your list."

"How about we take the bottle into the bathroom?" Riley suggested. Her eyes lowered to Quinn's lips. "We can toast to rare wines, hot showers, and everything that feels right."

52

RILEY

"*R*iley!" Lila came tearing up to her and gave her a hug.

"Oh! Hi, honey. Look at you!" Riley stepped back and put her hands on Lila's shoulders. "You're so pretty, just like a princess."

"Aunt Quinn bought me this dress," Lila said with a toothless grin. "It's a fairy dress, but Mom won't let me wear it to school."

"I don't think any of your friends wear fairy dresses to school now, do they?" Mary kissed Riley on her cheek and pulled out a chair for her. "It's so nice to see you again."

"Thank you so much for having me." Riley greeted Rob, then Tommy, who walked into the kitchen with an iPad in his hands. "What are you playing there, Tommy?"

"It's a racing game. I'm really good at it. I'm number three in my league."

"Please put that away, Tommy," Rob said. "No games at the dining table, you know the rules."

"But I haven't finished yet and if I stop now, I'll—"

"I'm serious, Tommy." Rob took the iPad from him and

placed it on top of the fridge where he couldn't reach. "You can have it back after dinner."

Tommy sat with a sulking expression and crossed his arms. "You never let me do anything."

"Poor boy. Must be so hard for you," Quinn joked, jutting out her bottom lip. She glanced at Riley, put her hand on her thigh under the table, and mouthed, "Are you okay?"

Riley smiled and nodded, a little nervous for the night ahead. Not because Mary or Rob made her feel uncomfortable, but she knew bringing her here was a big deal to Quinn.

The kitchen was cozy and messy, a typical space for people with kids. It was cluttered with toys, there were drawings on the fridge, held down with novelty magnets, and a big calendar on the door was full of scribbles. The sink was overflowing with mugs and plates, and a fresh lick of paint on the wall still showed the outline of a marker where one of the kids had drawn on it. "You have a beautiful home," she said to Mary.

"Thank you. We love it, although I apologize for the mess." Mary placed a big, wooden chopping board with antipasti on the table and sat down with a content sigh. "And it'll be even better now that we can afford to do some work on it." Smiling, she gestured at the wall. "That includes repairing all the creative damage these two have done over the years."

Riley laughed. "I'm sure it came at a good time."

"Yes, it's definitely cause for celebration," Rob said. "Our parents couldn't join us tonight, but we'll all get together next time. Dad has a pickleball tournament, and he likes to have a drink with his team after the game, so Mom's driving him. Now, we don't have Champagne in the house, I'm afraid, but we do have a splendid Barolo that's been waiting to be sampled at a special occasion, and it pairs perfectly with the buffalo mozzarella."

"It all looks delicious." Riley handed him her plate, and he filled it with marinated artichokes, mozzarella, caper berries, mortadella, and tomato salad. There was fresh rosemary ciabatta on the table with olive oil and pesto, and a selection of grilled vegetables. She closed her eyes as she took a bite of the mozzarella, followed by a sip of the full-bodied red wine Rob poured her. "You're right," she said. "This is heavenly."

"You've come on a good night." Mary passed her the grilled vegetables and the bread so she could help herself. "We normally keep it simple. It's easier with the kids."

"I don't want that. I want pizza," Tommy complained.

Lila looked at her brother and nodded. "I want pizza and ice cream. I haven't had ice cream since—"

"Since yesterday, so stop sulking and eat your vegetables," Mary said through a mouthful as she pointed her fork at the children. "One day, you'll both learn to appreciate good food, and you'll thank me for not raising you on bland beige deep-fried garbage." She turned to Quinn and Riley and studied them with curiosity. "So, tell me. What's been going on with you two? You look..." She chuckled as she glanced at the kids to make sure they weren't listening in. "Cozy."

Riley noted she was leaning into Quinn and backed away a little. She hadn't realized she'd been doing it all along, as it had become a comfortable habit. She loved the body contact, the warmth it brought her, and how it made her feel to have Quinn close. The urge to constantly have her near was a new and wonderful sensation, but it was also out of character for her, and seeing Mary stare at her like she could read her mind startled her a little. She waited for

Quinn to reply, but Quinn looked equally taken aback, so she smiled goofily at Mary and kept silent while Quinn did the same.

"Okay, that says enough." Rob laughed. "Whatever this is, I'm happy for you."

"Yeah. It's clearly not meant for kids' ears," Mary chipped in. "Let's continue this conversation later."

"What's not meant for kids' ears?" Tommy looked at them quizzically. "Tell me! I'm not a baby!"

"Okay, Tommy. You're right, you're not a baby," Mary said. "It seems that Aunt Quinn and Riley like each other. That's what we were discussing."

"But they're friends." Lila's innocent look was incredibly sweet as she stuffed a piece of bread into her mouth. "Of course they like each other."

"It means they have sex, dumbo." Tommy rolled his eyes at his little sister. "Women can have sex too. Ilse and Patty in my class have sex all the time."

"Oh, do they now?" Quinn laughed. "Are you sure about that? They're only eight, right?"

"I'm sure. They told me so," Tommy said matter-of-factly. "They kiss each other on the mouth. It's gross." He stuck his index finger down his throat and gagged. "And now they're in love. Eww!"

"How are the renovations coming along, Riley?" Rob tried to change the subject, clearly shocked by how clued-in his son was. Lila was giggling and kept repeating the word "sex," while her poor father had broken out in a sweat.

Although Lila's antics did make her chuckle, Riley attempted to ignore her, following her parents' lead. "Very well, thank you," she said. "My sister and my niece are coming to visit, so I'm trying to speed up the process. Why don't you come over when she's here? Her daughter is the same age as Lila, so they can have a play date."

"Yeah, we definitely will. Did you hear that, Lila?" Mary asked, trying to distract her daughter from the new word she'd learned. "Riley's niece is your age. You can play together."

"We can do sex." Lila was giggling so much she almost fell off her chair. "Sex, sex, sex!"

Tommy nudged his sister. "Stop it, you're gross."

"Oh, boy." Mary sighed and covered her face in her hands. "And so it begins..."

"She'll get bored of it soon enough," Rob said optimistically.

"I doubt it. She's been repeating the word 'flirting' all week." Mary got up to check on her lasagna in the oven. "How do other parents deal with stuff like this?"

"There's only one way..." Quinn pulled Lila onto her lap and started tickling her until Lila screamed. "I'll tickle it out of her!"

Riley laughed as she watched Quinn and her niece together. It was a beautiful, sweet sight, and she felt a warmth deep in her core, a new sensation that she couldn't quite dissect. Something about seeing Quinn being so great with children pulled at her heartstrings and sparked thoughts she'd never entertained before. What would Quinn be like as a mother? What would *she* be like as a mother? She pushed those thoughts to the background and parked them for later. She had enough to process as it was, and even beginning to think about such a serious subject was too much for now.

53

QUINN

The little townhouse in the city center of Mystic was picturesque and had lots of character. Wedged in between a coffee shop and an artisan candle shop, the two-story property had two bedrooms and a roof terrace that looked out over the high street.

"It's sweet, right?" Lindsey tapped the mantel over the fireplace. "It doesn't get any better than this. It's rare that houses come up for sale on the high street, so you're lucky your bestie is a realtor."

"Yeah, it's really nice." Quinn liked the exposed brick walls in the living room and the open fireplace that would be cozy in winter. The en-suite master bathroom had a spacious bath and a walk-in shower, and the recently renovated farmhouse kitchen was charming and in excellent condition.

"And you know what the best thing is?" Lindsey pulled her over to the window and pointed to the realtor's office opposite. "Look, that's my desk right there. We can wave at each other!"

Quinn laughed. "That's the best thing? You spying on me?"

"I think of it more like social control," Lindsey said with a grin. "So? Are you interested in putting an offer in? I could show you more properties, but this one is a gem. Besides that, I know you so well, and therefore I know what suits you."

"I'd have to think about it. I wasn't exactly planning on buying anything *right* now."

"Okay. But I'm not speaking as a realtor chasing commission. I'm speaking as your friend, and I'm telling you, this will be snapped up in days once it officially goes onto the market. That's the only reason I insisted you come here today."

"I can see that. It's absolutely stunning, but I'd still have to think about it." Quinn hesitated. "I don't know what it is, but something's holding me back."

"Is it Riley?" Lindsey asked, tilting her head as she looked at Quinn. "If it works out between you two and you decide you'd rather live somewhere together, you can always rent this out to tourists. It will make you a fortune in summer. Or maybe Riley would like to live here too, eventually. I think she feels a bit lost in that big house."

"It's way too early for conversations like that."

"Sure, but you can't deny it's been on your mind. There's no shame in admitting that." Lindsey's smile softened. "Look, here's what I think. Talk to Riley about it. Not about moving in together or anything like that, of course. Just tell her you've seen a property you like. It's what you do when you're dating. You talk about things."

Quinn nodded. "I will."

"Just don't wait too long because—"

"I know, I know. It will be gone." Quinn didn't like the

pressure, but she knew Lindsey was only trying to help. Glancing around the living room, she tried to imagine herself living here. Apart from Aster house, she'd never lived anywhere other than on campus and on her narrowboat, and it would be nice to have more space again. "Well, I'd better get back to work, but thank you so much. I really appreciate it."

"You're welcome. Message me if you have questions," Lindsey said as she let them out. "What are you up to tonight? Are you seeing Riley?"

"Yes, I'm seeing her later. I was worried maybe we were jumping into this too quickly, but the truth is, we want to see each other, so it seems silly not to."

"I don't think there's anything wrong with that. It's cute." Lindsey put an arm around Quinn's shoulders and squeezed her. "I loved seeing you so happy with her."

Quinn smiled at her. "Are you still messaging with that catfish?"

Lindsey gave her a playful slap. "Marcellus is not a catfish!" She laughed. "Okay, maybe he is. He kept putting off our date, so I gave him an ultimatum. I told him I wasn't interested in a WhatsApp relationship and if he was hoping for any chance with me, he'd have to meet me in person."

"And?"

"And he agreed to meet me for a coffee on the weekend. Let's hope he shows up."

"Will you be okay? I'm a little worried. I can come along and hang around in the background, like we discussed?"

"Nah. It's fine. He suggested we meet for a coffee at the bakery, and Martin said he'd look after me." Lindsey chuckled. "It's probably best if you stay away from him."

"Yeah." Quinn frowned. "I didn't know you and Martin were close. You never mention him."

"We're not *that* close, but we always have a nice chat when I'm there, and I told him I had a date. Besides, why would I mention him to you? It's still a sore subject."

"As long as you don't think I'll have a problem with you and Martin being friends. That would be silly," Quinn said. "I mean, it's unlikely we'll ever hang out together, the three of us. The guy hates me. But whatever you do is your business."

"I know that." They crossed the road and Lindsey lingered in front of her office. She seemed lost in thought as she eyed the bakery at the far end of the high street. "I don't understand why he's still single, he's such a nice guy. Not bad looking either."

"How much do you like him?" Quinn asked. "Are you attracted to him?"

"God, no. I've known him since high school. I don't see him that way. He's far too familiar." Lindsey waved it off and smiled. "He's just a nice guy who bakes delicious cookies."

"You'll have your love for cookies in common." Quinn shrugged and gave her a grin. "And with your undying love for them, on paper, it's a match made in heaven."

"Will you stop it!" Lindsey hissed when a couple passed them. "Someone might hear you. You know how people talk." Her phone pinged, and she gasped. "Oh, God. I forgot I was supposed to meet someone regarding a rental. I'd better fly." She raised her voice and looked over her shoulder as she ran toward her car, parked out front of her office. "Think about the house. I don't want you to miss out and regret it!"

54

RILEY

"I think Mindy will like this." Riley wiped her hands on her jeans and smiled as she looked around the room. "I'm pleased with how it turned out."

"You've outdone yourself," Quinn said, stepping inside. "The transformation is astonishing."

Riley felt proud as she took in her hard work from the past days. The walls in Quinn's old bedroom were stripped and painted a beautiful shade of light blue. White linen curtains graced the big windows; underneath them stood a beige antique chaise longue she'd bought in the second-hand furniture store and a coffee table with some books and a vase filled with white roses. She'd painted the big closet white, and she'd borrowed a huge, four-poster bed from the basement, which was topped with a new mattress and white and blue bed linen. She'd used her own art from New York on the walls, as the modern, neutral-toned paintings looked nice in here, and she'd adorned the bed with decorative pillows from the hardware store. There was a pretty dressing table with a velvet stool, a large antique mirror, and the nightstands had cute little reading lamps that projected stars onto the ceiling. It wasn't necessarily a children's room, but she was sure Mindy would be delighted with her dressing table and big-girl bed that could fit at least seven kids her size. The off-white rug that covered most of the floor was thick and soft with a subtle light-blue speck running through it, and it was the finishing touch that brought everything together in perfect harmony. The light was beautiful in Quinn's old bedroom, Riley noticed, as the sun shone through the windows, but best of all was the view over the yard and the river. "You must have loved this room."

"Yeah. It feels peaceful, doesn't it?"

Riley nodded. Having Quinn here had taught her to appreciate the house, and now that it was slowly coming together, she felt more and more at home in the mansion she'd so regretted buying only two and a half months ago. "I haven't started on the adjacent bathroom yet, but that's a big job, so it'll have to wait. It's working, and it's clean."

"She's going to be so happy." Quinn turned to the door-frame and placed a hand on her heart when she spotted the ridges. "You left my markers."

"I painted over it very lightly, then removed the paint from the ridges," Riley said. "I managed to restore the writing next to it too. It took me ages because I had to use a safety pin."

"That's so sweet. You didn't have to do that." Quinn inched closer and cupped Riley's face.

"I did have to. It's your history, and it's one of the things that make this house special, even to me." Riley leaned in to kiss her, and as their lips brushed, warmth surged through her. "I want you to know that I respect your history, and I'm seeing Aster House in a different light, now that I know you better." She smiled shyly. "I'm crazy about you, Quinn." Riley wasn't one for throwing her feelings on the table, but it was easy to be open and honest with Quinn, and she wasn't afraid to be vulnerable around her.

"I'm crazy about you too, babe." Quinn ran her fingers through Riley's hair and met her eyes. "How could I not be?"

Riley went weak at her gaze. The impact those eyes had on her was something she might never get used to. "I'm so relieved you're okay with my changes." She paused. "I've been thinking a lot lately, about the house..."

"What do you mean?"

"Income-wise. I'll be okay for the coming ten years, but if I want to live comfortably long-term, I'll need some form of income. And I was wondering if it might be an idea to turn Aster House into a guesthouse, just for the summer seasons. If I had it to myself in winter, it wouldn't be a huge commitment."

"A guesthouse..." Quinn pursed her lips as she pondered over that. "You mean like a bed-and-breakfast?"

"Exactly. Just a peaceful place to spend the night for people who visit Mystic." Riley shrugged. "I have to be careful not to get too stressed, but I already have a cleaner, and if I hire an additional housekeeper, I could easily handle it."

"Huh." Quinn frowned. "I wonder why none of the previous owners have thought of that. It's a great idea."

"Really? You think so?"

"Yeah. Aster House has the perfect layout and all the amenities anyone could want. A beautiful yard, it's on the water and walking distance from the city center..." Quinn shot her a mischievous smile. "And, if you really wanted to make the most out of it, you could even have a little prohibition-inspired bar in the basement. People would love that."

Riley laughed. "Who wouldn't get excited by entering a bar through a bookcase, right?" She pulled Quinn closer by her waist and kissed her again. "I love your idea, and I'll definitely give it some thought. How was your day, by the way?"

"Not as productive as yours, but it was good. My team installed a kitchen, and in my break, I met Lindsey to look at a house. She called me this morning because she'd just received a new listing and she thought it would be perfect for me."

"Oh? I didn't know you were actively looking," Riley said. A hint of unease tugged at her, and she wasn't sure why.

"I'm not." Quinn shrugged. "But I figured there wouldn't be any harm in viewing it. It's a nice town house."

"Just nice? You don't sound too keen."

Quinn ran her hands over Riley's behind and raised her eyes to the ceiling as she let out a deep sigh. "I don't know. On paper, it's perfect for me, but I wasn't really feeling it."

"Because it wasn't Aster House?" Riley asked, immediately regretting bringing it up. She didn't want the house to stand between them, yet she suspected it was inevitable. They were dating, but *she* had what Quinn wanted. Therefore, the balance was somewhat off, and sometimes that made her uncomfortable.

"No..." Quinn hesitated, then smiled and shook her head. "It has nothing to do with Aster House. I just wasn't feeling it."

55

QUINN

*I*t was one of those days to remember, Quinn thought. She put an arm around Riley and kissed her temple as they walked toward Mystic town. It was the first evening of the year that she didn't need a coat or a cover-up, and with the sun setting over the river, Riley by her side, and a free weekend ahead of them, she couldn't be happier. The town lay quietly along the riverbank as the shops were closed now, and the restaurants along the pier were getting ready for the evening, their staff arranging furniture underneath the heaters on the terraces and bringing out blankets.

"It's a beautiful town," Riley said. "I can see that now."

"Does it feel like home yet?"

"You know what? It does." Riley smiled as she looked up at her. "It's my first real home since I left my parents' house." She paused. "It's strange. New York feels like a distant dream now, like it only happened in my imagination. I never took the time to go for a walk there or even take in my surroundings. I like being more mindful."

"I'm glad you like it here," Quinn said. "I obviously want

you to stay." She pulled Riley close, cherishing the smell of her shampoo and the warmth of her body as they crossed the drawbridge, passed the ice cream parlor, and continued onto the high street. "Can I show you the house I looked at? It's been on my mind. I seem to be a little drawn to it after all, and it's not far."

"Of course. I'd love to see it." Riley took in a deep breath. "The town smells different today."

"Spring is in the air. It's my favorite time of the year." Quinn noticed the crowns of the trees along both sides of the street were full and green now, their branches reaching out like arms with bony fingers that almost met in the middle. "Mystic will be flooded with tourists soon. You'll be surprised to see how busy it gets." Quinn narrowed her eyes as they passed the bakery. She tended to avoid looking in, but knowing Lindsey had a date there earlier, she couldn't resist glancing through the windows. "Wait! That's Lindsey. Why is she still there?"

Riley followed her gaze. "Hmm. She had a date, right? I only see Martin."

"Maybe her date left when Martin closed up." Lindsey and Martin were sitting at the window table, and the sign on the door was turned to "closed."

"Or maybe Marcellus stood her up," Riley said. "I wouldn't be surprised. He's clearly not who he says he is." She stopped and looked over her shoulder. "Poor Lindsey. Should we ask if she wants to join us for dinner later?"

Quinn lingered on the spot, then shook her head when she saw Lindsey laughing. "No. She looks fine to me, and something tells me we should leave them alone."

"What? You think they like each other?" Riley lowered her voice and her eyes widened. "He was very chatty with her last time I met her there, but I didn't get a flirty vibe from their conversation. He's single, right? Or did he meet someone after..." She winced and stopped herself.

"After Rebecca? Not as far as I'm aware." Quinn took her hand and grinned. "Who's the gossip now, huh? You've only just moved here and you're already speculating about possible matches."

Riley chuckled and rolled her eyes. "Oh, God. You're right. I'm turning into a gossip."

"Don't worry, it's cute." Quinn stopped and gestured to the house next to the candle shop. "That's the one. What do you think?"

"That one? Oh wow, it's gorgeous. It's got character, and I love the blue windowsills and the old brick facade. I get why Lindsey wanted you to see it." Riley glanced through the windows. "It looks like the owners are still living there."

"The owner is an older lady on her own looking to downsize as she has trouble with the stairs. She's not in a rush to sell, but Lindsey thinks it will be gone as soon as it officially goes onto the market."

"So you're contemplating going for it now?"

"I don't know. I just feel like I'd be crazy not to," Quinn said. "It's the sensible thing to do."

Riley nodded, and she looked like she wanted to say something but then changed her mind.

"You disagree?"

Riley shrugged. "I know I'm not one to speak, as I let my assistant pick my home, but if your heart's not in it, maybe it's better to wait? I bought Aster House on a whim, and I regretted it the moment I stepped through the gates." She smiled. "I don't regret it anymore, of course. I met you, and that's been...well, honestly, it's been the best thing that ever happened to me. But just think about it."

Quinn returned her smile and cupped her face. Hearing

Riley say that made her melt, and she was still pinching herself at how lucky she was to have met her. "I adore you," she whispered and kissed her softly. A couple with a dog she vaguely recognized passed them, but she ignored them, and Riley didn't seem to mind either as she pulled her in and kissed her back.

Riley moaned softly as she broke away. "Every time you kiss me, I go a little crazy," she whispered. "I don't know how you did it, but you have me, completely." Her expression turned serious as she met Quinn's eyes. "If this is as real to you as it is to me..." She took her hands and hesitated. "Well...then maybe it's not a bad idea to wait with buying a place. We might want to live together, depending on how it goes between us."

Quinn nodded. "Yeah. I've been thinking about that too, but I thought it might be too early to bring it up. I'm glad you mentioned it."

"So you're saying that's something you might consider?"

"Of course. I want to be with you all the time."

"Okay..." Riley's smile widened, and her eyes sparkled with joy. "I happen to have a very, very big house that you happen to love."

Quinn's heart skipped a beat, and she squeezed Riley's hands. "I don't want you to think I'm with you for the house. We could look for something together in future and—"

"Hey, I know you're not with me for the house," Riley said, interrupting her. "We already spend most nights together, and the house is growing on me. I'd even go as far as to say I'm starting to love it, and if we both love it, then why would we even think about moving somewhere else together?" She paused. "We'll probably both need some time, but the house isn't going anywhere, and I'm not going anywhere."

Quinn's lips parted, and she stared at her while thoughts clouded her mind. It wasn't as much the house that had her head spinning but the fact that Riley was just as serious about her, and that she wanted them to have a life together. Searching for words, it took her a while to realize someone was calling her name.

"Quinn! Riley!"

She looked over her shoulder to find Lindsey crossing the road.

"Hey, lovebirds!" Lindsey's cheeks were rosy as she smiled at them. "Were you showing Riley the house?"

"Yes, we were just out for a walk and—"

"And?" Lindsey asked eagerly, fixated on Riley. "What do you think?"

Riley bit her lip, suppressing a grin. "I...uhm...I think it's beautiful." She was blushing and avoiding Lindsey's gaze, focusing on her feet.

"See? I told you she'd love it." Lindsey turned to Quinn, clearly clueless to the fact that she'd just interrupted a very personal conversation. "Have you thought about it? It's going on the market in three days, so you'd better make up your mind."

Quinn shook her head. "It's not for me, but someone will love this home very much."

"Right." Lindsey looked puzzled. "Are you sure? It would be so perfect for you."

"I'm sure. But thank you for showing it to me; I appreciate it. By the way, I saw you at the bakery with Martin. Did your date ever turn up?" Quinn asked, changing the subject. "Was he real?"

"No, he wasn't who he said he was." Lindsey crossed her arms. "But it's fine. At least I know now."

"I'm sorry, babe." Quinn pulled Lindsey into a hug. "Are

you okay?" She had a feeling Lindsey was hiding something. "Would you like to come for some food with us? We were thinking about having pizza."

Lindsey hesitated. She was obsessed with food and generally suffered from fear of missing out, so the fact she even had to think about it was suspicious. "Okay, why not?" she finally said. "As long as we don't talk about Marcellus. I just want to forget about him."

56

RILEY

"Thank you so much for your help today." Riley rinsed the last paintbrush, wound some plastic wrap around the bristles, and threw it into the bucket on the kitchen counter. "I'm so relieved it's all ready. I've been nervous about seeing my sister again. At least their rooms are one thing less to worry about, and with two more weeks to spare, I might even have time to spruce up the kitchen."

"Anytime, babe." Quinn wrapped her arms around Riley from behind and kissed her neck. "I want you to have a good time with them. They're going to love it here." Her lips traveled down to Riley's shoulder, and she tightened her grip, splaying her fingers wide over Riley's ribcage.

Riley shivered as Quinn brought her mouth to her ear and bit her lobe. "You drive me crazy when you do that. It's... mmm..." Her voice trailed away as Quinn lowered a hand to her behind and squeezed it hard. "It's so sexy."

"I'll show you sexy," Quinn whispered, slipping her hand into Riley's jersey hotpants. "You drive *me* crazy when you're wearing skimpy outfits. I've been fantasizing about bending you over this counter all day."

"Oh yeah?" Riley moaned as she pressed her behind against Quinn's pelvis. The warm hand that wandered lower set her on fire, and she was wet and throbbing with anticipation. Doing up the rooms together had been fun, but Quinn's strong arms had been terribly distracting as she assembled her sister's bed, the flex of muscles under smooth skin fully visible with her dressed in a white tank top and jeans. Knowing Quinn appreciated her skin on display, Riley had worn hotpants and a loose jersey sweater that hung off one shoulder. The whole day had been a string of flirtations and make-out sessions in between painting and decorating, and by now, she was so fired up she thought she might burst if Quinn touched her where she needed it most. "What's been stopping you?" she asked in a breathy voice.

"I'm asking myself that same question." Quinn ran a hand up and down Riley's back as she pushed her over the counter. Her touch was gentle but firm, and it made Riley's knees weak. Quinn was assertive, in charge and confident in a way she'd never known with her lovers, and that drove her wild as Quinn took her hands and placed them on the counter.

"Keep them there. I love it when you bend over," she said. "Your ass is just exquisite." Riley felt movement against her ear, and she knew Quinn was smiling. "What do you want? Slow and gentle or fast and hard?"

Riley closed her eyes and moaned at her words. "Fast and—" She gasped when Quinn's hand slipped into her shorts again without warning, this time from behind. Entering her slowly at first with two fingers, Quinn sighed.

"You're so incredibly wet, Riley. Is that for me?"

"Uh-huh." Riley moaned as Quinn's fingers filled her, then withdrew before she started fucking her. With deep and deliberate thrusts, Quinn pushed herself against Riley while she wedged her other hand underneath her top and bra to caress her breasts.

"Is that good?" she asked, pinching her nipple.

"Yes... Ahh..." Riley didn't know what to do with herself as she felt Quinn's fingers filling her over and over, and already, something big was building. "Don't stop," she pleaded while her nails scraped over the wooden surface. She lowered her forehead onto the counter and clenched her teeth as Quinn moved her hand down to her clit while she penetrated her from behind. It was carnal desire in its purest form, and the need for release was tugging at her as she pushed back against Quinn's fingers, her moans growing louder and louder.

"Come for me, baby." Bending over her and scraping her teeth over the sensitive skin of Riley's neck, Quinn pushed deeper and curled her fingers when Riley's breaths became heavy and ragged.

Riley's core tightened, and she shut her eyes as she crashed into an explosive orgasm. Knowing she was too weak to stand, Quinn held her up as she trembled in her arms. She brushed her lips along Riley's neck, cupped her chin, and turned her face to place soft kisses on her temple and her cheek.

"Good call on the counter," Riley said with a chuckle, rubbing her cheek against Quinn's as she caught her breath. She was flushed and buzzing and shuddering from the aftershocks. Only Quinn could do this to her, make her feel like the entire world revolved around them. She gasped when Quinn pulled out of her and caressed her behind. Turning them around and pushing Quinn against the counter, Riley went down on her knees and started unbuttoning Quinn's fly. "I think you'll like the counter too."

Quinn groaned when Riley tugged her jeans and her boxers down in one quick motion. "Oh my... Wait!"

"Wait for what? Are you going to say you don't want this? Because I know you do..." Riley ran her hands up Quinn's legs and brought her mouth between her thighs. She loved how Quinn tasted, and how she bucked against her tongue when she devoured her.

Quinn didn't answer, but her body language told Riley she wanted it very much. Throwing her head back, Quinn took in a quick breath and raised her face to the ceiling, clasping at the edge of the counter until her knuckles turned white. "Fuck!"

Riley's lips curled into a smile as she attacked her with her tongue, cupping her behind and squeezing her cheeks, pulling her in as close as she could. If someone had told her she'd grow to love the taste of a woman so much only a few months ago, she wouldn't have believed them, but now it was all she wanted. Quinn had finally given in to her, and Riley wanted to give her as much pleasure as she could. She wanted her all the time, night and day. Every time they met, she felt this potent tug to be as close as she possibly could to her, and she'd come to realize that there was something incredibly beautiful about pleasing a woman. It felt far more intimate than with a man, and she knew instinctively what Quinn liked. They were intuitive together; she loved to surrender, and Quinn loved to lead. Even now, Quinn's fingers laced themselves through Riley's hair, setting the pace as her moans grew louder. The explosion that followed made Riley feel more accomplished than any big contract she'd ever signed, and the pure delight of hearing Quinn cry out fired her libido all over again. Riley felt Quinn's orgasm everywhere. Against her lips, in her core, in her heart, and in her soul. Quinn's energy poured into her, filling her with hope for their future. Because she could envision that now, and it promised to be beautiful and exciting.

Gathering her thoughts, Riley slowly got up and straightened herself, then inched close and rested her forehead against Quinn's. Quinn smiled through heavy breaths and grinned as Riley ran her hands over her behind. "You are so gay," she murmured.

"I know." Riley chuckled. "It's the best thing that ever happened to me."

57

QUINN

"This is so funny." Lindsey stood next to Quinn as she steered her narrowboat across the river. "It must be the easiest way of moving home by far."

Quinn laughed. "I was wondering what I needed to arrange, then realized all I had to do was sail over to the other side. I'm not moving, though. I'll keep my stuff in my barge, but it's just more convenient when I don't have to keep driving back and forth into town since I spend most of my time here anyway."

"Sure. You keep telling yourself that." Lindsey winked at her. "It's a beautiful coincidence that you fell for the woman who bought your dream home, who also happens to live a five-minute boat ride away. If I didn't know better, I'd think you planned it."

"You know I didn't."

"Of course, but it makes me wonder about fate and destiny and all that kind of stuff. Maybe you were meant to meet."

"Maybe." Quinn would be lying if she said she hadn't considered that. Her path had crossed with Riley's at the right time in both their lives and aligned seamlessly as if, indeed, they were meant to meet. If there was such a thing as destiny, then this was it, and Quinn genuinely wanted to believe that. "I'm blessed, that's all I know for sure."

"And now you get to enjoy your blessed lives together." Lindsey grinned and ruffled a hand through Quinn's hair. "Speaking of coincidences, that was a weird date the other night."

Quinn furrowed her brows. "I thought he didn't show up?"

"Yeah, about that. He *was* there. I was a bit over-whelmed, so I had to let it sink in before I told you. The guy I've been talking to, the one who calls himself Marcellus? Turns out it was Martin."

"Martin was the catfish?" Quinn stared at her friend in disbelief. "Why? He could have just asked you out."

"That's what *I* said." Lindsey sighed. "He told me he's been into me for a while. He had a fake profile on the dating app, which he only used for casual chatting, but then he saw me on there and decided to reach out." Lindsey paused. "And after a while, we'd talked so much that he was scared to admit it was him. He said he was worried I'd laugh in his face if I found out it was the local baker rather than some world-traveling hotshot."

"Wow. I didn't see that one coming."

"Me either, obviously. Martin was the last person I expected to like me. I've known him all my life."

"I can only imagine. Was it weird?"

"Yeah. I was there waiting for my date, and when Marcellus didn't show, Martin closed up the bakery and confessed. He apologized like a million times, so I didn't have the heart to stay angry. You should have seen him. He was so distraught."

"And how do you feel about *him*?" Quinn asked, steering the boat toward Aster House. "Do you think he's attractive? He's not bad looking, right? That's what you said."

Lindsey blew out her cheeks and shrugged. "I never thought of him that way. He was always Rebecca's husband, and after that, he was poor Martin whose wife had an affair with you. Even though we were on friendly terms, our worlds didn't exactly mix harmoniously."

"And that's my fault." Quinn sighed. "I hope he can forgive me one day."

"He's long over Rebecca, and I don't even think he still holds a grudge against you. Not that we discussed that," Lindsey added. "Anyway, I agreed to meet in a few days, and in the meantime, I need to have a serious think about this."

"What does your instinct tell you?" Quinn asked. "Forget about the absurdity of the situation, just focus on your gut."

The corners of Lindsey's mouth pulled up into a small smile as she stared at the riverbank. "Well, I like him as a person. He's got a nice smile, and he makes great cookies."

"Cookies is more than you had in common when he was pretending to be Marcellus," Quinn joked, in two minds about the situation. For years, she'd avoided Martin in social situations, yet she wanted Lindsey to be happy. They kind of made sense together, and deep down, she knew Martin was a good guy. "Be grateful he's not an athletic lawyer," she added. "I know you. You would have spent the rest of your life trying to be someone you're not."

"I'm aware I tend to do that," Lindsey admitted. "I bend over backward to make men think I'm perfect for them. It's pretty fucked up."

"It's not fucked up, it's human." From a distance, Riley waved at them, and Quinn's heart skipped a beat when she caught a glimpse of that beautiful smile.

"Welcome to your new home." Lindsey waved back at her.

"Hey, as I said, it's not permanent," Quinn reminded her. "Having my barge there also means I can sleep on it if either of us needs space." In the past two weeks since they'd first brought up the topic, she and Riley had talked a lot about living together. Spending most nights together, not much would change, other than that her barge would be closer and she'd have her things at hand. She'd already crossed the river a few times, but the weather didn't always lend itself to sailing, and there hadn't been electricity at the Aster House jetty until today. Until she'd built a dock, the two sturdy poles sticking out of the water would suffice to keep the barge in place. "Think of it as a trial run."

"Trial run my ass. Once you're moored, you'll never leave. You two are way too smitten with each other to mess it up," Lindsey said. "I'm so happy for you."

"Thank you." Quinn wasn't worried about messing it up, but she *was* worried that it might be too soon. However, Riley was right; they'd both wasted years working toward goals that in hindsight were not important in the grand scheme of things, and it was time that they started living their lives to the fullest and enjoyed every moment together.

58

RILEY

"*W*elcome home." Riley pulled Quinn in to kiss her, then gave Lindsey a hug. "Lindsey, how nice of you to help Quinn with the strenuous move," she joked. It was an exciting day, and she'd been giddy for hours while waiting for them. She hadn't lived with anyone since she'd divorced her ex-husband. She'd always been fine on her own, but since meeting Quinn, she wanted to be with her all the time, and knowing they would wake up together every morning was a glorious prospect.

"Thank you." Quinn stared up at the house, then laughed as she glanced at her boat over her shoulder. "Well, I guess that's it."

"Who said moving is one of the most stressful life events?" Lindsey quipped. "By the way, am I interrupting a romantic moment here? I just realized this is a big day for both of you, and I'm kind of crashing it. Is this when you'd normally step through the front door and have wild sex in the hallway? Because I can walk back if you—"

"Don't worry, there will be plenty of time for wild sex in

the hallway later," Quinn interrupted her and shot Riley a wink.

"So true, so please stay," Riley said with a chuckle, her cheeks flushing pink. She pointed to the table on the riverside. "Quinn told me you were coming, so I have coffee ready, and I baked a chocolate cake."

"You bake?" Lindsey stared at the questionable-looking concoction. "I thought I'd smelled something delicious."

"I do now. I'm aware it looks like a big turd rather than a cake. It's my first attempt, but I promise it tases nice." Riley was proud of her turd, and she'd been surprised when she tasted it. She used to be a perfectionist and wouldn't have dreamed of baking in her former life; not unless she was able to create a masterpiece. No, she would have ordered a cake from the best baker in New York, but now, simply good enough was an achievement, and she'd enjoyed the process as much as the mediocre result.

"Best turd I've ever tasted," Lindsey said, breaking off a piece and closing her eyes as she savored it.

"Not with your fingers!" Quinn stared at her in comical horror. "There are plates and forks on the table. Why do you always have to stick your hands in everything?"

"Okay, Mom. Hold your horses," Lindsey said, licking her fingers.

"I'm not being a *mom*. I'm simply asking you to respect Riley's home and cake and show some manners."

"No need for manners," Riley interjected. "Please attack it as you wish, and this is your home too now, Quinn. It's not *my* home, it's *ours*."

Quinn shrugged and smiled at her sheepishly. "Thank you, babe. I'll need some time to get used to that, I suppose." Without thinking, she scooped a finger through the chocolate icing and sucked it into her mouth.

"Are you serious right now?" Lindsey nudged her. "You're such a hypocrite."

Riley threw her head back and laughed. "Will you two stop it? You sound like an old married couple." Quinn and Lindsey's innocent bickering always amused her, and she smiled as she pulled out a chair for Lindsey and poured her coffee, then plated a huge slice of cake for her. Although technically today was no different from yesterday—Quinn had been here almost every night—it *felt* different, and Aster House had a different vibe to it. The yard was gorgeous in the wind-free, sunny morning; the river lay serenely before them, the water softly lapping against Quinn's barge. Climbers were starting to cover the back wall of the house, blending it with its surroundings. There was something about the back door and the windows at the rear of the house that reminded her of a face and today, it seemed to be smiling, welcoming home a long-lost loved one. She could sense the house's energy now; it was a good energy. It was happy to have Quinn back.

"She started it," Quinn retorted playfully, pointing at Lindsey. "By the way, babe, this is so good." She moaned as she took a big bite of the cake. "Seriously good."

"You like my cake..." Riley locked eyes with Quinn, smirking as she said, "That means I might be able to hold on to you."

"Hold on to her?" Lindsey snorted. "Quinn is so smitten with you that you couldn't get rid of her if you tried. She talks about you all the time, and I'm telling you, my bestie is—

"Okay, okay." Quinn arched a brow at Lindsey. "Can someone please give her more cake so she'll keep quiet for a minute?" She turned to Riley, who was sitting next to her, and placed a hand on her thigh. "All joking aside, Lindsey's got a point. It would take a lot to keep me away from you."

Riley leaned into her, and words couldn't describe how happy she felt in that moment. She finally had an idea of what it was like to have a real home and a real life, and that was all because of Quinn. "Same here," she said, blushing even harder when Lindsey peered around Quinn to meet Riley's gaze. "And I can't believe I'm saying this, but you couldn't pry me away from Mystic either. I love it here, and I love Aster House."

And I love you, she wanted to add, but she wisely kept that to herself. *Did* she love Quinn? She felt these over-whelming emotions every time she saw her, and yes, it felt like love. She felt it deep within her, this beautiful but also terrifying sense of compassion, admiration, and adoration; a sense that she may not know how to carry on if she lost her. Her years of solitude were in the past, and even though the future was unknown, she was excited for it. Riley's life had always been mapped out down to every minute detail; now, before them lay an unknown road they would explore together. She would walk with Quinn, follow her, for as long as Quinn would let her.

59

QUINN

*I*t still hadn't sunk in that she was living here now. All these years Quinn had been working toward one goal only: making Aster House her own. The moment she'd given up on her dream and accepted her fate, she'd fallen head over heels for a beautiful woman, and here she was, waking up in her childhood home. It was surreal, but Riley's steady breathing grounded her. She looked angelic in her naked pureness, only partially covered by the sheets. With one arm draped over Quinn's waist, a thigh resting on her legs and her hair tousled, she was the most stunning vision Quinn had ever laid her eyes on.

"Good morning." Riley smiled sweetly as her eyes fluttered open. "Did you sleep well?" She shifted and scooted under the covers, aligning her body with Quinn's.

"I did, babe. This is nice." Quinn took Riley in her arms and brushed her lips over her forehead. "Are you looking forward to seeing your sister and Mindy tomorrow?"

"Yes. I can't wait."

"Good. Would you like me to stay on the barge? I can be

out of your way. That's what the boat is for." Quinn grinned. "For our trial period."

"No, I want you to get to know them." Riley kissed her. "I'm entirely comfortable introducing you to Jane and Mindy. If anything, it will be more of an adjustment for Jane than it will be for me, as she only knows me as the stern, straight, and distant workaholic."

"A stern, straight, and distant workaholic... I have trouble seeing you that way." Quinn smiled against her lips. "Especially the straight part," she joked.

Riley chuckled. "Well, the workaholic part is most certainly true. I used to get up at six a.m. every morning. I'd go to the gym, then head to the office where I worked for about fourteen hours straight before I'd have a working dinner either alone, with clients, or with my assistant. I had no time for anything or anyone unless it was work related, and my sister always called me out on it." Riley yawned and stretched out before she curled up against Quinn again. "You're the missing part of my life I didn't know I needed, and Jane will see that. She'll adore you."

"I'm sure I'll like her too." Quinn kissed her cheek. "How about we get my family over for a barbecue while they're here? The weather will be beautiful this week, and Mindy can play with Lila. I'll organize it if you like." She hesitated. "Maybe toward the end of the week? To give Jane some time to get used to you having a female partner before bombarding her with your new in-laws?"

"Thank you, that's very sweet of you." Riley nuzzled her neck. "Do my new in-laws know they're *my* in-laws yet?"

"No, but I'm meeting them for a coffee this morning. Will you come with me?"

"While you tell them?" Riley blushed. "Are you sure?"

"Yes. I don't think they'll be surprised. They've seen me

around you, and they noticed my barge was gone from the dock in town. My mother messaged me yesterday, so I told her I'd explain everything over a coffee. They all love you. You have nothing to worry about."

"Then why don't you ask them to come here instead?" Riley suggested. "So, you're a barbecue kind of woman, huh? There's so much I still don't know about you."

"Who isn't?"

"Me," Riley admitted. "It will be a first for me."

"What?" Quinn laughed. "You've never been to a barbecue?"

"No. Unless Korean barbecue in a restaurant counts." Riley shrugged. "So you'll have to help me out."

"I know my way around a grill. There's nothing better than smoking coals and the smell of burgers on a nice sunny evening. If you don't have a barbecue, I can borrow my brother's."

"I don't, but I'm happy to buy one," Riley said. "If you man the station, I'll do the prep."

"Sure. Or we could get one together?" Quinn suggested, realizing she'd never purchased anything with a lover. Not even a set of coffee mugs. She'd kept her cards close to her chest and now was the time to start sharing.

"If you're not sick of shopping with me." Riley smirked. "Now that you're living here, we need to make Aster House your home as much as mine, so if you want a bigger TV in the bedroom or a toolshed in the yard, we'll make that happen. Anything you want."

Quinn kissed Riley's forehead and smiled. "Honestly, a toolshed would be a dream. I've never had anywhere to store my tools properly." She paused and reminded herself that although she loved living here, they shouldn't rush things. "But let's take it slow and see how we go first. I don't want you to feel like I'm taking over in any way."

"And I don't want you to feel like it's *my* house," Riley said. "I want you to feel like it's *our* house." She hesitated. "You're right. Let's see how this goes, but later this year, if it still feels right and you still want to be with me, then maybe..."

"What?"

"Well, maybe you could put your name on the deed, so we'll own the house together. If you'd be interested in that," she quickly added. "No pressure. I don't need the money, but since you have the capital now and you've always wanted to buy it..."

Quinn's eyes welled up as she stared at Riley in adoration. It wasn't even the fact that she'd have the chance to get Aster House back in her family; knowing that Riley wanted to share this dream with her choked her up.

"What I want is to be with you," Quinn said softly. "But yes, of course I'd love to own the house with you eventually." Her phone lit up, and she hesitated when she saw it was a message from her mother. "She wants to meet me at ten."

"Go on, tell her that's fine and that I'll be joining you," Riley said, glancing at her screen.

"She's going to be over here a lot once I tell her we're together and that I've moved in with you. You know that, right? She has no idea what to do with herself now that she's not working anymore. That's why I've been putting off telling her. I guess I just wanted to stay in our private bubble for a little longer."

"I love our bubble too, but it's time you burst it. I don't mind having your mom here. I like her, and she even offered to help me with the renovations."

Quinn laughed. "See? That's what I mean. I swear, once

she feels comfortable here, you won't get rid of her easily. I love Mom, but she gets too involved sometimes." Her phone lit up again, but this time, it was ringing.

Riley shook her head and grinned. "Let's get this over with." She took the phone from her and answered, "Riley Moore, Quinn's girlfriend speaking."

60

RILEY

"And just like that, I have another daughter-in-law." Audrey looked emotional as she hugged Riley tightly. "I never thought I'd see the day."

Her father wasn't shy of a squeeze either, and he rubbed Riley's shoulder after he finally let go of her. "Welcome to the family, Riley."

"Thank you." Riley chuckled nervously. As bold as she'd been on the phone, now she didn't quite know what to say. "It's nice to see you both again." She held up two mugs and smiled. "Coffee?"

"Yes, please!" Audrey walked over to the kitchen window and peered out. "Did you give up your mooring space, Quinn? Are you neighbors now or have you moved in? Why didn't you tell us?"

Riley glanced at Quinn, who blew out her cheeks while her mother fired off an arsenal of questions. "I'm telling you now, aren't I? And no, I didn't give up my mooring space. I'm just here now...sort of."

"Hmm..." Audrey smirked. "I knew it," she said. "I called it, didn't I?"

"Yes." Her father laughed. "She called it." He turned to Riley. "So, how long have you two been dating?"

Riley frowned as she dug through her memory. They'd only been together for about five weeks officially, but things had started way before that. "I'm not sure," she said. "It's been a whirlwind, and it's all a bit of a blur."

"That's what love does to people." Audrey let out a sigh of delight. "Isn't this wonderful? We're sitting in the kitchen of Aster House with the lovely new owner who's dating our daughter. You're special. I could tell right away. Quinn is lucky to have you."

"I'm the lucky one." Riley gave her a sweet smile as she put down their coffees, then continued to make two for Quinn and herself while Quinn sliced the chocolate cake Riley had made. Her second attempt looked more like a cake and less like a turd but tasted just as delicious as the first. "She's amazing and I'm crazy about her," Riley added, then bit her lip and grinned when Quinn blushed and smiled at her sheepishly.

"Aww!" Audrey placed a hand over her heart and leaned into her husband. "Young love. Those were the days, right?" She patted his shoulder. "Sometimes I wish I could go back to that romance-filled era."

"Hey, I still buy you flowers every Tuesday," he protested. "And I cook for you all the time."

"That's true. He gets me flowers on his way back from pickleball practice on Tuesdays," Audrey admitted. "I know I'll get white roses at eight p.m., and that's very sweet, but the spontaneity is somewhat lacking, don't you think? And you're the chef in the household, so it only makes sense that you cook." She pointed at Quinn and continued before her husband had a chance to get a word in. "Enjoy the honeymoon phase, honey. And try to avoid routine because before you know it, you'll get the same flowers every week and you'll only have sex once a month for ten minutes on Saturday night. *If* you're lucky," she added. "And then it becomes this thing where you just do it to—"

"Mom! I don't want to hear about your sex life!" Quinn shot her mother an incredulous look. "And neither does Riley."

"But, honey, I'm just explaining how important it is to keep intimacy—"

"Audrey..." Her husband stopped her. "Quinn is right. This is not the time or place to discuss such things."

Riley listened with fascination and bemusement. Quinn had warned her about her mother, but she never imagined her to be so straightforward. Apparently, now that she was part of the family, nothing was sacred.

Audrey held up a hand. "Okay, okay. I thought we were all open-minded people here, but let's drop the subject." She turned to Riley. "Anyway, now that you're dating Quinn, we'll have plenty of opportunity to talk among ourselves."

"Of course, anytime, Audrey," Riley said with a chuckle. She didn't mind Audrey being intrusive; she liked her and had felt a connection with her from the first moment they'd met. If anything, it was funny to see Quinn cringe as she plated the chocolate cake. "I'm just here working on the house, so drop in anytime you want."

"Don't give her ideas," Quinn warned.

"Oh, stay out of it." Audrey gave her daughter a playful slap on her behind, then took two slices of cake to the table and sat down. "Surely, Riley could do with some help. How's the renovation going? It's looking great, by the way."

"Thank you, it's going well," Riley said. "Quinn's been really helpful. In fact, she's been a lifesaver, but there's still a lot to do. I'm not in a rush. All in due time, but eventually,

I'd love to start a bed-and-breakfast here, which means I'll need to get everything looking beautiful and in perfect working order."

"A bed-and-breakfast? I love that idea!" Audrey clapped her hands together. "It's brilliant. Who wouldn't want to stay in a mansion along the river rather than in one of the hotels in town?"

"That's what I thought," Riley agreed. "Aster House is a romantic place. I can see couples coming here. I'm not sure if I'm suitable to work in hospitality, though. I've never done anything like that."

Audrey waved it off. "There's nothing to it, honey. I can help you. I'll teach you all the tricks of the trade, and if you ever need a part-time employee, I'm your person."

61

QUINN

Quinn pulled the knot tight and leaned on the swing with her full body weight to make sure it was secure. It was just like her old swing that used to hang under the exact same willow, big enough for two adults or three kids. She vividly remembered the day her grandfather had built the original one. She and her brother were sitting on her grandfather's knees, holding on to the sturdy ropes while they swung higher and higher. She remembered their laughter, his laughter, and her grandmother yelling at him to be careful. Her brother had lost a tooth to the swing, and she'd broken an arm one summer, but that didn't stop them from getting back on it, always begging their grandfather to join.

Years later when she was older, the swing had become a place for her to retreat and gather her thoughts; a silent companion that cradled her. She'd found solace under the branches of the willow tree, pouring her emotions into the whispering breeze. This place had absorbed her laughter, caught her tears, and soothed her heartache. Maybe one day, it would do the same for someone else.

When she sat on it and started swinging, a wave of nostalgia washed over her. The rhythmic motion, a dance between earth and sky, lifted her and set her mind adrift. Flashbacks of long, beautiful summers and memorable days with her family made her smile. With each forward arc, she felt a release as she soared through the air. Quinn had no idea how long she'd been swinging back and forth by the time Riley came out with a glass pitcher of freshly squeezed lemonade and two tall glasses.

"Babe, you finished it. It's gorgeous!"

"Thank you. Want to try it with me?" Quinn stopped the swing, scooted over, and waited for Riley to place the beverages on the table. She was wearing a white cotton summer dress that ended just above her knees and a gray cardigan that covered her arms. Barefoot and fresh-faced, she looked angelic in front of the lowering sun that radiated around her.

"Are you sure it will hold both of us?" she asked.

"Positive. Come here."

Riley approached her with a teasing grin and instead of sitting next to Quinn, she hiked up her dress and straddled her. "Is this what you had in mind?"

"Not quite..." Quinn moaned when Riley shifted closer, pushing herself into her. Quinn's core tightened at the sensual sight and the pressure of Riley's pelvis against hers. "But I'm not complaining." She ran a hand over Riley's bare thigh from her knee upward, stopping just before the edge of her panties. "Maybe I should have gotten one for the bedroom after all."

"I told you so." Riley cupped Quinn's face and ran her tongue over her lips, smiling when Quinn let out another soft moan. "I guess this swing will have to do for now." Her eyes were sparkling with mischief, and she bit her lip as she ground into Quinn.

Their bodies entwined in an embrace. Quinn kept one hand on the rope while the other slipped underneath Riley's dress to caress her back. Riley's hair swayed around them, and every time they moved back, Quinn caught a waft of her fruity shampoo. They fell into a passionate kiss, and she closed her eyes, reveling in the moment. She felt dizzy, but she couldn't stop kissing her, and hungry for more, she tugged at Riley's dress. "This needs to come off," she murmured against her mouth and held Riley so she didn't fall while she took it off. They laughed when Riley tossed the dress behind her and it landed on a branch instead of on the lawn. "No bra?" Quinn arched a brow as her gaze was drawn to Riley's bare breasts, and instinctively, she leaned in to fold her lips around a hard nipple.

"Who needs a bra? It's not like there's anyone here..." Riley pushed her chest forward and let out a strangled cry when Quinn bit her softly, teasing her with her teeth. She ground into Quinn, her body rolling as she arched her back. Everything about her was sensual and seductive, and as she inched back to look at her, Riley found her mouth again. They fell into a heated make-out, and Quinn felt like a fantasy she never knew she had was coming true. A beautiful, near-naked woman was straddling her, teasing her with her lips and grinding into her each time they swayed back. She couldn't take it anymore; she had to have her.

"I think we should move to the lawn," Quinn whispered, frustrated she wasn't able to use both hands.

"I like your thinking," Riley said.

Overcome by lust, she wanted to be all over Riley, on top of her, inside her. Scraping the sole of her sneaker across the ground, she brought them to a halt and grinned when Riley got off her and wiggled her hips as she walked away from the shade of the tree, where the grass was thicker and greener. Her ass looked exquisite in the white, lace panties that only scarcely covered it, and when Riley lowered herself onto the lawn and lay back, Quinn couldn't get off the swing fast enough.

They both turned their attention to the drive when they suddenly heard a car coming up the drive, followed by another car.

"Fuck!" Riley slammed a hand in front of her mouth. "I forgot Gareth and Tammy were coming."

"Oh, shit..." Quinn's eyes widened as she saw Gareth's truck pull up, followed by Tammy's little Renault. She turned to Riley, who got up and covered her breasts with one hand while she tiptoed underneath the branch to grab her dress. She, too, had forgotten Tammy was coming in for a quick tidy and clean prior to Jane and Mindy's arrival tomorrow, and the fact that Gareth would arrive at his usual time to water the plants hadn't even crossed her mind.

"Help me, Quinn. Don't just stand there." Riley chuckled, jumping up and down. "I can't reach."

Springing into action, Quinn got back on the swing and raised herself onto her feet, pumping it until she went high enough to jump off and grab hold of Riley's dress in the process. It tore at the neckline, and although the dress came down, a piece of white fabric remained hanging from a stub on the branch. "Sorry, I ruined it," she said with a goofy grin when Riley scrambled to get it on. "But I like the lower neckline."

Riley laughed and shook her head as she covered her face in her hands. "God, I'm so embarrassed. Have they seen me?"

Quinn noted both Gareth and Tammy had stepped out

of their vehicles and were pretending to busy themselves with something in the back of Gareth's pickup. They normally greeted them when they arrived, but they were making a point of avoiding contact. "I think so." She closed the distance between them, pulled Riley into a hug, and the absurdity of the situation made her laugh. "You in your panties, your dress in the tree, me on the swing trying to retrieve it. At least it will give them something to gossip about."

"Are we going to be the talk of the town now?" Riley blushed profusely when she finally found the courage to look up and wave at Gareth and Tammy, who waved back.

"Yes," Quinn said as she raised her hand and smiled. "Tomorrow, everyone in Mystic will know why you have a swing in your yard."

62

RILEY

"Mindy!" Riley bent down to pick Mindy up and spun her around in her arms.

Mindy studied her with adorable, furrowed brows. "You look different."

"Do I?" Riley smiled and kissed her cheek. "Well, it's been a while. You look different too. You're a big girl now."

"You do look different," Jane agreed, closing the car door. "Wow. This is quite the house." She shielded her eyes from the sun as she looked up at Aster House. "I remember you used the word 'estate,' but you never mentioned it was the size of a small castle. And the yard... It's never-ending."

"It's crazy what you can get for your money once you move out of New York." Riley put Mindy down and hugged her sister, closing her eyes as she squeezed her tightly. It felt like a pivotal moment, like this was a chance to start over and she was on parole somehow. She was going to get through her parole, no matter what. From the corner of her eye, she saw Mindy running around the house.

"There's a sea!" the little girl yelled.

"Don't go there, honey, the river is dangerous." Riley ran

after her niece and caught her, and Mindy screeched when she tickled her. "We can go feed the ducks together later, but let's put your things inside first."

"Jane stared at her and frowned. "You're not wearing heels," she said. "No, strike that. You're barefoot. What's with the new look?"

"I'm comfortable barefoot."

"I can see that. Do you live here all by yourself?" Jane asked.

"No, not anymore." Riley's lips stretched into a wide smile as Quinn came out of the house. They'd been adding last-minute touches to the bedrooms, and Quinn had stayed behind to fluff up the pillows and put some toys in Mindy's room, as Jane and Mindy had arrived earlier than expected. "This is Quinn. She moved in with me last week." She took Quinn's hand when she joined them and leaned into her. "Quinn, this is Jane, my sister, and this little chipmunk is Mindy."

"Hi, Quinn. It's so nice to meet you." Although Jane seemed full of enthusiasm, there was also a hint of confusion in her expression as she glanced from Riley to Quinn and back. "Riley's never introduced me to any of her friends. You must be close if you're living together."

"Actually, Quinn and I *are* together," Riley said, and she noted it rolled off her tongue easily. She'd had no trouble being open about them so far, and now, even with her own sister, it seemed so straightforward. "She's my partner," she clarified when Jane gave her another puzzled glance while stroking Mindy, who was clinging to her leg at the sight of the stranger.

Jane let out an uncomfortable chuckle, then slammed a hand in front of her mouth when she realized Riley was serious. "Oh, I'm so sorry, I didn't mean to laugh. I just thought you were..."

"Joking? No, I'm not." Riley shot her sister a sweet smile to put her at ease. "I'm with Quinn and I've never been happier."

"So you're...gay?" Jane whispered.

"Yeah, I am."

"Okay...well, I'm super happy for you. For you both. I mean, if this is what you want, then..."

Quinn, who clearly felt the tension in the air, kneeled in front of Mindy. "Hi, there. I heard we had a big girl coming to visit, so we made you a big-girl room." She winked. "The bed is so big, I bet you can't get onto it."

"Sure, I can." Deciding she trusted Quinn, Mindy inched away from her mother and gave her a toothless grin. "How big is my bed? This big?" She spread her little arms wide.

"Oh, it's much bigger than that. It's a giant's bed," Quinn joked.

"She's right. There's a huge four-poster in there," Riley said. "We thought she might enjoy sleeping in it."

"She'll love that." Jane stared at Riley and Quinn again, then shook her head and laughed. "Forgive me if I'm a little short of words. You kind of dropped a cannonball on me. Besides that, you look totally different, so I might need to process this before I'll be able to have a normal conversation."

Riley laughed too and put a hand on Jane's back. "That's okay. Why don't I show you to your rooms so you can freshen up, and then we can have some food in the yard by the river?"

"If you take them upstairs, I'll get dinner ready," Quinn said. "Do you guys like pasta?"

"Thank you, we love pasta. And I promise I'll be back to

my normal self in a bit. I'm just surprised, that's all." Jane grinned sheepishly. "My stern and highly unromantic sister is suddenly gay and in love and lives in a castle. It's a lot to process."

"No worries," Quinn said with a chuckle. "I totally understand. We'll catch up later."

"I want to see my room!" Mindy yelled. "Are we sleeping in the castle?"

"You sure are. Want to see your big-girl room?" Riley took her little hand as they headed inside. As much as she'd hated the house before, now she felt proud at hearing Jane's gasps and comments about how grand and beautiful it was.

"This is amazing." Jane stared up at the enormous chandelier. "How is it at night?" she asked, lowering her voice when Mindy ran up the stairs ahead of them.

"It was a bit scary in the beginning," Riley whispered, "but I understand the house better now, and having Quinn here makes a big difference, of course."

"She seems nice. How did this happen? Have you always been into women?"

"No, but I never knew myself that well, I suppose. Quinn is special, and this isn't a phase, in case you're wondering." Riley opened the door to Mindy's bedroom first, and Mindy gave an excited shriek when she spotted the huge bed with stuffed animals and presents on top.

"Is this for me?" she asked, climbing up the small stepladder Quinn had placed next to the bed, as it was too high for her to get onto.

"Yes, that's all for you, honey. And your mom's room is next door, so if you get scared, she's really close and you can always go sleep with her."

"No, I want my own room." Mindy grinned.

"Please don't encourage her. I need my sleep," Jane

283

joked. "The room is gorgeous, by the way. This is so sweet of you."

"I should have put more effort into seeing you and Mindy a long time ago. I'm sorry it took a change of lifestyle to make me realize that."

Jane nodded and studied her intently. "You seem happy."

"I am." Riley smiled. "I'll fill you in over dinner, but let me show you your room first." She walked out and opened the next door, which led to one of the bigger bedrooms in the house. It looked pretty and romantic, and she'd treated it like a hotel room, with toiletries, towels, a robe and slippers, and local magazines on the nightstand. It was a good practice run to gauge how much work it would be to get it ready for paying guests, if that was what she decided to do, and she'd enjoyed the process.

Jane looked seriously impressed as she stepped inside. "My God, Riley. It's like a room in a five-star resort."

"Not quite. The bathrooms still need a lot of work, but I'm getting there." Riley laughed when Jane climbed onto her own high bed and lay back with a sigh. "Take your time. I'll go help Quinn in the kitchen. There's no rush if you want to take a nap. We can look after Mindy."

"No way. I'm hungry, and I can smell something delicious cooking." Jane glanced out of the window and spotted the table that was laid out by the riverside. "Do your thing, we won't be long."

63

QUINN

"*W*ine?" Quinn held up a bottle of red.

"Yes, please." Jane nodded eagerly, then raised her face skyward and took in a deep breath as she blinked against the sun. "It's lovely out here—please excuse my outfit. I was planning on getting dressed after my shower, but this robe was so comfortable I didn't want to take it off." She ruffled a hand through her wet hair and closed her white robe farther. Mindy was wrapped in a robe too; Riley had bought one in her size that matched Jane's, and she loved wearing the same as her mother.

"No need to get dressed around Aster House," Riley said. "It's not quite bikini weather yet, but that's all *I'll* be wearing when it gets warmer. I might even get my first tan."

"Is that so?" Quinn looked Riley over, picturing her in a bikini and the tan lines underneath. She was dressed casually today, as she hadn't had time to change yet, but she looked gorgeous in her linen pants with rolled-up hems and a simple white T-shirt.

"Uh-huh." Riley blushed and glanced at Mindy, who was

on the swing and out of hearing range. "I just ordered one for the summer. I think you'll like it."

"I'm sorry, but this is so weird," Jane said with a chuckle. She turned to Quinn. "I'm not used to seeing Riley flirtatious. She's all giddy and girlie around you. It's like she's a different person."

"I *am* a different person." Riley placed a hand on Quinn's thigh and squeezed it. "It's been a strange couple of months. Surreal even, but they've also been the best months of my life."

"Aww, thank you, babe. You know I feel the same." Quinn felt a happy glow spread through her. Hearing Riley say that meant everything, and the fact that she was so relaxed about them while her sister was around gave her so much hope for their future. This was what a real relationship felt like; togetherness, family, and sharing everyday moments that would shape their lives and form beautiful memories. Her mother was beside herself when she'd told her about Riley, and she'd arranged to get everyone together on Sunday including Lindsey. Jane, who'd been utterly shocked at first, was slowly getting used to the new Riley, and Quinn suspected she liked this version of her more.

"You look so comfortable together," Jane continued, clearly still not grasping the change in Riley. "And I have to say it again. You're barefoot. I mean, when did I ever see you without your high heels apart from when we were kids?"

Chuckling at Jane's observations, Quinn plated eggplant and tomato pasta for her and Mindy, then grated some parmesan over the dishes and sprinkled them with fresh basil.

Jane turned toward the swing and raised her voice. "Mindy, come eat your dinner, honey!"

"As I said, I needed a change." Riley twirled her wine

around in her glass and smiled at Mindy, who came tearing up to them.

"Burnout?" Jane asked.

"Something like that." Riley took a sip, avoiding her gaze.

Quinn looked at Riley sideways as she plated for her. She didn't want to interfere, but she wondered why she refused to tell her sister the truth about her heart condition.

"Like what?" Jane's question was interrupted by Mindy, who climbed onto Riley's lap.

"I want to sit here. Can I sit with you, Aunt Riley?"

"Of course you can. Do you want a spoon?"

"No, I can eat with a fork. I'm five!" Mindy clumsily speared her fork through her pasta and immediately dropped half of it over Riley's pants before it even reached her mouth.

"I'm so sorry." Jane beckoned Mindy over. "Come sit next to me, honey. You're ruining Aunt Riley's white clothes."

"It's okay, it doesn't matter." Riley waved it off and laughed when another heap of spaghetti landed in her lap. "You're doing so well, Mindy. I can't believe how good you are with your fork." She kissed the top of Mindy's head.

Quinn's heart swelled at seeing Riley's love for her niece. She could relate to that; she loved Lila and Tommy with all her heart, and she loved spending time with them and spoiling them when their parents weren't watching.

"If I finish my food, will you come on the swing with me?" Mindy asked Riley.

"Of course! It's a cool swing, isn't it?" Riley glanced at the double swing under the biggest willow. "Quinn made it. She's very good at making things."

Mindy nodded while she focused on her pasta. "It's big

like my bed." She looked up at Quinn, then gasped when an idea suddenly hit her. "Can you make a pool?"

"A pool?" Quinn laughed. "It takes a lot of time to build a pool, but we could order one?" she suggested, turning to Riley. "It's supposed to get warmer this week."

"Please don't go to any trouble," Jane said. "I saw there's a community pool in town. I can take her—"

"Yes, a pool!" Mindy bounced on Riley's lap, causing the pasta on her fork to land everywhere, including on her dress and in Riley's hair. "Can we have a pool? Please?" she begged, drawing out her voice and putting on her most manipulative cute-angel face.

"Oh, boy, here we go..." Jane sighed and shook her head. "You'll certainly need a dip after dinner, but it will be the bathtub kind, I'm afraid. I think Aunt Riley might need one too."

Riley chuckled. "It's all good," she said. "I'll tell you what. If you eat all your pasta, we'll have a look online for pools after."

What followed was an explosion of excited shrieks before Mindy started stuffing the food into her mouth like her life depended on it. Quinn took a sip of her wine, watched her in bemusement and smiled when she locked eyes with Riley. There was so much more to discover about her, to discover about each other, and so much they hadn't discussed. Children, for one. Did *she* want children? Did Riley? Watching her with Mindy sparked questions as much as it made her crave more, but more of what, she wasn't quite sure.

64

RILEY

*R*iley understood what Quinn meant now when she'd described her childhood at Aster House. It was adorable to watch Mindy and Lila play on the lawn. They'd spread out a blanket and were playing "family picnic" with two dolls and a stuffed animal, and they were terribly serious about it, insisting the dolls would eat their vegetables and drink their milk so they'd grow big and strong. Lila kept begging Tommy to be the father, but he refused and told them it was a stupid game.

It wasn't just Riley who was amused; listening in on them made everyone at the table laugh. She was siting among Quinn's parents, Mary and Rob, Lindsey, and Jane, who seemed to be having a great time, and of course, there was Quinn by her side. She loved seeing her sister so animated, and the few days she and Mindy had been here had been healing to Riley. The heavy weight of guilt in her gut was slowly subsiding, and she and Jane were getting to know each other all over again. Her sister was kind and surprisingly fun, and Riley wondered why she'd never come to that conclusion before. She'd always seen Jane as a chore;

someone she had to keep in contact with because it was the right thing to do. How selfish and foolish.

"Eat your spinach, Britney," Mindy said, stuffing a few sprigs of grass into the open mouth of one of the dolls. "You can't leave the table before your plate is empty."

"She's been so difficult lately," Lila said, shaking her head. "I'm having a really hard time with her."

Mindy nodded and let out a dramatic sigh. "Kids are always difficult at this age, but it will get better. Just give her some time."

At that, the whole table burst out in floods of laughter. Mindy and Lila were so engrossed in their game they didn't realize they were the center of attention until Tommy pointed it out.

"Stop talking like Mom and Dad, Lila. You sound like a grandma," he said, looking up from his video game for a split second.

"Hey, I'm not *that* old," Mary exclaimed, turning to her son.

"And I'm the grandma, but I sure as hell don't sound like that either," Quinn's mother chipped in. She looked at Quinn and narrowed her eyes. "Do I?"

"They must get it from somewhere." Quinn grinned and held up both hands. "Anyway, I'm staying out of this. I think the burgers are ready, so I'd better go check on them."

"Avoiding confrontation, huh?" Mary raised a brow at her. "Just like in high school when you never picked sides."

"Hey, I'm a lover, not a fighter." Quinn shot Riley a wink as she got up, and Riley followed her to the barbecue by the water's edge. It was their first purchase together, and Riley loved the big workspace it came with. Already, she knew they were going to get a lot of use out of it.

"Need some help?" she asked, inching close. "I can unwrap the corn and the baked potatoes."

"Yes, please. I put dishes underneath. You can use those." Quinn kissed her and put an arm around her as she flipped the burgers and inspected them. "It's a good day, right?"

"Yeah. I think everyone's having a really nice time." Riley met her eyes and smiled. "Thank you."

"For what?"

"Just for being you, your amazing self. You have no idea how much your energy lifts me." Riley blushed as they were about to fall into a kiss. "Okay, maybe we should wait because if I start kissing you now, it will be a proper smooch." She focused on the corn instead, shifting them to a dish.

"A proper smooch, huh? I wouldn't say no to that." Quinn grabbed her behind and Riley shrieked, slapping her hand away. Behind them, the kids were giggling at the sight, and Mindy yelled at them to behave.

"Sorry!" Riley shot them a grin. "Who wants burgers?"

"Me, me, me!" Tommy held up his hand.

"I want pizza," Lila protested.

"That's not happening today, Lila. Have you ever seen a barbecued pizza before?" Quinn asked her niece, who furrowed her brows, considering that question. "Exactly, I don't think so. Now come here and help us get the plates to the table. Britney can have a burger too."

"I want to help!" Mindy joined them and carefully walked away with the corn dish Riley handed her. She took her task very seriously, her tongue sticking out as she went on her tiptoes to place it in the middle of the table, then gave everyone a piece, including the two dolls who now had a prime seat at the head.

Riley plated the rest of the vegetables and tossed the salads while the kids served the burgers. The chatter and laughter around her warmed her, and once again she was filled with a sense of belonging. She was part of a family, and that was something she truly appreciated. Mystic had been a godsend. It was the community she never thought she needed, the support system she now embraced and treasured. It felt like she'd been destined to end up here, in this place randomly chosen by her assistant, and that she'd been destined to meet Quinn. Otherwise, what were the chances of finding such happiness? Aster House was no longer intimidating. It was a warm home. It was where she belonged.

65

QUINN

"*L*ook at her, she's exhausted." Quinn pointed to Mindy, who was sleeping on the blanket next to her doll.

"She's had such a fun day," Jane said, wiping the table after they'd cleared it. "And so did I. I'm still amazed at how nice it's been, and I was thinking... Well, I was thinking maybe Mindy and I could stay a few more days if you guys are okay with that? It's good for her to be outdoors so much, and I haven't seen her this animated in a long time."

"Of course. We'd love to have you here longer. Right, Quinn?" Riley shot Quinn a beaming smile, and Quinn returned it. She could tell by the tone of Riley's voice that she was touched to hear her sister was enjoying herself.

"Absolutely. I've loved getting to know you." She frowned when Riley suddenly reached for her chest and swallowed hard. "What is it? Are you okay?" Her first thought was that there might be something wrong with Riley's heart. "Is it—"

"No!" Riley quickly said. "It's just indigestion." She narrowed her eyes at Quinn, a clear warning not to bring up the subject. "I've been eating richer foods since I moved to Mystic. Pasta, barbecues, cake, pizzas... I got some pills last week, but I'm out of them."

"Tell me about it." Jane rolled her eyes and remarked to Quinn, "She used to live on sushi and green salads in New York. The few extra pounds look good on you, Riley. You look much healthier." She rooted through her purse and held out a box. "Here, take these. I have a spare strip in my suitcase. I get indigestion too. It must run in the family."

"Thank you." Riley took one and sighed. "I should probably get back to salads, which I love, by the way, but ever since I started considering food as something enjoyable rather than just fuel, I've been having these cravings." She turned to Quinn. "It's your fault. Your barbecue and pastas are addictive."

Quinn laughed, but she wasn't quite at ease, and she was grateful when Jane picked up Mindy so they could have a moment alone.

"I'll take her to bed. God, she's getting heavy." Jane groaned as she pushed her daughter, who continued to sleep, farther up her hip. Mindy's head fell onto Jane's shoulder, and Jane brushed her hair away from Mindy's face and kissed her cheek lovingly. "I won't be long."

Quinn waited until she was out of hearing distance, then rubbed Riley's shoulder. "Are you sure it's not your heart?"

"Positive. My betablockers are working, and anyway, indigestion feels entirely different from tachycardia."

Quinn nodded, somewhat relieved. "Are you ever going to tell Jane?"

"I will." Riley's gaze shifted to the back door. "Just not yet. I don't want to dampen our lovely time with something so serious, and she'll just worry about me when there's nothing to worry about. I've been fine for months. Jane was worried sick when our father got admitted to the hospital. I guess as a nurse, she feels responsible for everyone's well-being, and she blamed herself that she hadn't seen it coming."

"I get it," Quinn said. "That's a lot of pressure on her, but you shouldn't keep health problems to yourself."

"Even if it causes Jane sleepless nights? Even if it means she'll go out of her way to check on me every day and panic when I don't pick up my phone?"

Quinn nodded.

Riley sighed. "Okay, I'll tell her before she leaves. I promise."

"Please do. If I were Jane, I'd want to know."

"What about Jane?"

Riley startled and straightened herself when her sister approached. "I was just saying how nice it's been to see you and Mindy," she said, painting on a smile. "I feel like I'm getting to know you all over again. Isn't that crazy?"

"Totally, me too. And I'm loving Riley 2.0." Jane sank onto the couch next to the dining table and propped her feet on a stool. "Want to have a nightcap together? It's so quiet without screaming kids around, and the view is gorgeous." She spread her arms. "I mean, look at this."

"I know, I feel very lucky," Riley said, sitting next to her and propping her feet up beside her sister's. "You know you're welcome here anytime, right? Whenever you need a break."

"Thank you. You know what? I'll take you up on that offer. I feel like I'm on vacation, but it doesn't come with the stress of being somewhere with a child and having to entertain her."

Jane looked at Riley affectionately, and Quinn smiled, seeing the love between them. It was a peaceful night, and the sudden silence was indeed a welcome break. The river lay still, and there was a gentle rustling in the trees overhead.

"How about a glass of port?" she suggested. "I have that nice bottle from when Grandma was here." She shook her head when Riley was about to get up. "Stay there and let those pills do their work. Would you like a cup of chamomile tea instead? It might be better with your indigestion."

"Yes, please. You're the sweetest." Riley blew her a kiss, and Quinn beamed as she walked to the back entrance of the house and heard Jane whispering, "I fucking love that woman. If you ask me, she's the best thing that ever happened to you."

It was a great week. Riley's sister approved of her, and Mindy had taken a liking to her too, following her around with her dolls all weekend. Furthermore, her parents were delighted that she'd finally found someone to settle down with. It felt like everything was naturally falling into place, as if it was written in the stars that she would be with Riley. A destined journey of two lives intertwining. It was almost too good to be true.

RILEY

"*C*an we go set up the pool now, Aunt Riley?" Mindy stuffed the last piece of toast into her mouth and pointed at her plate. "I've finished my breakfast."

"Sure, we can, if your mom is okay with it."

"Why not?" Jane said. "It's going to be the first warm day of the year, and I wouldn't mind going in there myself. If I'll fit in," she added with a chuckle.

Riley laughed when Mindy sprinted toward the big box leaning against the kitchen counter. It was way too heavy to pick up, but she kept trying anyway, pulling at it with her full body weight. It was going to be warmer today, and the pool Mindy had picked was most certainly big enough to fit all three of them.

Mindy had been up at the crack of dawn, waiting for the delivery, waking them up each time she heard a noise. When it finally arrived by courier at eight a.m., Riley had no choice but to make breakfast so they could get their day started. "Can you swim?" she asked.

"I can with armbands." Mindy turned to Jane. "Mom, where are my armbands?"

"They're in the big suitcase, honey. Go get them. Your swimsuit is in there too." Jane finished her coffee, got up, and sighed as she glanced from the box to Riley and back. "You think we can do this? No, wait," she corrected herself. "We *have* to do this. Mindy's mood depends on it, and I don't want to have a sulking child on my last few days here."

"Come on. I've decorated half the house. I'm sure I can manage to get a simple paddling pool up and running." Riley yawned as she picked up one side and waited for Jane to take the other side.

"Are you tired?" Jane asked. "You keep yawning, and it's making me yawn too."

"A little," Riley said, noting her body felt achy. It wasn't just the yawning; faint spells of dizziness had bugged her all morning, but she'd ignored them. She had no reason to be tired; if anything, she'd had lots of rest while Jane and Mindy were here. A little voice in the back of her mind told her to see a doctor and have herself checked out, but she was having such a nice time with her family that she didn't want to ruin their carefree vibe now that they were finally getting on so well.

Although she'd had dizzy spells many times before and felt fine the next day, they were still warning signs, so just in case, she stopped halfway down the hallway. "Hang on, I forgot something." Riley went back and grabbed her phone from the kitchen table before they headed into the yard. Perhaps she'd get a quiet moment to call the doctor's practice to make an appointment for next week, after Jane and Mindy had left.

"Right. Where shall we set it up?" Jane asked, panting as they put the box down to rest for a beat. "And why is it so heavy? I thought it was just an inflatable paddling pool."

"No, it's a puncture-resistant base attached to a metal

frame, and it's quite big," Riley said, hoping it came with a clear manual. Feeling light-headed, she blew out her cheeks, then painted on a smile. Nothing was going to ruin this beautiful day, and she was going to be fine.

"Yay! I'm going to swim!" Mindy came tearing out in her swimsuit. In her rush, she'd put it on back to front, and she looked adorable, waving her armbands in the air. "Can we put it under the swing, Mommy? I want to jump in the pool from the swing."

"I don't think that's safe, honey," Jane said with a chuckle as she looked her over. "You might hurt yourself."

"But I can swim!" Mindy jutted out her bottom lip.

"I know you can, but you're also a bit of a monkey, and I don't want you landing on the frame."

"How about by the river next to the seating area?" Riley suggested. "Then we can keep an eye on her while we're having sundowners later. Maybe under the—" She stopped herself when she suddenly felt shaky. The tremble that grew in her limbs made it hard to stand. *Fuck. It's happening again.* Cold sweat broke out as she sank onto the lawn and held her chest. Her heart was beating abnormally fast, randomly skipping a beat every few seconds. It was bad, and she knew it.

"Riley, what's going on?" Jane kneeled next to her and held her with a worried frown between her brows. "What's wrong?"

"It's my heart," Riley said through heavy breaths, barely able to get the words out. So many things went through her mind in that moment. Her previous cardiac events had been scary too, but she'd felt invincible and had dealt with her recovery like it was one of her projects, never really admitting what was at stake: her life. But things had changed, and she couldn't die now. Not when she was finally, truly happy.

She had Quinn, she had a home, and she had her family. She could see her future so clearly, so vividly, and that future was threatening to slip away. Most of all, she loved Quinn, and she needed a second chance to tell her that. She couldn't breathe through the panic and pain that spread through her chest.

"Ambulance..." she whispered, barely mustering the energy to pull her phone out of her back pocket. She held it out for Jane, then dropped it when pins and needles set in, turning her hands numb.

Jane patted her cheek. "Okay, stay with me, Riley. I'm calling an ambulance now. Anything I should know? Would it be quicker if I just drove you to the hospital? I have no idea where it is."

Riley couldn't answer. She heard Jane's voice, but she sounded so far away. Was she walking away from her or was Riley slipping away herself? Opening her mouth to ask the question, no words came out, and Riley's mind went blank.

67

QUINN

*R*ushing through the hospital corridors, Quinn couldn't think straight. She kept asking people for the cardiology department, but the building was a maze, and she couldn't find it. She'd driven here in a state of panic, most likely picking up some speeding tickets on the way. If only this was a nightmare and she'd wake up and everything would be okay. But despite her confusion, it felt too real to be a nightmare. "You need to come to the hospital," Jane had told her. "It's Riley. It's her heart." Quinn had been at work when she received the call, and she still had paint stains on her hands and work jeans.

"Please, I need the cardiology department," she yelled when a nurse passed.

"You're here. Try to concentrate on your breathing. You're about to hyperventilate." The nurse patted Quinn's arm. "Come with me." She led the way to the reception desk, which was hidden in a nook around the corner. "Calm down, please, so I can help you. Who is it you're looking for?"

"Riley Moore. She was admitted about an hour ago."

LISE GOLD

"She's in room seventeen," one of the other nurses, who had overheard the conversation, said. "But they're doing some tests on her, and she's not currently allowed any visitors. You can wait outside her room, though. There's a seating area and a coffee machine opposite."

"Is she going to be okay?" Quinn turned to the clerk. "Can you tell me how serious it is?"

The clerk typed something into her computer and squinted as she read the notes on the screen. "We can't tell you anything until she's been fully examined, I'm afraid. One of our cardiologists will fill you in as soon as we know more." She smiled apologetically at Quinn. "Are you family?"

"I'm..." Quinn swallowed hard. "I'm her partner. Her sister, Jane Moore, is already here. She's the one who called me."

"Right. Well, if you take a seat outside Miss Moore's room, we will update you as soon as we have any news." She pointed to the left corridor when Quinn was about to walk the wrong way again.

"Thank you." Quinn fought back her tears when she met Jane's eyes. Jane was sitting in a chair with Mindy sleeping on her lap, and she looked like she'd been crying.

"Hey there," she said with a sad smile.

"Hey." Quinn gave her a careful hug so she wouldn't wake up Mindy. "What happened? How is she?"

"I don't know any more than you do," Jane said. "One moment she was fine—or at least, I thought she was fine, albeit a bit tired—and the next she collapsed on the lawn, clutching her chest. She passed out for a little while, but she was completely lucid by the time the ambulance arrived."

"Was she talking?"

"Yes, but she was weak, and her heart rate was through

the roof. I'm a nurse, but for the first time in my career, I panicked because I couldn't do anything to help her." Tears trickled down Jane's cheeks, and she sniffed. "I'm usually so calm in life-threatening situations, but this is Riley, my sister, and I didn't know what to do..."

"Hey, you couldn't have done anything. She needed a cardiologist, medication, and intensive care. That's not something you can give her in the backyard," Quinn said, putting an arm around her. She was grateful to hear Riley was lucid, but that didn't take away the knowing feeling of doom in the pit of her stomach.

"Maybe, but it sucks to feel so helpless. She said it was her heart, and to me, it looked like it was her heart, but..." Jane hesitated and narrowed her eyes at Quinn. "Do you know something I don't?"

Quinn sighed and decided Jane had a right to know, even if it came from her. She was Riley's sister, after all, and she was terrified. "Riley has the same heart condition as your father," she said. "She's on medication, and she thought it was under control. Clearly, that wasn't the case."

"Oh my God..." Jane slammed a hand in front of her mouth, causing Mindy to stir against her. "Why didn't she tell me?"

"I don't know. She didn't want you to worry, I suppose. Or perhaps she didn't want to put an extra burden on you, as she felt guilty for being so flaky. I know that bothered her —that she hadn't put much effort into your relationship. She's had a lot of regrets since she moved to Mystic." Quinn shrugged. "A change to a slower pace of life can do that to people. She had a lot of time to reflect."

"So that's why she sold her business..." Jane rested her hand on Quinn's. "I asked her about it a couple of times, but she kept giving me vague answers, so I drew my own conclusions. I figured it might have been a failed relationship that drove her away from New York." She shook her head. "I couldn't have been more wrong."

"Yes, she had to slow down drastically, and she did. That's why I don't understand why—" Quinn stopped herself when a doctor came out of Riley's room. "Miss Jane Moore?"

"That's me." Jane held up a hand. "And this is Quinn Kendall. She's Riley's partner."

He gave them both a polite nod and a smile. "Hello, I'm Dr. Norwich, one of the cardiologists here. Based on her medical history and initial tests, it seems that your sister... and your partner," he added, turning to Quinn, "Has suffered an episode of ventricular tachycardia. In itself, it's not normally life-threatening, but as you probably know, Miss Moore's episodes are far more extreme, and this latest one has, again, left some damage." He held up a hand when Quinn looked at him with despair. "However, it's likely she will make a full recovery, and we will do our very best to find out why this has happened again despite her medication. For now, please wait here, or go home and try to distract yourself the best you can. It might take a while. We'll call you as soon as we know more and she's strong enough to have visitors, as we need to prevent her from getting overly emotional."

68

RILEY

$\mathcal{T}$ears trickled down Riley's cheeks when she heard Jane and Quinn talking to Dr. Norwich in the corridor again after five long hours of waiting. She'd missed them both more than she'd worried about herself. Once again, she was in a cardiology wing, but this time, she wasn't alone, and she was so grateful to be alive.

It wasn't stress that had caused her heart to go into extreme arrythmia. Tests had shown she was low on electrolytes, magnesium specifically. She'd been taking medication for heartburn, which had led to hypomagnesemia, and as her heart was already sensitive, that had triggered an episode of ventricular tachycardia. The good news was that she was going to be okay, and her heart would likely repair itself as long as she stopped taking heartburn pills. She vaguely remembered doctors telling her to watch out with certain medication, but the heartburn pills had seemed so innocent that she hadn't given it a second thought.

"Babe!" Quinn walked into the room, and she was crying. "Babe...can I hug you?" she asked, glancing over the wires attached to Riley's chest and the tubes and IV going into her wrists.

"Yes! Come here." Riley clumsily spread her arms and embraced Quinn when she bent over and brushed her cheek against hers. With that embrace, all fears of uncertainty she never knew she had were erased as she wallowed in a cloud of comfort. "I'm so glad you're here."

Quinn lifted her head and wiped her cheeks. "Babe, I was terrified I was going to lose you." She hesitated, meeting Riley's eyes and carefully taking her hand. "I can't lose you. I love you."

Riley stared at her for a beat before she too, started crying. "I love you too," she said, feeling her words deep in her core. She felt so much love for Quinn, and she'd felt it for a while. "I love you," she said again. "And I'm not going anywhere."

"Don't you dare, I need you." Quinn cupped her cheek. "How are you feeling?"

"Not too bad. Just tired and achy." Riley closed her eyes and leaned into Quinn's touch. Something was going against all rules of life because, despite her physical discomfort after nearly dying, she'd rarely felt happier. Quinn loved her, and that filled her with such warmth that nothing else mattered. "I assume Dr. Norwich filled you in?"

"He did," Jane, who had just witnessed their intimate exchange, chipped in before she looked from Quinn to Riley and back. "You guys are so sweet together. I totally get it now." She walked over to Riley and kissed her forehead. "How are you feeling, sis?"

"Okay. Glad to still be here." Riley smiled widely. "They're keeping me for a few days to monitor me and make sure my magnesium levels go back to normal, but if everything's okay, I can go home soon."

"I'll stay here with you, if they'll let me," Quinn said and held up a hand when Riley was about to protest. "No discussion. I'm not leaving your side."

Tears burned again at the corners of Riley's eyes, and she nodded. "Thank you." She shifted her gaze to the door, then looked at Jane. "Where's Mindy?"

"She's in the corridor." Jane checked her drip and continued as she studied the screen next to Riley's bed. "She fell asleep, and the clerk offered to look after her for ten minutes. I wasn't sure if seeing you like this would traumatize her, so I thought it might be best to keep her out."

"Do I look that bad?"

"No, not at all. Just a lot of tubes." Jane smiled as she looked her over. "So, this isn't your first time, huh? I wish I'd known. I'm a nurse, for God's sake. If I'd known you had heart problems, I would have never let you take those heartburn pills." She took Riley's hand, careful not to interfere with the tubes. "Why didn't you tell me?"

Riley shrugged. "At first, I didn't want to bother you because I'd neglected our relationship. And then when I finally saw you again, we were having such a nice time that I didn't want to ruin it with a serious conversation. You're a worrier, and you shouldn't be worrying about me."

"But I *want* to worry about you, and I want you to share what's going on in your life. Isn't that the whole point of rebuilding our relationship? Sharing stuff? What if I was going through something difficult? Wouldn't you want to know?"

Riley winced because her sister was right. "Of course I'd want to know, but I don't feel like I deserve your support," she finally said through sniffs. "I wasn't there for you when you went through your divorce, and I didn't realize how lonely you must have felt until I was all alone myself. I've neglected you and Mindy, and I'm so, so sorry..."

"Don't be. The past is in the past, and today we're starting over. Clean slate, okay? No looking back." Jane gave her a sweet smile. "And talk to me about whatever is happening in your life, good or bad. Will you do that for me?"

"I promise I'll talk to you," Riley said, feeling the heavy weight of guilt lifting off her shoulders. She'd never noticed how heavy that weight was until it evaporated. "But that's it. That's the whole truth. My heart is the reason I sold my company and moved to Mystic. As you know, my condition is generally not life-threatening providing I take it easy and live a healthy life, which I do."

"Then I hope you'll continue to take care of yourself. Hopefully, this was just a one-off, so stay away from those damn heartburn pills." Jane had fallen into nurse mode, and it was sweet to see her like that. Riley could imagine her at work, talking to her patients in the same stern and pressing manner. "I'm glad Quinn is living with you. At least she can keep an eye on you."

"Me too." Riley looked at Quinn lovingly and was instantly caught in her gaze. She couldn't have escaped if she'd wanted to.

Clearly aware she was crashing a moment, Jane straightened herself. "Well, I'll take Mindy back to the house and Quinn will stay here with you. I want to make sure everything is tidy and ready before we take you home. I'll cook you some healthy food and prepare a comfortable seating area outside where you can relax and sleep whenever you feel like it."

"That's so sweet, but I swear I'll be okay," Riley protested.

"Last time I was discharged from the hospital, I felt fine and went straight back to work."

"Yeah, well, that's not happening this time."

"She's right," Quinn said. "You're going to rest, recharge and repair that beautiful, kind heart of yours." She brushed a hand through Riley's hair and kissed her. "I'll get you some lunch now. The hospital food looks awful. What do you feel like?" She continued before Riley had the chance to answer. "You're not allowed phones or iPads in here, but can I get you some magazines?"

69

QUINN

"How did you manage to provoke such a change in Riley?" Jane asked, throwing chopped tomatoes into a bowl. She, Mindy, and Quinn were cooking together while Riley was sleeping upstairs. She'd taken charge, for which Quinn was grateful. A seasoned nurse through and through, Jane was the kind of woman who knew how to handle stressful situations. She'd made sure Riley was comfortable before putting Quinn to work, giving her instructions behind the cooker while Mindy stood on a chair by the counter peeling clementines.

"I didn't," Quinn said. "I've only known the way she is." She turned to Jane. "Is this the moment you tell me you'll kill me if I ever hurt your sister? Because I won't. I meant what I said. I love her."

"I know you do." Jane chuckled and shook her head. "And no, I'd never threaten you. In fact, I want to thank you. She seems so happy, and I suspect that has something, if not everything, to do with you."

Quinn smiled. "She makes me happy too." She paused and turned to Jane. "Do you think she'll be okay? Long-term, I mean? She was so lucky you were there. I can't stop thinking about what might happen if she has another episode while I'm at work and she's alone and—"

"Hey, you can't think like that," Jane interrupted her. "You'll drive yourself crazy. Who knows? Anything can happen in life, but I wouldn't worry too much. She's recovering really well. Just make sure she stays away from pills she shouldn't be taking—although I'm sure she's learned her lesson—and that she keeps stress levels to a minimum." She offered Quinn a reassuring smile. "Really, she'll be okay."

Quinn nodded. "Good. That makes me feel better, coming from a nurse."

Jane patted her arm. "By the way, I was getting some groceries in town this morning, and I'm pretty sure a woman was talking about you and Riley in the dairy aisle." She shrugged. "Obviously, no one knows I'm her sister, so she didn't suspect anything when I hung around pretending to inspect every single type of fruit yogurt."

Quinn frowned. It was likely the word about Riley's health scare had gotten around. "What did she say?"

"Well, she's talking about the swing in your yard and..." Jane gestured to Mindy and lowered her voice. "A dress in a tree. That's all I can say for now."

"A dress in a tree? That's weird." Quinn tried to keep a straight face.

"They think you use the swing for certain activities," Jane clarified and raised a brow. "You know, of the adult kind."

"Oh..." Quinn felt her cheeks burn. Of course everyone was talking about the incident. There was no way Tammy hadn't told her sister, who was the town's gossip, and it was likely Gareth had told his girlfriend, who wasn't shy to share a good story either. "I have no idea what they're talking about," she said. "They're probably making it up. It happens. There aren't many same-sex couples in Mystic, so they're probably just speculating."

"That's sad. Doesn't it bother you?"

"No. I'm used to it, and I doubt Riley will bat an eyelash either." Quinn composed herself and changed the subject. "What about your father? How's he doing?"

Jane narrowed her eyes and stared at her for a beat, clearly deciding whether she was telling the truth or not. "He's much better now that he's made some drastic lifestyle changes, but it wasn't easy getting there. Mindy and I moved in with him for three months to keep an eye on him and make sure he ate healthy and got enough exercise. It wasn't that long after Mom passed away, so he needed the company anyway. I think having Mindy there was a good distraction for him. I still worry about him—he's not getting any younger, after all—but he's picked himself up well, and he has a social life." She sighed. "I'm glad Riley is finally planning on visiting him. He misses her."

"Yeah, I know. She asked me to come with her."

Jane's eyes lit up. "You should! You guys can stay with us. We live very close to Dad."

"Thank you. Only if it's no trouble for you." Quinn laughed when Mindy let out an excited shriek.

"Yes! Can Quinn sleep in my room, Mom?" she asked. "Please?"

"I think Quinn and Aunt Riley would prefer the guest room, honey." Jane chuckled as she grabbed a cucumber from the bowl of vegetables in front of her and started cubing it. "Needless to say, it's nowhere near as fancy as this house, and the suburbs aren't exactly inspiring. We don't have a swing either," she added with a cheeky grin, "but we'll have fun. After all, it's all about family and being together. I like that you're a family person. It must be nice to have a big family."

"It is, and I love them," Quinn said, ignoring the swing comment. "And now I have a lovely sister-in-law too. And you," she said, pinching Mindy's cheek.

"Yeah. I feel like we've bonded." Jane chuckled and nodded toward Mindy, who'd started dissecting the clementine, poking her fingers into the flesh to take out the seeds. Juice was running down her arms and soaking into her sleeves. It was the only job they could think of to keep her busy that didn't involve knives or anything she could break.

"Like this?" Mindy asked, holding up a deflated wedge attached to a piece of skin.

"Perfect." Quinn handed her a plastic picnic plate. "Why don't you arrange them on here and give them to Aunt Riley when she wakes up?"

Mindy seemed to like that idea and took great care in lining up clementine wedges around the edge of the plate. "It's a fruit salad," she said with a serious frown. "I need something to put in the middle."

"How about some strawberries?" Quinn opened the fridge and handed her a box. "Take the green top off and make them look pretty."

"You're good with kids," Jane said. "Have you ever thought about having children?"

"I don't know. It would be nice, I guess. I never saw myself having a family, but now…"

"Are you reconsidering?" Jane arched a brow at her. "What about Riley? Have you spoken about it?"

"No. It's a little too soon for that. I haven't even given it much thought myself." Quinn paused. "But I suppose the idea has been growing on me."

"Hmm..."

"What?" Quinn asked, glancing at Jane sideways.

"Well, I couldn't ever imagine Riley as a mother, but she's actually really good with kids. Mindy loves her. Don't you Mindy?"

"Yes. She got me a pool." Mindy smiled widely as she held up her fruit salad that looked like it had been pre-digested. "Can I take this to Aunt Riley now, Mum? I want to be a nurse like you."

70

RILEY

*W*alking out into the yard, Riley's steps were steadier, a testament to her growing strength. The world had beckoned her, a symphony of birdsong and the touch of a gentle breeze through her bedroom window drawing her outside. Her heart was beating with vigor, and the weight of the past few days slowly lifted, replaced by a renewed sense of purpose. With each step, she embraced life, vowing to savor every beat, every breath, forever grateful for everything she had. She'd needed her three days in bed; her recovery was much slower this time, but now she was sick of staring at her iPad, the TV, and the ceiling.

Taking in a deep breath, she raised her face skyward. Wisps of cotton-like clouds floated lazily, casting shadows over the lawn. One plump and billowy cloud resembled a lion, its mane floating behind him, and nearby, a cluster of smaller clouds danced together in a ballet against the blue backdrop. The air carried the zesty tang of newly sprouted leaves, and there was a distant aroma of a woodfire coming from a neighboring house. A subtle tingle crossed her flesh as if the sunbeams were caressing her. Riley soaked up the day. Her senses felt stronger, or perhaps she was just more mindful now.

Turning the corner, her lips curled into a smile when she saw Quinn by the water's edge. She was drinking coffee and reading a newspaper. As if sensing her presence, Quinn looked up. Warmth blossomed in Riley's chest as their eyes met, and captivated by the beauty of the simple morning scene, she took her in.

"Good morning, beautiful," Quinn said, patting the seat next to her. "You're up."

"I've had enough of my bed. It's not the same when you're not in it."

Quinn kissed her cheek and put an arm around her. "I heard Mindy running around early this morning, and Jane was still in bed. I didn't want her to wake you, so I took her outside." She pointed at her barge, where Mindy was sitting behind the wheel. "It's Captain Mindy now, by the way."

Riley laughed. "Let's hope she doesn't sail away."

"It's safe. I'm keeping an eye on her. She promised to stay inside and shout out of the window when she wants to come off." Quinn studied Riley. "How are you feeling? Be honest."

"Actually, I feel really good." Riley tilted her head and brushed her lips against Quinn's. "Let's wait and see what they say during my checkup next week, but I'm not tired or dizzy anymore."

"That's great, but make sure you don't take on too much. I'm keeping an eye on you."

"You're sweet." Riley scrunched her nose and smiled. "Is Jane still sleeping?"

"I think so."

"Hmm. She never sleeps in." Riley frowned as her eyes darted to the driveway. "Her rental car is gone."

"Oh!" Quinn shrugged. "She must have gone out to get groceries or something."

"But she would have told you, right?" From the way she avoided her gaze, Riley had a feeling there was something she wasn't telling her. "Quinn? Look at me, Quinn." She put a hand on her arm. "Where is Jane?"

At that moment, they heard the front gates open, and Jane's car turned up the driveway. "There she is. See? Everything's fine." Quinn gestured to the car. "She brought a guest. Why don't you go and see them? I'll get Mindy from the barge."

"What?" Riley narrowed her eyes as she started walking toward the car. Jane came out first and opened the passenger's door.

"Dad?"

Riley stopped for a moment and swallowed hard. He looked so much better than last time she'd seen him; much stronger, a little tanned, and he straightened himself and beamed when he spotted her.

"Riley!" He waved at her and spread his arms. "Come here."

Riley did something she never thought she'd do. She ran up to him, flung her arms around his neck, and burst into tears. "Dad, you're here."

"Yes, I'm here, my girl."

"I'm so sorry," she said through sniffs, clutching him. "I haven't been there for you, and I'm so, so sorry."

"From what I've heard, you've had some rough times yourself." He stepped back and cleared his throat. "You should have told me, kiddo. Jane called me, so I had to come. She just picked me up from the airport."

"Thank you. It's really good to see you." Riley wiped her cheeks. Yes, she should have told him and Jane. She should have shared her life with them, the good and the bad. She should have understood how important family and mutual support was, how precious time was, and how precious life was. It wasn't too late. "I love you, Dad," she said.

"I love you too, honey." Her father smiled at her, then glanced up at Aster House. "Look at you. My little princess in her castle. How are you feeling?"

"Good. Much better." She smiled bravely. "I'm going to be okay, Dad. How are you?"

"Not too bad either." He winked at her. "Turns out one is never too old to learn a new sport. I've been playing pickleball."

"*You're* playing pickleball?" Riley chuckled. Her first thought was to suggest he could play with Quinn's father before she remembered he had no idea she was living with a woman. She looked over her shoulder when she heard Quinn and Mindy approaching and widened her eyes at Jane.

"Don't worry, I already filled him in," Jane said with a grimace. "I thought it might be best to tell Dad about you and Quinn so you wouldn't freak out when he suddenly showed up. I hope that's okay. I've been reading up on this stuff, and it's not okay to 'out' someone but I—"

"No, it's fine," Riley interrupted her. "If you're okay with it?" She turned to her father, unsure why she'd said that. It wasn't like she needed his permission, but she wanted him to be comfortable.

"I'm still shocked," he admitted. "But I'm just glad that you're okay, and I want to meet your lady friend." He rubbed her shoulder. "I assume that's her, with little Miss Mindy in tow?"

Riley had no chance to answer because Mindy screamed at the top of her lungs, "Grandpa!"

Her father bent over to pick Mindy up. "Hey there, Mindy chubby cheeks. I thought I'd join you on your vacation. Is that okay?"

Mindy giggled as he kissed her cheeks and tickled her. "I have a pool and a boat!" she yelled. "Will you come on the boat with me, Grandpa? It's a cruise ship, and I'm the captain and Quinn is the co-captain." She tapped the white baseball cap she was wearing. Quinn had written the words "Captain Mindy" with a marker; Riley had a feeling Mindy would even wear it to bed.

Her father laughed, and it felt so good to hear that familiar, roar of joy again. Riley hadn't heard him laugh since her mother was alive, but he was in good spirits today.

"Well, that sounds exciting." He smiled at Quinn. "Will you introduce me to your co-captain first?

71

QUINN

"*R*iley looked so much better." Lindsey glanced at Quinn sideways as she steered the car toward the drawbridge. "And how nice that her father was there. I loved meeting him."

"Yeah, he's a great guy. They're actually a lot more alike than I thought they'd be. They have the same mannerisms, and even their laugh is the same, although his is quite a bit louder." Quinn opened the window to let in the river breeze. "So, since you whisked me away, are you going to tell me where we're going?"

"Not yet. I don't want you to run off."

"Well, that's filling me with confidence," Quinn said, arching a brow. "Should I just jump out now?"

"Don't be so dramatic, it's not a big deal." Lindsey turned onto the high street and stopped in front of the bakery. It was normally closed on Sundays, but Quinn saw the lights were turned on.

"No. Seriously, Lindsey. You can't do this to me." Quin shook her head and held up a hand. "I am so happy for you and Martin. I genuinely mean that, but he's not going to want me there."

"How do you know? It was his idea." Lindsey switched off the engine and turned to her. "Look. I want Martin to be a part of my life. I mean every part of my life, and that includes you. You're my best friend, and I want to be able to invite you over to dinner and bring him to social events without having to worry about tension. He's willing to talk and make amends because he's a good man and he wants me to be happy." She paused. "So will you please do this for me?"

Quinn blew out her cheeks and covered her face in her hands. "Are you sure he wants to talk to me? I know you so well. You tend to make things up to get your way."

"Yes. I'm sure." Lindsey jutted out her bottom lip, and Quinn caved in.

"Five minutes," she said. "But if it gets awkward, I'll excuse myself, okay? He's got every right to hate me, and I've accepted that."

"He doesn't hate you. At least, not anymore," Lindsey added with an uncomfortable chuckle. "Come on. Five minutes."

An hour later and Quinn was still at the bakery. Martin, of course, had no idea she was coming; he'd thought he and Lindsey were going to bake a chocolate cake together for Lindsey's mother's birthday. As expected, Lindsey's prepared speech had been highly awkward, and the start of their conversation had been rusty, but they'd said what they needed to say, and Quinn appreciated being given the time to make a genuine apology.

"Again, I'm so sorry," she said. "Nothing I can say or do will turn back the clock. I acted selfishly, and there's no excuse for that."

"I don't want to go back." Martin shrugged. "I want to be with Lindsey, not with my ex-wife. I'm very, very fond of Lindsey. I have been for a long time," he said, turning to Lindsey with a shy smile, "and although I'm also a little angry that she lured me into this situation, it was probably time we talked because she's right. If you're her best friend and I'm her..." He hesitated. "Partner?"

Lindsey giggled like a schoolgirl and nodded.

"Okay, well, if I'm her partner," he continued with flushed cheeks, "then we should move forward and leave this behind us."

Quinn leaned back and let out a sigh of relief. "Thank you," she said, hoping he could see how sincere she was.

Martin stretched his hand out over the table. "Friends?"

Quinn shook it. Friends might be a stretch, she thought, but if Martin was willing to extend an olive branch, she'd happily embrace it. "Friends."

Lindsey sat at the end of the table, beaming like a talk-show host who had just resolved a lifelong feud, but the only thing Quinn and Martin had in common right now was that they were both irritated with her for lying to them.

"Lindsey told me you'd moved into Aster House," Martin said. "You're dating the New Yorker—is that right?"

"Yes, Riley Moore. She's my girlfriend." Quinn wondered if Martin might be worried that she'd take off with Lindsey too. Obviously, that would never happen; they were friends and not in the slightest attracted to each other, but it wasn't unthinkable that he might still see her as a predator and keeping his enemies close. More than anything, she wanted to reassure him. "I love her," she added. "I hope we'll grow old together." She meant it from the bottom of her heart, and Martin's expression softened.

"I'm happy for you." He eyed her curiously. "I didn't take you for the settling-down type."

"I never met someone I wanted to settle down with." Quinn bit her lip and internally scolded herself. She didn't want to give him the impression she'd stolen his wife just for fun. "Rebecca and I were never meant to be," she finally said. "But she was gay, trust me, and although what we did was wrong, it would have happened sooner or later, only with someone else."

"I know." Martin straightened himself and took a deep breath. "And that chapter of my life is over now. I want to start with a clean slate, with Lindsey." He scooted his chair over, put an arm around Lindsey, who was visually melting on the spot, and leaned into her. "So from Lindsey's partner to her best friend, let's bury the hatchet."

72

RILEY

"You know what I'm thinking?" Riley pulled Quinn into the hallway and smiled at her suggestively. They'd just waved off Jane, her father, and Mindy, and a blissful silence had settled over Aster House. It was the silence she'd hated before, but now she welcomed the privacy after a month of visitors. Due to her heart problems, Jane and her father had decided to stay longer, and although she loved them dearly, she was glad they had the space to themselves again, especially when Quinn was looking the way she was.

"What *are* you thinking?" Quinn turned them around and pushed her against the wall.

"I'm thinking you look yummy in those shorts and that tiny bikini top," Riley said, teasingly wedging her fingers between Quinn's hard stomach and the waistband of her shorts. She'd missed being able to be so free with her, to flirt and play throughout the house. It was sinful for Quinn to dress like that while she was lounging in the yard, and she'd longed to touch her for hours, anticipating the moment they'd be alone.

"Yummy?" Quinn arched a brow.

"Yeah. I want you." Riley's breath hitched when Quinn ran a hand under her tank top and over her breasts, skimming her sensitive nipples that immediately rose to her attention. She shivered, and her eyes fluttered shut for a beat.

"I want you too..." Quinn bit Riley's bottom lip softly and tugged at it. "Right here, right now," she whispered, trailing kisses down Riley's neck, tracing a path to her collarbone.

The wetness of Quinn's mouth left a zinging sensation on Riley's skin, and needing to feel the pressure of her body, she tugged Quinn closer and bucked her hips forward. Every time with Quinn still felt like the first time, and her heart was racing with intoxicating desire.

Quinn tugged at the hem of Riley's top, and she lifted her arms so she could take it off. Riley unbuttoned Quinn's shorts in return, then clumsily fumbled with the zipper that got stuck halfway. "Take them off," she begged. She needed to feel her skin, to feel her close, but pushed her back so she could look at her.

Quinn was a vision of strength and grace, her body barely covered by a cobalt-blue triangle bikini that accented her sculpted form. Her arms were toned and strong, hinting at a sensual power she could unleash at any moment. Her abdomen was etched, her waist trim and slender, her physique a result of years of physical labor. Subtle muscles graced her thighs, firm and defined, and Riley couldn't wait to have those muscles between her legs. She was a woman who embodied both strength and femininity, but what Riley loved most about her was that look in her eyes and that captivating aura of sexual energy that told her Quinn wanted her just as much.

"God, I love looking at you," she murmured, knowing she'd never grow tired of the sight.

"You're beautiful." Quinn pulled down Riley's shorts, and Riley stepped out of them, basking in the sensation of skin on skin as they came together, their lips meeting in a sensual collision.

Riley cupped the back of Quinn's neck, pulling her tighter against her as their tongues met in a passionate dance. Every kiss, every touch, every caress heightened her desire. She had so many years to make up for. Perhaps that was why she always felt insatiable around Quinn, who had awoken a whole new side to her; a side she never knew she had.

Quinn's hands roamed over her behind, following the path of her curves. Anticipation was swirling between them when Quinn stepped back to catch her breath and look at her. "Lie down," she said, pointing to the rug in the hallway. "Unless you prefer the bed?"

"No." Riley bit her lip and grinned as she inched away and lowered herself onto the rug. She didn't care where they were as long as she didn't have to wait. Lying in her white, lace bra and panties as Quinn's eyes caressed her body, she yearned for closeness and release from the throbbing sensation between her thighs that left her trembling.

Closing the distance between them, Quinn's small breasts rose and fell with every breath. Standing over her, she looked Riley up and down, then tugged at the drawstrings of her bikini until it came undone and fell off her.

Breathless while gazing at her, Riley was burning to have her close. "Come here."

Quinn bent down and crawled over her, steadying herself on her hands and knees. "I still can't believe you're mine," she said, inhaling against Riley's temple before she shifted her mouth to her lips. "It blows my mind every time I'm with you." She shifted so her knee rested between Riley's legs, putting pressure right where Riley needed it before she brought her full body weight down.

Riley let out a deep sigh, basking in the euphoria of their love and connection that knew no boundaries, no limitations, and they both moaned as they sank into a sea of wonderful sensations. She knew Quinn could feel how wet she was, how much she craved her, and when Quinn pushed into her, Riley's whole body jerked with ecstasy. The delicious pressure and the deep kiss that followed made her delirious with lust. Quinn took her hand and laced their fingers together while her other hand drifted down over Riley's waist and hips, curling inward.

Quinn's behind was firm under her fingertips, and Riley felt her muscles tense as she squeezed her flesh. Spreading her legs, she welcomed Quinn's hand that caressed the inside of her thigh, slowly moving up to find her slick with arousal. Her light touch made her gasp against Quinn's mouth, and when Quinn built up pressure and ran her fingers through her folds, Riley dug her nails into Quinn's behind and moaned loudly. Her other hand squeezed Quinn's, trembling in her grip.

Kissing her fiercely, Quinn entered her, then carefully added another finger, and fucked her slowly and deeply while riding Riley's leg. She licked her lips, and a moan escaped her as she thrust into her.

"Lift your hips," Riley whispered and moved her hand in between them to caress Quinn's wet, swollen center. Her arousal made Riley squirm; nothing was sexier than Quinn's pleasure. Her beautiful face glistened with a sheen of sweat, her eyes dark and determined, and behind her, the crystals of the ceiling chandelier reflected the late-afternoon sun, causing specks of light to dance over her hair as they found a lazy rhythm together. When Riley circled her clit, Quinn let out a hoarse cry and bucked against her, clenching her jaw.

Hungry to possess all of her, Riley sought her mouth again and relished in their intimacy. Her core tightened, she was floating, and everything apart from them blurred into insignificance. She was close and so was Quinn; she could feel it in her movements that became faster, and she could hear it in her erratic breathing.

"Come with me, baby," she murmured, grasping Quinn's hair.

Quinn nodded and her mouth pulled into a smile as she pushed deeper, penetrating her harder and faster until Riley let go and exploded, her muscles jerking tightly around Quinn's fingers. They tensed, clasping each other, and Riley felt not only her own pleasure but also Quinn's climax coursing through her veins. She loved this woman more than anything, and lying on the hallway floor with Quinn's fingers still inside her, she felt happy tears stinging the corners of her eyes. Emotions caught up on her as she processed her family's visit and the moment she thought she might not live to see another day. She'd been blessed. She had a new life, a new forever love, and a new sense of gratitude for every breath she took and every moment she was alive. This time around, she was going to make it count.

73

QUINN

Quinn's day had started out uneventfully with her commute to site; a lovely building in the city center of Mystic that her team was converting into three apartments. She'd worked hard all day, then stopped by Lindsey's place on her way back to Aster House where she'd had a cup of tea and cake with Lindsey and Martin. They seemed so comfortable around each other now, and Quinn was slowly getting used to seeing Martin as her best friend's partner rather than someone who wanted her gone from the planet.

As always, she was looking forward to coming home to Riley. That was the best part of her day: finally holding her again. Riley hadn't joined her at Lindsey's house because she was busy putting together ideas for her bed-and-breakfast with Quinn's mother, who was keen to be a part of it.

The sun was already low as she crossed the drawbridge, but the August heat was still sweltering this year. That was unusual for Connecticut, but she loved their long nights in the yard on the riverbank. They'd even had fireflies by the swing under the old willow, and a flock of ducks and two swans had made the water's edge their home, demanding breakfast each morning. There were butterflies, birds, and otters, and they were graced with regular visits from a badger whom they'd named Lindsey because it made a habit of stealing cookies from the pantry when they left the door open.

As she drove through the gates and up the drive, something was different. There was a certain scent in the air that triggered her to look closer, and as she turned her gaze to the lawn, she saw thousands of little purple buds poking through the green. As always, she hadn't seen it coming.

In the years prior when she'd driven by the house, she'd always stopped by the gates to admire the spectacle, but she wasn't an outsider anymore. It wouldn't be more than a few days until the yard would be transformed into a dreamscape.

"Did you see it?" Riley said as she came out to greet her. Quinn got out of her pickup, and Riley flung her arms around her.

"Yeah. It's started." Quinn smiled and kissed her softly, then turned to view the beauty that had emerged from the other side of the lawn.

"They're everywhere and materialized out of nowhere," Riley continued. "This morning it was still green and when I came out a few hours later, the whole color scheme had changed. And not just a few either. It's like they all collectively woke each other up." She shook her head and knelt down to examine the buds. They were purple, pink, and white, but Quinn knew the purple would take over. It had always been that way. "I've never seen anything like it."

"You haven't seen anything *yet*. Wait a week and you'll really be blown away."

"It's so much more impactful than in the pictures." Riley

took her hand and squeezed it. "It's already a masterpiece. I feel so lucky to live here."

"So do I." Quinn took her in her arms and kissed her forehead. "Do you want to have a drink on the front steps?"

"Yes." Riley grinned. "I already chilled a couple of beers. I'll have one with you." She wiped her forehead. "I was going to make herbal tea, but it's so warm, I need something cold." A strand of hair was stuck to her clammy forehead, and Quinn brushed it away. Riley was tanned now, and she had a healthy glow to her cheeks.

"A cold beer sounds perfect," she said. "Are you okay having alcohol since you have your hospital appointment tomorrow?"

"Yes, it's fine as long as I don't have too much." Riley let go of her and sprinted up the steps into the house. "Stop worrying so much about me. How many times do I have to tell you?" she yelled over her shoulder. "I'll be back in a minute."

"Okay, okay." Quinn chuckled as she sat on the steps. She would always worry about Riley, but knowing she was now having checkups every few months rather than twice a year made her feel a little better. "Are you nervous?" she asked when Riley came back out and handed her a beer.

"About tomorrow? I feel fine, so no, not really, and besides, the excitement of this manifestation..." Riley gestured to the lawn. "It took my mind off it." She leaned into Quinn. "You?"

"Of course. It's been bugging me." Quinn shrugged and pressed the cold bottle against her neck before she took a sip. "You seemed fine before, and then..." She winced. "Then I almost lost you."

"You won't lose me. Hey..." Riley met her eyes and cupped her cheek. "I promise that from now on, I'll let you know if I feel something's not right. No matter how much I know you'll worry about me. I'll tell you everything."

"Please. That will make life easier for me." Quinn wrapped an arm around her and pushed away negative thoughts as she pulled her close. All she wanted was to sit here with Riley and enjoy the miracle of nature unfolding in front of their eyes. It would be a memorable day, and she wanted it to end on a good note. A hopeful note. "How was your session with my mother?"

"It was great. She had so many good ideas—things I would have never thought of myself. We'll move the big desk from the office into the hallway and use it as a reception desk, as it suits the style of the house, and she suggested turning the office into a communal space for the guests so we won't have to give up our privacy by letting them use our living room. She also suggested signing deals with local restaurants who can deliver so I won't have to worry about arranging dinner for them." Riley paused. "I really want to try this. I think I can make it work with her help. I won't have to do much myself. Tammy can take care of the changeovers, and your mother can take care of the reception desk part-time, so all that's left for me to do is cook breakfast and be available when your mom's not here. Frankly, I can't wait to start welcoming people to this special place. It should be shared."

"I love that," Quinn said. "And Mom knows what she's talking about. She's got over forty years of experience and knows the tourist scene in Mystic inside out. Thank you for letting her be a part of this. She really needed something to focus on."

"I need her too," Riley said. "And she's lovely."

"Well, I'm glad you like my mom and that you found

something you're passionate about. Just don't work too hard."

"I won't." Riley nuzzled Quinn and kissed her, and Quinn let out a long sigh of contentment.

As the day drew to an end, a tranquil stillness settled over the grounds, only broken up by the faint chirping of crickets and the distant call of a lone bird. The world seemed to hold its breath, caught between day and night, and as the last embers of daylight slipped away, the color purple slowly faded with the dying light. The show was over, but only for today.

74

RILEY

"Miss Moore..." Dr. Norwich's voice was calm and upbeat, which somewhat reassured Riley. He looked like he hadn't slept much with his messy hair and the heavy bags under his eyes, or maybe he'd just jumped out of bed. His stethoscope was hanging low on one side, almost dropping off his shoulder, and although Riley and he hadn't had that much interaction last time she was here since the nurses and junior doctors did most of the communication, she felt connected to him, and she trusted him. He had saved her life, after all; he was the reason she was still here. She'd been fine yesterday, but this morning she'd woken up slightly anxious, with numerous what-ifs running through her mind. What if she needed surgery? What if they'd found underlying issues? Other faults with her heart? They were all viable scenarios, she'd been told.

"Yes?" Riley braced herself, leaning into Quinn, who was squeezing her hand hard. Although she tried her best to hide it, Riley could tell Quinn was even more on edge than she was; she'd been fidgety since they'd arrived.

As her cardiologist was running late, she and Quinn had

been sitting in the waiting area, worried something might be wrong. The waiting was the worst, speculating about reasons for the delay in nervous anticipation.

There was no sign of bad news in Dr. Norwich's expression, though. He simply excused himself and told them he was very busy.

He glanced down at her medical file before he met Riley's eyes again. "I've reviewed today's test results, and I'm pleased to inform you that everything seems to be stable. Your recent blood works were positive too. I'll go over everything with you in detail later. I just wanted to give you the good news before delving into facts. Your medication is effective, and I am optimistic that, in combination with a healthy lifestyle, regular monitoring, and good communication with our healthcare team, you will be able to live a normal life providing you keep your stress levels to a minimum. You're required to attend your scheduled checkups, and don't hesitate to reach out if you experience any concerning symptoms or changes in your condition. Anything, no matter how small or insignificant it may seem. We're here to help you every step of the way."

"Thank you." Riley let out the breath she'd been holding, and she felt Quinn's tense body relax against her.

"Needless to say," he continued, "you'll need to keep a close eye on the list of over-the-counter medication you're supposed to stay away from. No exceptions." He arched a brow at her. "And no more than one coffee a day and avoid any type of energy drinks. That includes herbal energy teas to be on the safe side."

"Of course." Riley nodded. "I'll be careful from now on."

"According to my notes, this is exactly what you were told the last two times you were dismissed from NYU Langone in New York," he said matter-of-factly. The underlying message in his words was clear: she hadn't listened before, and he wasn't convinced she was taking his advice seriously now. "You've been very lucky three times, but your luck won't keep you going forever."

"I hear you, and you're right," Riley said. "I wasn't focused on myself back then, but things have changed." She wasn't sure how she could explain to Dr. Norwich that her life felt more valuable this time around. That she didn't just have herself and her business to live for. Her autopilot existence was a thing of the past, and now she cherished each moment and each breath because she had love, a home, a family, and a community. She even had little new pleasures such as fresh bread in the mornings, barbecue nights with loved ones, long walks along the river, animal friends who demanded her attention, mood boards that would soon manifest into beautiful spaces, and a field of asters right on her doorstep. She had magic in her life, and she had time; lots of time to be enjoyed in a slow, mindful pace.

"I'll be careful. I have to be." She smiled as tears stung the corners of her eyes. The weight that had been pressing on her shoulders was gone, and she felt a serenity only relief could bring. "I want to live. I really do." As she said it, Quinn squeezed her so tightly she could barely breathe, and she wrapped her arms around Quinn in return and met her eyes that were loaded with emotion.

"You're going to be fine, babe," Quinn said, then turned to Dr. Norwich. "I'll watch her like a hawk, I promise."

"Good. I have a feeling you might be the first to talk some sense into Miss Moore," Dr. Norwich joked. He observed their exchange with fondness, then beckoned them to follow him as he walked ahead through the long corridors of the hospital that seemed far less daunting now.

Riley took Quinn's hand and realized that, for the first

time, she felt stronger with someone else by her side; much stronger than when she was alone. She'd always thought she was invincible, but she needed the support. Quinn was her rock, and Riley would be Quinn's support in return, in whichever way she could be. It was a beautiful feeling, knowing she wouldn't have to face her struggles alone. They were allies in a world that would throw them curveballs, but their love would be an unwavering beacon in the darkest of times. With Quinn, her burdens seemed lighter and her challenges more conquerable. Everything was easier, and, most of all, better with love.

EPILOGUE

QUINN - 1 YEAR LATER

"*This* is it. The house is yours too now." Riley took Quinn's hand and looked up at Aster House. "How does it feel?"

"Surreal," Quinn said, following Riley's gaze. It was a very special day, and she was hoping it would become even more memorable. They'd just returned from their lawyer's office to add her name to the deed. She'd bought herself into Aster house and they were now joint owners. It was still hard to grasp that her childhood home was back in her family. "But it feels right," she continued. "Not just the house, of course. It feels right to do this with you, to build a future together."

"If our future looks like this, then it couldn't get any better," Riley said sweetly, leaning into her. "I love our home, and I love you."

August was warm and broody and Mystic was bustling with happy tourists and events. It had always been Quinn's favourite month; the month that the asters thrived, covering the front yard in a sea of purple. It was a spectacular sight, and she cherished it each day she left the house in the morning. She and Riley usually had coffee together on the front steps, and in the past weeks, they'd watched the patches of purple spread until every inch of the yard was in bloom, only leaving the network of stone paths free to cross the lawn.

"I love you too." Quinn wrapped her arms around her and pulled her in. "Are you ready for our first guests?"

"As ready as I can be." Riley chuckled. "I have no idea what I'm doing but the rooms look beautiful, and the yard is perfect. Other than welcoming them with a big smile, I don't think there's much else I can do."

"It will be fine, I'm sure. And we've only taken bookings until late September. If you don't enjoy hosting, you'll never have to do it again," Quinn said. The bathrooms and the office – that was now a communal chill-out space for their guests – were ready, and they'd be renting out four rooms and Quinn's barge in the coming six weeks to see if it would be something Riley would like to pursue going forward. Now fully booked, they'd been surprised at the over-whelming interest, even for the barge. There was still a lot of work to do on the house but there would be plenty of time over winter to build a bar in the basement and a pool in the back yard. As they were standing there, holding each other and embracing the special moment, the image of her great-grandparents in front of Aster House on the day they moved in, crossed her mind. It was taken on the same date, eighty years ago. Quinn had enlarged the photograph and it was proudly hanging in the hallway, alongside other pictures of her grandparents, her mother, and herself while they lived there. She'd specifically chosen today to sign the deed as the date felt symbolic. "I want to take a picture of us," she said, pulling her phone out of her back pocket.

"Okay. A selfie?"

"No, I'll put it on the timer. Stay there." Quinn headed over to a nearby tree, balanced her phone on a branch and turned it slightly until she had a good view of Riley in front of the house. She set it to ten seconds, ran back and put an arm around Riley, the same way her great-grandfather had done with his wife. "Smile, babe."

"You don't need to tell me to smile. I'm already as happy as I can be." Riley rested her head against Quinn's shoulder and they both smiled widely. It was a great picture, Quinn saw when she went to retrieve her phone. The light hit the house beautifully, and the asters came up to their calves. Riley was wearing a floaty, white summer dress and Quinn was in her denim shorts and a white T-shirt. It wasn't their Sunday best, and nothing was staged like the picture of her great-grandparent's, but this was a different era, and thankfully, a time where a same-sex couple could safely settle down in Mystic. Much had changed, but Aster House hadn't changed. It had withstood decennia of cold winters, warm summers, many storms and two floods, and its walls were still sturdy as ever. The asters continued to bloom every year without exception, transforming the yard into a surreal display of pure beauty.

"Does it feel more like your home now?" Riley asked. "Because it's official?"

"It always felt like home to me, but most of all, home is where you are," Quinn whispered, nuzzling Riley's hair. In the past month, they'd had big get-togethers on Sundays, with her family, their friends and her grandmother who now came to Aster House once a week. It had a calming effect on her, and even though she didn't always understand the context of the situation and rarely recognized them, she felt connected to the house and loved being here. Riley's father had also visited them a few more times, along with

Jane and Mindy. The house had been healing for them; a place to connect and re-connect with their family, their loved ones, and with themselves.

There was a lot of love between those walls but the love she felt for Riley overshadowed everything, and it was the forever kind of love. They'd spoken about children and hoped to have a family of their own. If they did, Quinn would make sure they grew to love the house as much as she did. It would be a haven for them, a place they would miss when they went off to college or moved away from Mystic to pursue their dreams. And the house would always be here when they returned, welcoming them with open doors, waiting for a new generation and many more to come.

There was only one thing left to do; something Quinn had been wanting to do for a while. Her great-grandmother's ring was in her pocket, and Riley gasped when she got down on one knee and took her hand. "Beautiful, wonderful Riley," she said, nerves coursing through her as she took it out and looked up at the woman she adored. She'd secretly had the ring altered so it would fit Riley, and although the weeks waiting to get it back had been agonising, the local jeweller had returned it in sparkling condition. Her hand was trembling, but she didn't care as she continued. "I hope you know how much I love you, and I'd spend eternity with you, if I could. I promise to always be there for you, to love you and support you until the day I die. I promise to protect your heart in every way I can, and that I will spend my days determined to make you smile." She choked up when Riley nodded before she'd even asked the question. "I truly believe that we were meant to meet, and that you are the only one for me on this planet, because why else would our paths have crossed in this bizarre way?" Swallowing hard, Quinn paused and held up the ring. Her hand was shaking so badly now, she could barely manage to put in on Riley's finger, and she chuckled nervously when it finally slid on and graced her hand. "Will you please marry me?"

"Of course." Riley burst into tears as she examined the ring and nodded again. "Of course I'll marry you; I thought you'd never ask." She fell around Quinn's neck, sniffing against her shoulder, and Quinn squeezed her tightly, lifted her off the ground and spun her around. Their future was unknown, but their love was as strong as the walls of Aster House. There would be laughter and joy, and there would be pain. But whatever happened, they'd get through it together, and Aster House would never lie dormant again.

AFTERWORD

I hope you've loved reading *Along The Mystic River* as much as I've loved writing it. If you've enjoyed this book, would you consider rating it and leaving a review? Reviews are very important to authors and I'd be really grateful!

ABOUT THE AUTHOR

Lise Gold is an author of lesbian romance. Her romantic attitude, enthusiasm for travel and love for feel good stories form the heartland of her writing. Born in London to a Norwegian mother and English father, and growing up between the UK, Norway, Zambia and the Netherlands, she feels at home pretty much everywhere and has an unending curiosity for new destinations. She goes by 'write what you know' and is often found in exotic locations doing research or getting inspired for her next novel.

Working as a designer for fifteen years and singing semi-professionally, Lise has always been a creative at heart. Her novels are the result of a quest for a new passion after resigning from her design job in 2018. Since the launch of Lily's Fire in 2017, she has written several romantic novels and also writes erotica under the pen name Madeleine Taylor.

When not writing from her kitchen table, Lise can be found cooking, at the gym or singing her heart out some-where, preferably country or blues. She lives in London with her dogs El Comandante and Bubba.

ALSO BY LISE GOLD

Lily's Fire

Beyond the Skyline

The Cruise

French Summer

Fireflies

Northern Lights

Southern Roots

Eastern Nights

Western Shores

Northern Vows

Living

The Scent of Rome

Blue

The Next Life

In The Mirror

Christmas In Heaven

Welcome to Paradise

After Sunset

Paradise Pride

Members Only

Under the pen name Madeleine Taylor

The Good Girl

Online

Masquerade

Santa's Favorite

Spanish translations by Rocío T. Fernández

Verano Francés

Vivir

Nada Más Que Azul

Luciérnagas

Hindi translations

Zindagi